DUSTING

DUSTING

N.J. Bruett

iUniverse, Inc.
New York Lincoln Shanghai

DUSTING

Copyright © 2006 by N.J. Bruett

iUniverse books may be ordered through booksellers or by contacting:

iUniverse
2021 Pine Lake Road, Suite 100
Lincoln, NE 68512
www.iuniverse.com
1-800-Authors (1-800-288-4677)

ISBN-13: 978-0-595-38748-9 (pbk)
ISBN-13: 978-0-595-83130-2 (ebk)
ISBN-10: 0-595-38748-9 (pbk)
ISBN-10: 0-595-83130-3 (ebk)

Printed in the United States of America

For Abbie, Dave, and Greg, of course. Without you, there is no point.

Close your eyes, think lovely thoughts, and suddenly you're flying.

—Peter Pan

These murders would not have been possible without the multiple rescues of my manuscript from cyber-space performed by my family, the creative touch of the embezzlement scheme suggested by a dear mortgage broker, and the original inspiration from three sharing friends. You know who you are.

Immeasurable gratitude is owed to Linda Wigglesworth. What would I do without you?

Finally, I send a prayer to Angel Beaune, the only one who eagerly listened to every word, whenever I needed fresh ears, and kept my toes warm, too.

NJB

Born in New Jersey, Nancy Jelliffe Bruett is living her adult life in a town on the New England sea coast. She remains married to the same man for over thirty years, and is blessed to have her two adult children nearby. Her incorrigible, eclectic friends provide the author with both inspiration and tasty food for thought.

Chapter One

There is something ghoulish and vulgar about being the first to arrive at a funeral, especially when you're merely acquaintances of the deceased, not family, or really even friends. Without question, Stephen and I were guilty of poor taste, but we were doing our best not to be hypocrites.

We had agreed to meet an hour before the memorial service at the church's inconspicuous basement door. The pews would soon be filled by mourners, mostly insincere and publicly pious, and we fully intended to appreciate the show. I parked next door to the church in a friend's driveway. My winter coat was tightly wrapped around me as I cut through the arborvitae that separated the two properties. I had done this countless times over the years to disguise my frequently tardy arrivals.

Stephen was waiting for me in the recess of the church's cellar door. I had an old set of keys, given to me during my stint as a Sunday school teacher. I lost no time unlocking the door and closing it tightly behind us. We embraced in the dark basement.

"Do you think anyone saw you, Laura?" Stephen's whispered voice did not mask his anxiety.

"No. What about you?"

"I don't think so. Donald dropped me right at the door on his way to work."

"Good. Take my hand and I'll get us out of here."

Unfortunately for Stephen, he obeyed my request. I proceeded to crash into stacks of folded chairs, send coat racks on wheels spinning into collapsed card tables, and eventually knock baby Jesus out of his manger, where he had been peacefully resting in anticipation of the next Advent season.

"Ow! Oh, shit! Cripes!"

"No Laura, I think you mean 'Christ'. I caught him on the first bounce, though."

"Sorry. I don't remember this basement being so dark or crowded. Oh, here we are."

We had arrived at the stairs that led from the basement, past the vestry, and up to the balcony. I fervently hoped the balcony was still deserted. It would no doubt fill with people before the ceremony commenced, but I had special seats in mind. We encountered a closed door at the top of the stairs. Before opening it, I turned to Stephen and placed my finger in front of my mouth, signaling for quiet. He nodded. We tiptoed into the balcony. Below us, florists were busily placing opulent arrangements on the altar and at the stained glass windows. Soon enough the extravagant flowers would be as dead as Grace Rogers. Like cats stalking an unsuspecting bird, Stephen and I crept on all fours along the last row of the balcony.

"Damn," I said as I felt a run scamper up my pantyhose.

"Tsk. Tsk. Language."

"Who made you Pope?"

When reaching the center aisle, we stopped. I turned back the rug at the top of the aisle, revealing a door. We carefully lifted the trap and climbed down eight stairs, into a projection room. Stephen reached up and quietly closed the door above us.

This space was used for the spotlight on the annual Christmas pageant and occasionally for slide presentations of the Holy Land, or other tedious vacations church-goers are so anxious to inflict on others. Annually, after the church's potluck supper, a film strip chronicling the good deeds the congregation's pledges had made possible the previous fiscal year would be shown and then new pledge cards would be distributed. But otherwise, the space went unused. Stephen and I sat down behind the one way glass, overlooking the main floor of the church. We were both flies on the wall and free to whisper and point.

I looked over at my friend of more than twenty years. He was oblivious to his beauty and natural grace. He moved with the ease of Cary Grant and even sweat pants managed to look elegant on him. Stephen's hair was thick, shiny, and naturally streaked blond, just like his well-shaped eyebrows. He was one inch over six feet, with broad shoulders, and what I believe the younger generation calls washing board abs. His legs and arms were muscular and each year I unashamedly look forward to seeing him in his summer wardrobe. Stephen's facial features were chiseled; high cheekbones, straight, well proportioned nose, sensuous lips, a strong, square chin, and the brownest, most deeply set eyes I have ever seen. Dark-eyed blonds are unusual, and the combination is not easily forgotten.

Stephen accepted his appearance, without being the least bit impressed with it. When he wasn't cleaning houses, he was teaching aerobics. I had met Stephen when he was ten and I was a thirty-five-year-old mother of two. It was school vacation and he was accompanying his father, Mack Macomber, on rounds as an appliance repairman. Our washing machine, which was on the second floor, had overflowed the day before, creating a real mess. The water had leaked through to the living room below, soaking the rug and a water stain was drying on the ceiling. Stephen and his father went upstairs to fix the washer, while I finished in the kitchen. Eventually, I checked on their progress and noticed the door to the walk-in closet was open. Because I'm not the most organized homemaker, I like to keep my closet doors closed. As I started to shut the door, I noticed Stephen was inside, trying on my new pair of Ferragamo three inch heels. When he saw me, the look of fear on his face eliminated any annoyance I might have had.

"You have good taste," I said. "Those are the best shoes in this closet."

"I'm sorry. The door was open, and I just walked in."

"What's going on out there? Stephen, what are you doing now?" His father shouted so sharply that Stephen cringed.

"Everything's fine, Mr. Macomber. I asked Stephen to help me rearrange some of the boxes in this closet, if you don't mind."

"Oh, no. Go ahead. It's the perfect job for you, isn't it Stephen?" There was cruelty in Mr. Macomber's voice and Stephen cringed again.

When the repairs were finished, I wrote a check to Stephen's father and asked if I could hire his son for the rest of the day, if it was all right with both of them, of course.

"It suits me just fine," Mr. Macomber snapped, not waiting to hear what his son thought.

Stephen stayed that afternoon, and two afternoons a week for the next seven years. He was good company and always willing to help. Even when Stephen was ten, we had great conversations. I eventually realized that his parents, April and Mack, neither planned nor wanted him. His mother resented his inconvenience to her acting career. In reality, April May, her professional name, was a model working mostly at the convention center for boat and automobile shows. April May was usually bikini-clad, but with time, she had been increasingly asked to wear the larger-than-life bright costumes of Big Bird or Mickey Mouse. Rather than blame this turn of events on her impressively increasing girth, she held Stephen responsible for ruining her image as a sex symbol. Mack Macomber lost interest in his son when it became clear that the only spectator sport Stephen enjoyed was figure skating, especially the men's competition.

For my part, I looked forward to afternoons with Stephen. My children Abbie and Dave loved him like an older brother, and Stephen felt the same. We discovered a mutual affinity for cooking. My husband Greg especially appreciated the evening meals that Stephen and I prepared. When Stephen turned sixteen, he learned to drive in my car; his parents seemingly oblivious to his age. He started spending two nights a week with us, so we could enjoy his culinary creations together. Once Stephen graduated from high school, he found himself unwelcome in his parents' home. He moved in with us graduation night and stayed three years. He supported himself by cleaning houses, but Stephen was also attending night school, and by his twentieth birthday, he was an accredited aerobics teacher and personal trainer. Once Stephen had a steady income, he left us, but thankfully, he only moved two towns away. All this time, Stephen was my friend. I was never a mother figure, or even an adult to his role as child.

In the twenty-one years since meeting Stephen, my beloved Abbie and Dave have appropriately flown their mother's coop, and my husband Greg, at the tender age of fifty-five, shocked all of us by dying on a business trip to Vancouver, when a heart attack left him dead before he hit the hotel room floor, or at least that's what the coroner told me.

Stephen and I make an unusual couple. I could be his mother, but we don't look a bit alike. I am a foot shorter than he is, small-boned, and will never be described as a hard body. My hair is L'Oreal blonde, but my eyes are gray, not deep and dark like Stephen's. I am doing my best not to become dowdy, but find myself spending increasing amounts of time researching plastic surgery. If I were in show business, I would insist on airbrushed portraits, Vaseline on the lens, and under no circumstances would I ever take off my clothes.

The reason Stephen and I were attending the funeral of Grace Rogers so surreptitiously was that Stephen had discovered her body. Grace lived in a gracious modern mansion, built into the cliff of our seaside New England village of Magnolia. The Rogers had been Stephen's clients for less than a year. Thursday was their usual cleaning day and when Grace did not respond to Stephen's knock on the front door, he let himself in with the key she had given him. Stephen had keys, or knew the whereabouts of the spare, to most of his customers' homes.

Nothing struck him as unusual. When he entered, he called out loudly to announce his arrival. He had started his usual routine; kitchen, bathrooms, bedrooms, main floor, and vacuuming last. At the Rogers' home, just before vacuuming, Stephen always meticulously cleaned the sliding glass door, which led to an impressive deck, overlooking the Atlantic. The salt spray from the ocean below played havoc with the windows, so Stephen took special care to wipe the outside of the glass, and that is when he had seen Grace. She was splattered far below the deck on an outcropping of ledge.

Stephen had the presence of mind to dial 911 before climbing down the steep cliff to the body. Unfortunately, there was no doubt that poor Grace was dead. Her neck was broken and her skull was smashed. A few curious seagulls were already inspecting the body when the police and ambulance arrived. The facts that Stephen had found the body, and also had a key to the house, caused the local constabulary to question him. By the second interrogation, the police were already hypothesizing that Stephen had fought with Mrs. Rogers, eventually throwing her off the deck.

"What reason do they give for the fight, Stephen?" I asked when he phoned me at my home following his second interrogation.

"To quote them, 'We're the ones asking the questions here, Stephen.'"

"Maybe they feel Grace left one crumb too many on the dining room rug, causing you to snap into a murderous rage."

"Oh, God, Laura. Don't let them hear that. It could put an idea in their communal heads."

Stephen nervously brushed the dust from our balcony crawl from his impeccably creased gray slacks. I looked at my pantyhose and noticed both shins now sported runs. Stephen noticed, too, and raised his eyebrows.

"If you laugh, I swear I'll fart in your face when we crawl out," I warned him. "Did the police tell you anything at all?"

"I do know that they've ruled out any sort of accident because the 'victim' was not wearing a coat. Because it's February, the police have surmised that no one would stand on a windy balcony overlooking a frigid ocean without a coat. They've also ruled out suicide because Grace's last phone call was less than a half-hour before I let myself in and it was to her travel agent, finalizing the details for her annual trip to Jamaica with her sister." I raised my eyebrows and Stephen added,

"The Rogers' yacht winters in Jamaica with its Captain, and the sisters luxuriate on board two weeks each year. Who would confirm travel plans minutes before hurling herself off a cliff. It's a valid point. Besides, no note has surfaced."

"Let me get this straight. After tossing the lady of the house over the cliff, the police think you cleaned meticulously, except in your panic you forgot to vacuum, and called 911 prematurely."

"Pretty much, except they've unearthed what they consider a motive. The Rogers were three months late paying my bill. If I murdered every slow paying client, Jack the Ripper would pale by comparison. Most of my 'carriage trade' customers are slow payers, but Magnolia's finest didn't want to hear that."

I hated seeing the discouraged slump in my friend's shoulders as we sat side by side. Stephen and I had spent the weekend between Grace's death and this funeral comparing notes on Grace Rogers. Neither of us knew her well, but we both liked her. She was a quiet, glamorous, and a seemingly lonely married woman in her mid-thirties. She wore dramatic make-up and severe hairstyles, but the combination suited her. Grace's nails were as perfect as the jewels she wore on her fingers. Stephen told me that her closets were filled with expensive clothes, still bearing tags; a sure sign of loneliness.

Stephen's significant other, Donald, had started his career as a salesman at Armani's in Boston. He knew how to recognize the rich, compulsive shoppers, the women who were really looking for a friend and not a four thousand dollar ensemble. Donald had recognized that quality in Grace Rogers and profited from it. He was the one who had suggested to Grace that Stephen be hired as their housecleaner.

Grace was married to Sean Rogers, a handsome, wealthy, criminal lawyer who exuded charm and charisma. Sean was a decade older than his wife. The couple was childless and had filled their lives with possessions; a state of the art, eighty-foot yacht, complete with captain, a ski house in Vail, and a summer home on the Vineyard. Sean had a reputation as a philanderer. I cautioned Stephen not to take this gossip too seriously, as I suspected the source was envy and not evidence. Sean Rogers had received national notoriety for skillfully defending Mafia figures and earning both their acquittals and huge fees, rumored to be paid in cash.

After two days of speculation, and despite the authorities' theory to the contrary, Stephen and I decided that Grace had probably committed suicide. We wished she had left a note. At first, we thought maybe her death was somehow connected to her husband, but he seemed so genuinely devastated that we just didn't have the heart to seriously believe it. I had barely been widowed two years and Sean's misery looked real to me. Because he had successfully defended the mob, there was no reason for them to kill Grace. Stephen and I decided to keep open minds for the time being, but we felt a clue might be gleaned by spying on the mourners filling the church. I watch LAW and ORDER re-runs and I know that most murders are committed by someone close to the victim.

The first mourners to arrive were Christine Parker and Reverend William Andrews. Christine had been my across the street neighbor until a few years ago, when she and her husband had divorced and sold their house. I knew more than I wanted to about Christine and her ex-husband.

"Those hypocritical phonies!" I whispered. "They don't even know the Rogers."

"When has that ever stopped the good Reverend and his devoted 'flockette'?" Stephen whispered back. "I'm sure they're here to relieve our suffering, and not promote their piety. It's just a coincidence that they've chosen to sit second pew center."

Stephen and I frequently gossiped, but never about his clients. Somehow, that would have been unprofessional. After all, a housecleaner learns a lot about the people he picks up after. For example, I'm sure Stephen knew if a customer were secretly alcoholic and hiding bottles behind the curtains, or if there were too many unpaid bills on the desk in the study. While Stephen would never eavesdrop, he couldn't help but notice whispered phone conversations or arguments. I was also sure that more than one of Stephen's housewives had made a pass at him. Stephen was gay, but he was not effeminate. He had moved out of town a decade ago, and most of his customers were the newly rich, recent arrivals to Magnolia. They would have no reason to know Stephen's sexual persuasion.

Luckily for us, neither Christine nor the Reverend had ever been Stephen's employers, so we had always considered them fair game. Long before the Parkers divorced, I had noticed Reverend Andrews' frequent visits to Christine during the day. At first, I gave them the benefit of the doubt, but with time, and the Reverend's all night visits, when Mr. Parker was out of town, I changed my mind.

Reverend Andrews was still married to a painfully serious woman. I suspected his wife did not have much reason to smile. Christine Parker was not the Reverend's first infidelity. He had been forced to "retire" from Magnolia's Congregational Church four years ago for inappropriate behavior, involving another female parishioner, but he appeared undaunted.

"Oh, how charmingly appropriate. Today they've chosen their signature urban missionary outfits," Stephen said imitating the commentator of a haute couture fashion show. "Please note their stylish use of the mock turtleneck, giving the impression of a clerical collar, without the tiresome use of starch. Christine and William have also chosen to accessorize with, what would you say Laura, eight crosses between them? It's hard to tell from this distance, but I would definitely say eight. William's choice of the stylish black sneaker should not be overlooked nor should Christine's shoes. They are an exceptionally nice touch, and can be ordered over the web at Holyrosary.com." Stephen continued, referring to the sensibly tied, black, stacked heel shoes on Christine's feet.

I smiled and wrote their names in my notebook. This pair often paraded conspicuously at a church event. Funerals were their favorite, and they were always early arrivals. Their presence here today probably meant nothing, but Stephen and I could brainstorm about it later.

Next to enter the church were the Carlisles. They sat across from Mrs. Parker and the Reverend, conspicuously on the other side of the aisle.

"Leave it to those vultures," I said under my breath. As far as I knew, the Carlisles were barely acquainted with Grace Rogers or her husband. They were Magnolia's most aggressive realtors. I assumed they were positioning themselves to be the listing brokers, if the grieving widower decided to sell. I couldn't think of any other reason for them to be here, but I wrote their names in my notebook.

"Laura dear, the Carlisles aren't the only vultures here," Stephen whispered. I looked down and noticed Liz Hathaway sashaying down the center aisle. "Well, she's certainly dressed to kill. I believe I can smell her perfume from here," he added, as Liz paused at the second pew.

"She's trying to decide which side Sean will sit on. That little slut."

Liz Hathaway was Magnolia's most divorced citizen. She threw herself at rich men, but could never manage to be faithful after they married her. Consequently, her divorce settlements provided for living expenses, but not in the style she desired.

"If I wasn't under suspicion, I could really enjoy myself," Stephen muttered, as two more over-dressed and over-coiffed divorcees made their way to the front of the church. "That second pew is getting crowded."

We sat in silence as the organist started to play, and increasing numbers of people shuffled in. I didn't recognize half of them and assumed they must be business associates of Sean's. I wondered briefly how many had carried guns into church.

"Oh, my!" Stephen exclaimed, interrupting my thoughts.

My eyes followed where he was pointing. Walking slowly down the side aisle were April May and Mack Macomber.

"I haven't seen them in thirteen years. Mother seems to have put on some weight."

Chapter Two

Stephen and I were forced to admit that the service was impressive. There were no eulogies, but Sean Rogers had imported Bishop O'Malley for the occasion, and he spoke effectively about a life ended too soon, and how we should all make the most of every day because God may be calling us heavenward. It was your basic "Carpe Diem" theme, but extremely well-delivered. The preponderance of mob bosses in the Bishop's audience didn't seem to discomfort him.

Sean Rogers had also arranged for fifteen members of Boston's Handel and Hayden Society to sing the hymns, accompanied by Boston Symphony's chamber ensemble. Sean was dressed impeccably, from his platinum collar pin, to his gleaming Bruno Magli shoes. His face, however, looked like the wrath of God. His eyes were bloodshot and puffy, with prominent dark circles beneath them and his cheeks were wet with tears. He was either an actor worthy of the Oscar, or Sean Rogers was genuinely wracked with grief.

"That must have cost him a bundle," I said as we watched the church empty. We were waiting to sneak out of the projection room at the funeral's conclusion. Sean had extended an invitation to everyone to join him in Grace's honor at their home. I was looking forward to it, from a sleuthing point of view.

"Three things bother me," Stephen said, ignoring my comment. "If the Bishop were there, suicide must have been ruled out. Killing yourself is the only sin worse than being queer, or is it the other way around? So many rules. Anyhow, he's forbidden to preside over the funeral, or even allow the corpse in church, unless of course the deceased's family is both wealthy and generous. It also concerns me that Mr. Rogers has not asked me to tidy-up after the reception. It would be the natural thing for him to do. I think it kind of makes me look guilty."

"Unless, of course, he's guilty and is trying to throw suspicion on you," I interrupted. "Now what's the third thing?"

"What the Hell were my parents doing there?"

"Being supportive?" I ventured.

"Highly improbable. A keen desire to see me squirming is more like it. They probably think they'll inherit if I go to the gas chamber." Stephen sounded glum.

"You're not going anywhere, except Sean Rogers' with me."

"Ooh, do you think that's a good idea? I was thinking you could go alone and tell me about it. I'd be like the proverbial skunk at the picnic."

"Stephen, you can't let yourself think that way. You didn't do it and you can't start acting like you did."

Stephen knew I was right and with uncharacteristic slumped shoulders, he drove with me to the Rogers' home. The funeral reception was well attended and we had to park at the bottom of the hill and around the corner from the house. By the time we reached the front door, the first of the guests were already leaving.

"Now that wasn't my imagination. Those two glared at me," Stephen whispered out of the side of his mouth, after they had walked past. I shrugged, but he was right.

"We might as well get used to it. Just pretend you're Gregory Peck in <u>To Kill a Mockingbird.</u> Remember how the whole town hated him for defending that black man? But he showed them. You look like a blond Gregory Peck, you know."

"You're just trying to get into my pants," he said as we entered the house.

As bad luck would have it, the first people we encountered inside were Stephen's parents.

"I don't believe we've met," Stephen said, defiantly staring at his parents. "My name is Stephen Macomber."

"Very funny," replied his father. "We were hoping you'd have the good manners not to show your face here. You weren't at the church."

"We were in the balcony," I chimed in. "How are you both? Long time, no see,"

"Come on Mack," April May said, tugging her husband's sleeve.

"Leaving so soon, Mom? Don't you even want to know how I've been these last, oh, how long has it been Mommy dear, say thirteen years?"

"I don't want to know anything about you, Stephen. We know too much all ready."

"I didn't know you were friends of the Rogers," I interrupted.

"I've done some work for them," retorted Mack. "And being the father of a murdering pansy ain't gonna help my business any. You can't blame us for kissing ass and trying to disassociate from your friend here. Come on April. I don't want no one to see us talkin' to this fag."

"Kisses, Mummy," Stephen said watching them leave.

"You're bad, Stephen."

"Another touching Macomber family moment," Stephen said. "God it was great to see them. I'd forgotten just how wonderful my parents are. Maybe we can all do Thanksgiving."

"Come along, Mr. Peck. It's got to get easier from here."

"Just don't expect me to eat."

Sean was surrounded by condolence-givers, so we approached the not-so-Right Reverend William Andrews and his paramour Christine Parker. There was nothing wrong with their appetites. They had each helped themselves generously to the buffet that had been provided.

"I imagine they're trying to keep up their strength for later. That Christine is a lot of woman," Stephen muttered to me as we crossed the crowded room toward them.

I studied Christine Parker as we approached. Her appearance had not changed too much since her days as my neighbor. Christine was a big-boned, robust woman. She was almost five foot ten, wearing a size fourteen, or more, but she wasn't fat, just solid. I remembered being amazed by her ability to vigorously rake leaves, manipulate wheelbarrows filled with mulch up hills, and handle big shovels. I had watched her plant at least three trees single-handedly over the years. The woman was tireless. We were about the same age and the only real change I noticed in her appearance was that she was dying her hair a much darker shade than previously and the contrast of her coal black hair, bright red lipstick and abundant emerald green eye shadow unsettled me. Christine's new hair color had also inspired a new eyebrow artistry. The dramatic arch of her heavily penciled black brows gave Christine Parker a look of constant surprise.

The Reverend was also a large man. He was easily six foot three, with broad shoulders and a big head of flowing gray hair. His hairstyle was both premeditated and pretentious. I don't know why so many evangelicals insist on dramatic hair. Maybe they consider themselves in show business. I doubted that the Reverend was as physically fit as Christine, but not many of us are. There are some poor mortals who find being waited on uncomfortably embarrassing. Reverend Andrews was not part of that group.

"Hello, Christine. Reverend. Do you know Stephen Macomber?" I said pointedly ignoring my friend's comment.

"I remember Stephen from my time across the street from you, Laura," Christine replied, friendly enough. "How are you, Stephen?"

"I've been better."

"Yes, I understand you're the fellow who found poor Grace's body. That must have been a nasty shock," contributed the Reverend with his mouth full.

"I wouldn't want to do it again, if that's what you mean," Stephen offered.

"Now, my son, in my business you get used to death, but never violent death. I would be more than happy to counsel with you if you are troubled. I would like to think that my time spent with dear Grace gave her some peace during these past few weeks. Whatever you ask will remain between us, my son."

"Thanks for the offer, Reverend. No problems yet, but you'll be the first to know if things change."

"William means what he says, Stephen. He's soothed many a soul in his day. You can take it from me," Christine said saccharinely, gazing adoringly at the Reverend, but after glancing at her watch, she abruptly announced, "I think I'll help myself to dessert, William. Those pastries look DIVINE." They both chuckled, enjoying what I guessed was ecclesiastical humor.

"I'll come with you, my dear. We need to leave soon, anyway, if we expect to accomplish today's ministries."

Stephen and I briefly held each others' gaze. We'd never heard it called "ministries" before. Live and learn.

"So much to do, such little time," the Reverend added piously.

"Now aren't you glad you came?" I asked when the lovebirds were out of earshot.

"Suddenly I have the urge to gag, Laura. Somehow, I suspect the pastry tray is not their only indulgence. Love in bloom. I always find it uplifting."

"Do you think there's any chance that Christine found the Reverend soothing Grace's soul, Stephen? He did mention his 'time spent with dear Grace recently.' Did you notice the scratches showing just above Christine's mock turtle? She's strong enough to heave Grace off the cliff, too."

"It's an interesting thought, but I just can't feature Grace and the Reverend. I wouldn't put him past trying, but no way Mrs. Rogers would have any part of that. Maybe your old neighbor Mrs. Parker just has a cat who's a good judge of character."

I remained quiet and looked around the room.

"How do we approach the crowd with bulges in their armpits? If this were a professional hit, we'll never prove it," Stephen said hanging his head.

"Stand up straight right now, Stephen," I said quietly before continuing.

"Whatever you say, Mrs. Helmsley."

"Well, maybe we could encourage the police to investigate that aspect," I continued.

"Somehow, I just don't think that Magnolia's finest are up to the task, Laura. You didn't have the opportunity to spend quality time with them the way I did."

"Don't be so sure. Remember that big heroin bust last year? They had tips from the Feds about a sailboat in the harbor, but our guys pulled off the arrests. Maybe those glory days will encourage them to inquire more thoroughly about Mr. Rogers and his associates."

"I'll plant the thought in Detective Miller's mind at our next cozy interrogation," Stephen said, still scanning the room. "I'd like to make one of those femmes fatales from pew two for the crime, but tossing Grace off the deck just isn't their style. It would put their nails at risk."

"Now that's interesting," I mused. Stephen followed my gaze and noticed the Carlisles talking with one of the armpit holster enthusiasts. We walked toward them.

"Hi June. Hi Dick," I said. "Do you know Stephen Macomber?"

"Of course we do," the realtors acknowledged. "This is one of Sean's associates, John LoConte," Dick Carlisle said, introducing the big lug standing next to him. "Nasty business this," he continued pompously.

"Grace seemed such a gentle soul. She certainly had excellent taste," June added, looking around the home with dollar signs in her eyes. "Just look at the proportion of this room, and of course, east-facing is a view to die for." June was so busy calculating her commission, that she didn't even notice her unfortunate faux pas, but her husband did.

"Now, we must apologize for running, but we have showings all afternoon and keeping the customer waiting is a 'no-no' in our business. Good-bye all. We'll see you soon, John," Dick said ushering June out.

"Are you thinking of moving to Magnolia, Mr. LoConte," I asked after the realtors had left. "It's a quiet little town. We've never had a tragedy like this in the thirty years that I've lived here."

"Ya' nevah know. Sean told me real estate in a burg like dis is a money makin' proposition." He paused to look at his watch. "I gotta go. I got stuff to do."

"Nice meeting you, too, Mr. LoConte. Lovely fellow," Stephen said when John LoConte was out of hearing range. "We seem to be scaring people off, Laura."

"It's just that this is a Monday and people can't take the whole day off. Don't get paranoid on me. Everyone is leaving, not just the people we spoke to. We might as well face the music and give our sympathies to the widower."

Stephen and I slowly walked over to Sean Rogers. He was still surrounded by the women from the second pew, but he stopped mid-sentence when he saw Stephen.

"What are you doing here, you murdering son of a bitch. What did she do, catch you stealing? I want you out of this house!"

Suddenly the armpit bulge crowd had Stephen by the scruff of his neck and were roughly shoving him to the door and down the front steps. Stephen fell down the last three, landing on his hands and knees. I rushed to help him.

"I'm all right, Laura," he said. "Don't make it a worse spectacle than it already is."

"Spoken just like Gregory Peck," I said helping him up.

We walked to the car and I drove Stephen to the apartment he shared with Donald.

"Sean Rogers was way out of line, Stephen. I think he's hiding something."

"Give him the benefit of the doubt, Laura. His wife just died."

"Well at least try not to worry. We're going to figure this out. Have a good soak in the tub and call me in the morning."

My phone rang at 7:30 the following day.

"Have you seen the Globe?" Stephen asked without waiting for me to even say "hello."

"No, it's still on the front steps. I'll get it."

"Don't bother. I'm on my way over."

I hadn't slept very well the night before. I kept thinking about who might want to kill Grace Rogers. Despite what the police thought, surely it had to be suicide or some sort of tragic accident. Maybe Grace was a reformed smoker, who still snuck a cigarette now and then. I knew lots of people who would step outside their own homes to have a sly puff, and avoid leaving any telltale odor. Was there ice on the deck? Maybe Grace wasn't paying attention and she slipped over the railing. Maybe she slipped under the railing, or just maybe, she committed suicide. What did we really know about Grace? She and Sean had lived in town for two years. They had moved here from Chestnut Hill. The commute to Boston was longer, but the ocean views and easy summer yachting had wooed many a city dweller. Grace was not a New England native. The obituary said she was from Chicago and an alumna of Sarah Lawrence near New York City. Her parents were dead and, besides Sean, her only surviving relative was her sister, one Elise Sanderson of Lake Forest, Illinois. I wished I'd had a chance to meet Elise yesterday at the funeral, but I couldn't think which one she might have been. She wasn't in the pew with Sean and our abrupt departure had taken my opportunity away.

When I was five, our across the street neighbors were the Pritz family. They had a wonderful daughter Brenda who was ten years older than me, and an excellent babysitter. Mr. and Mrs. Pritz had grown up in Germany and had secretly worked against the Nazis. Brenda had been born in Germany and they moved to America immediately after the war. The Pritzes were perfect neighbors. Their kitchen door was always open to me, and Mrs. Pritz baked the most delicious cakes, cookies, and pastries I have ever eaten. There was a framed, needlepoint, German saying on their kitchen wall. I asked Mrs. Pritz what it was and she said her mother had made it for her family's bakery when Mrs. Pritz was a child. It translated to "We guarantee that everything contains pure butter."

Mr. Pritz was a talented gardener and their lawn was the greenest in town. He loved all children, especially Brenda. He used to rub our ears. It was odd, but comforting. One day Mr. Pritz went to his office in New York City, hung up his topcoat, and after wishing his secretary "good morning," he leaped out the thirtieth floor window. He didn't leave a note. All night I had found myself thinking about Mr. Pritz. Perhaps there was something in Grace's background that none of us knew, which would explain a suicide. I needed to talk to Elise.

Stephen arrived, bringing my newspaper inside with him.

"I'm screwed," he said handing it to me.

We had a very conscientious delivery person, who folded and placed the Globe inside a plastic bag, no matter the weather. I removed it and read the headline. "MAGNOLIA WOMAN STABBED IN THE BACK BEFORE BEING THROWN OFF CLIFF."

"Well, forensics took their time to figure that out," I said scanning the article.

"Gilbert Hospital isn't the biggest in the world. The body didn't arrive until late in the day Thursday, and I guess there were bodies ahead of Grace's. First come, first served, so to speak. No one performs autopsies over the weekend there. Keep reading. After yesterday's autopsy, Detective Miller searched the cliff and he found the murder weapon about twenty feet from the body in a crevice. It might have been thrown from the balcony, or the impact of the body landing dislodged the knife and it skittered further down the cliff."

"I don't suppose there were any fingerprints on the weapon."

"No such luck. They found blood on the railing and the rocks directly beneath the deck, though."

"Poor Grace. She must have run away from her assailant and onto the deck, but the murderer caught her at the rail and stabbed her. If he, or she," I shuddered to think, "were wearing gloves, this gruesome episode was premeditated. The killer was lying in wait. Grisly and sickening."

We were quiet, lost in our own bloody thoughts. I spoke first.

"Stephen, are you sure you didn't notice anything unusual when you entered the house? Did you pass anyone on the Rogers' road? According to the phone log, very little time elapsed between the conversation with the travel agent, the murder, and your arrival. The murderer was lucky, or this whole thing was carefully planned."

"I'm sure I didn't pass anyone on the road. Salt Hill is so narrow and winding that it's hard for cars to pass one another without someone pulling into a driveway. Every week I expect my car to be hit by one of those seventy thousand dollar rocket ships driven by Salt Hill's elite. Most of them seem to have been born with a silver right of way in their mouth. 'Yield' is not part of the life style.

"I'm sure there was nothing unusual in the house, either. It wasn't the first time that Grace was out and I was there by myself, but as a rule, Grace is home. The sliding door to the deck was locked. The killer took time to do that, I guess. I've been going over and over events in my mind, and the only thing out of the ordinary was the time of day that I arrived. The Hotchkisses are away for the month of February. Usually I clean them first, and go to the Rogers' later in the day, but I won't clean the Hotchkisses again until the last week of February. I was four hours earlier than usual at the Rogers'."

"Well, I'm glad you weren't four hours and fifteen minutes earlier than usual. You might have seen the murderer and there would have been two funerals yesterday, instead of one."

"Jesus, I hadn't thought of that."

I poured coffee for the two of us. Stephen was visibly shaken, a condition I hadn't seen him in since he was a boy. He leaned his elbows on the table and held his head in his hands.

"I've jotted down a list of things we need to do," I said sliding a copy of the list to Stephen. "Feel free to add to it."

"Find a lawyer," Stephen read out loud. "That's discouraging. Do you think I really need one?'

"Yes, I think you really need one. Greg had a great corporate attorney. Do you want me to ask who he would recommend?"

"That would be nice," Stephen answered without conviction. "Talk with Elise Sanderson," he continued down the list. "Grace's sister, yes?"

"Right. I didn't see anyone who might have been her yesterday, did you?"

"No, come to think of it, I didn't."

"I'll take that one, if you want me to. Sean may have prejudiced her against you already."

"Swell. Two for you. Find out if Christine Parker 'has a cat,'" Stephen continued. "Very subtle, Laura. I can do that. There was a message on our answering machine from the good preacher when I got home yesterday, imploring me 'to lean on him in my hour of need.' That man is sanctimonious. I'll return his call and set up an appointment. Christine speaks very highly of his ministries. I might enjoy myself."

"You just do that, my friend. You'll also have to tackle the next item and convince the police to look into Sean's alleged underworld connections. I have no idea how to do that, do you?"

"Heavens no, but maybe that hotshot lawyer you plan to find me can help, as well as this last item on your list."

"Ah, yes, the will. Is there money and who stood to gain?"

Stephen looked at his watch, gulped of his coffee and stood up.

"I can't stay any longer, Laura. I'm due at Genevieve Conlon's condo. Then I teach two aerobic classes, spinning and step. The paycheck must go on. I'll be home by 6:00, if you would care to join Donald and me for a glass of wine. I told Donald I'd be inviting you and he'd like to hear your views of this mess. The situation isn't easy on him, either."

"It's a date. Who knows, we might learn something between now and then."

Chapter Three

Stephen hated cleaning Genevieve's condominium. It was in a recently renovated and over-priced complex on the beach. The little colony had originally been occupied by an abundance of household servants at the beginning of the 1900's. Magnolia was part of Gloucester in the eighteenth and nineteenth centuries, but as the newly rich, fair weather aristocracy flocked to the breathtaking village, they chose to distance themselves from the bustling city and its immigrant fishermen. They craved a more prestigious summer address, so the village of Magnolia was established, named after the pungent and abundant Magnolia trees that flourished on its shores. The aristocracy even succeeded in attracting President Taft's summer White House, which encouraged even more lavish entertaining.

Weddings were especially popular, and of course, the additional staff needed housing, so a co-operative arrangement was struck among the village's summertime millionaires. As a result, a series of beachside bungalows was built. Unfortunately, these men were captains of industry, and not seafaring captains, or they would have known to build this housing further back on the beach. These homes flood most years, when the inevitable New England hurricane or blizzard strikes, and the normal twelve-foot tide can become a twenty-foot tide.

The location of Genevieve's home didn't bother Stephen. Genevieve bothered Stephen. She was a hard body, gym groupie. Jack Kerouac would have called her a "whore-bitch-destroyer." Genevieve had been divorced twice, with generous settlements. Stephen had met her last husband and he was a stand-up guy, but

Genevieve was demanding, in every way, and she simply wore men down. Her most recent husband was desperate for a divorce and finally agreed to give his wife of only four years fifty percent of his income. The poor sap was so grateful to be free that he referred to the settlement as a bargain.

Genevieve Conlon walked a fine line between being a ditz and "crazy like a fox." Stephen had no doubt that she could be downright scary if she didn't get her way. The second week that Stephen worked for Genevieve, she opened the door to him naked, and only when he immediately turned around to leave did she act flustered or surprised.

"Oh! Stephen, I thought you were Brett, coming back for more. I hope I didn't embarrass you," she had explained, as Stephen walked toward his car. "Don't leave Stephen. I'll put on clothes, if you insist."

"I insist," Stephen had replied loudly, with his back to her.

The next week, Stephen surreptitiously observed Genevieve's condominium from the safety of his car and noticed a living room curtain slightly pulled back, as though someone were peaking out. When he arrived at the front door, he found it ajar, and Genevieve called out for him to "come on in." Stephen walked in and found her precariously balanced on the kitchen stool, replacing track lighting bulbs in the ceiling.

"Here, let me help you," Stephen had said, as she started wobbling. When he arrived at her side, Stephen realized, too late, that Genevieve was not wearing underwear beneath her mini-skirt. Quick as a striking snake, Genevieve had clutched him for balance, and Stephen found his face was buried in her crotch.

"Oh, silly me," Genevieve had cooed, "I would have probably broken an arm if you hadn't arrived."

Stephen doubted it, and he began phoning Genevieve before he showed up for work, to ask pointedly if it was a convenient time for him to CLEAN.

The following week, Genevieve had left a dildo prominently displayed on her pillow in the bedroom, but there were no other distractions. However, that was the week that he and Donald both had noticed a car, just like Genevieve's, driving slowly past their apartment several times during the night, and a series of hang-up phone calls had begun, too.

"The weirdest stuff is happening to me and my roommate, Genevieve. We think we're being stalked," Stephen had told Genevieve the next time he worked. He had used his best imitation of an empty-headed, wide-eyed gay man. "Donald is reporting it to the police as we speak. Have you ever heard of such a thing? I imagine they'll trace our phone calls and keep track of drive-bys."

That was all it took to discourage Genevieve, but Stephen still felt repulsed by the woman, and he was uneasy in her presence. On his drive to her home, Stephen decided to give Genevieve his notice.

When he arrived, Stephen rang twice before Genevieve opened the door. He was relieved to see that she was completely dressed, right down to her sneakers.

"Good morning, Mrs. Conlon."

"Hello, Stephen. What's new?"

Stephen hesitated, remembering Laura's optimistic hope that they might know more by the cocktail hour. He wondered if a loose canon like Genevieve was crazy enough to kill Grace. Was it possible that somewhere in her warped persona, Genevieve was jealous of Grace? The thought was appallingly reasonable within the twisted confines of the woman Stephen knew. He wasn't convinced that Genevieve Conlon always operated in reality. Once he had accidentally vacuumed the cocaine she always left on a mirror beneath her bed and heaven knew she was strong enough to fling poor Grace off the balcony. This murder was making him paranoid.

"Poor Grace Rogers," Stephen began, in response to Genevieve's question. "Did you know her?"

"Barely. She struck me as entirely too dull for Sean. He may not know it yet, but better things are ahead for him. Mark my words. You clean for them too, don't you? What do you think?"

Stephen was taken aback; so much for not speaking ill of the dead.

"Well, yes I did, but I don't think Mr. Rogers is interested in my services any longer," Stephen said as he started dusting. "He wasn't exactly pleased to see me at Grace's wake yesterday."

"Really," Genevieve said, following Stephen into the next room. "Don't worry. Sean is just shooting the messenger. You found the body, right?"

"Well, yeah, I did."

"That must have been a rush. I bet Miss Prim and Proper was a real mess when you found her, wasn't she?"

Stephen didn't know how to answer. Genevieve was actually smiling as she imagined, or could she be recalling the dead victim. She knew Grace Rogers well enough to call her dull, prim and proper, while at the same time admiring Sean. None of this jibed with her original response of "barely" to Stephen's question; yet she wasn't at the funeral. Stephen wondered if Genevieve had been conspicuous by her absence. He also wondered how she knew that he cleaned for the Rogers, if she barely knew them. Stephen never discussed customers with other customers.

"I don't do funerals," Genevieve said, as if reading his mind. Stephen took a deep breath and decided to forge ahead.

"That's too bad. It was quite a production; Handel and Hayden, the Symphony Chamber ensemble, Bishop O'Malley, lots of over-dressed divorcees, men with shoulder holsters. Mr. Rogers looked like death himself. He pulled out all the stops, so to speak. I guess he really loved Grace."

"Oh, don't be so sure. I watched the crowd go in and out of church and none of those bimbos are Sean's type, believe me. I've talked to Sean since the murder. He doesn't sound grief-stricken to me."

"Oh, well I wouldn't know, of course. I'm glad you're helping him through it, though." Stephen was dumbstruck. Genevieve and this conversation were making him more than uneasy. It was definitely time to change the subject.

"There's something I need to tell you, Mrs. Conlon. I've decided to cut back on my house cleaning and concentrate on teaching aerobics. The gym is adding classes and they've asked me to give them more time, if I can."

"Oh, no! I really need you next week. My mother is visiting for her sixtieth birthday. I couldn't get out of it, and I'll go over the edge if I have to clean. It's bad enough she's staying three days. Give me a break."

"Anything for Mom," Stephen answered, but he was really thinking, "Just one more week. I can do that."

After Stephen had left for Genevieve's, I went to visit my father. He was in a nursing home a half an hour from Magnolia. Clark was almost ninety-four. My mother had died eighteen months earlier, but he hadn't noticed yet. At first, I would remind him, but it seemed to do no good. Eventually, I decided that being shocked several times a week by the news that your wife of nearly seventy years had died, was too mean, so we spoke as if Mom were having a nap, or grocery shopping.

"Hi, Pop," I said kissing him.

"Oh, hi Kiddo. What's new? Did you see your mother on the way in?"

"Just for a minute. She was headed out to do errands."

"Yes, I think she said she was going to the bank. How do you think she looks?"

"Maybe a little tired. What do you think?"

"I think she looks tired, too. Sometimes your mother does too much."

"You know Mom. So, how are you, Daddy? Are you keeping busy?"

"Yes, I start camp tomorrow. Did I tell you that Charlie Lemly is going to be my bunkmate again. He's the one who likes to catch snakes and knot them into empty socks. Remember last year when that blue racer got loose? That was a hell of a thing. Crazy Charlie," he said smiling.

I never knew exactly where on Memory Lane my father and I would land. I had visited him a few days earlier and he had been napping in his wing chair. I had pulled up a chair, put on his television and waited for him to wake up.

"Hi, Kiddo," he had said when he came to. "Have you been here long?"

"Just long enough to put on the mid-day news," I had answered. Clark then looked at the screen and seen footage of ex-President Clinton having a press conference on Park Avenue in New York City.

"I always wanted to be President," he had said. "But now I'm not so sure."

After visiting my father, I spent the rest of the day doing paper work. Also, it was February and I was starting to organize for the dreaded income tax. Late winter afternoons were becoming increasingly depressing for me. It was finally sinking in that no one would be returning home with news, or simply to enjoy my cooking and conversation. It was lovely to have Stephen and Donald's invitation, so I treated myself to a bubble bath and gussied-up a bit.

Stephen and Donald's apartment was the third floor of a nineteenth century Federalist brick mansion in Salem. The home belonged to Arrietta Bertram Endicott, the elderly great-great grand-daughter of Captain Josiah Bertram, who had commissioned the construction of the home one hundred-fifty years earlier. Miss Endicott lived graciously on the first two floors. Most of the mansions bordering Salem Common had been commissioned by affluent ship owners and privateers, who had grown rich from the far-eastern China trade. The town of Salem was made famous by its witch trials, but it was made rich by the China trade. Miss Endicott lived surrounded by valuable, museum quality heirlooms. She had already donated most of her family's antiques to Salem's Peabody-Essex Museum, and the ones that she chose to live with would go to the museum upon her demise.

I never minded walking the two flights up to Stephen and Donald's nest. The stairway was circular and wide. The balustrades were gleaming mahogany, and the steps were carpeted with a luxurious, and I suspected, original Oriental runner. I went back in time whenever I ascended that stairway and touched its massive banister. The hall at the top of the stairs was expertly paneled, had fourteen foot ceilings and one solid, oversized mahogany door. The entrance to Stephen and Donald's apartment was fitted with well-polished antique brass hardware and a large knocker, cast as a pineapple, the symbol of welcome in the original colonies.

Stephen's partner Donald answered my knock promptly and he pecked me on the cheek. Stephen and Donald had known each other for five years and had chosen this apartment three years ago. Strangely enough, it was another death that had brought them together, the death of Donald's mother. Donald needed help cleaning his mother's house before placing it on the market. Stephen's listing in the Yellow Pages as a "thoroughly honest" cleaner was just what he needed.

Donald was almost a decade older than Stephen, which placed him halfway between the two of us. Flecks of gray had recently started appearing in his hair and the effect was a handsome contrast to his still youthful face. Donald had been made regional manager for Armani's a year ago. The job included wardrobe, but when he and Stephen were alone, he preferred flannel shirts and jeans. In contrast to Stephen's dark eyes and blond hair, Donald was blue-eyed with dark hair. He was just under six feet tall and slighter than Stephen. Over the years, I had found him to be kind, calm, and wise. Probably because both of these men were staggeringly handsome, neither one seemed impressed by it.

I was pleased to see and feel the crackling fire in their large Count Rumford hearth. Their home was cleverly furnished to reflect its inhabitants. It was eclectic and comfortable. Their artwork was mostly photographic in nature and very interesting. Donald had a green thumb and the room boasted three large flowering hibiscus; pink, yellow and orange, strikingly grouped in a corner. The floor was hardwood and covered with multi-colored area rugs. The tall windows had folding shutters, and swags above them. Without any sense of pretension, the room simply felt right.

A bottle of red and another of white wine were already uncorked on the butler's table. Next to them, a heavenly aromatic fondue was bubbling, and a basket of freshly cubed French bread was waiting. Donald helped me off with my coat and Stephen handed me a glass of Toasted Head Chardonnay, my favorite. I helped myself to the fondue before sitting down in the platform rocker, next to the fire. Donald and Stephen returned to their overstuffed burgundy and cream striped sofa.

"Stephen, this fondue is celestial," I said with my mouth full. "What's in it?"

"A bottle of Guinness, a pound and a half of Vermont's finest extra sharp cheddar, and a touch of garlic."

"Grain, dairy, vegetable, and carbs. Sounds like health food to me," I said refortifying.

"To Grace," Donald announced, raising his glass.

"To Grace," we responded.

I broke the ensuing silence by asking Donald what he knew about Grace. He had known her the longest; before the Rogers had even moved to Magnolia.

"I don't suppose I actually knew much about her. I knew she was rich, married, and living in Chestnut Hill when we met. I knew she had fabulous jewelry, expensive, but elegant taste, and that she wore a European size forty-two. I suspected she was lonely and somewhat isolated. She never shopped with a friend, and I thought her facial expression seemed a bit sad. I can't recall ever having a substantive conversation with her. Every now and then I would talk her into trying on something daring. You know, a plunging back, or a high slit leg. She looked great in clothes like that, too, but in the end she would never choose to buy. Grace would say something like 'I don't think this would please Sean. I better not.' Almost as if she were frightened, but I never noticed any bruises and I was in a position to. You know how the devoted, gay young salesman is welcomed in the dressing room."

"Well, actually I don't. I'll have to get out more," I responded smiling. "By the way, have you seen our list of things to do? Would you like to add to it?"

"Stephen told me, and I don't have anything to add, but I think I can help with some of it. Two boyfriends before Stephen, I used to date a rookie in the Boston Police Department." Stephen rolled his eyes in my direction. "Hal was still in the closet then. In those days, you had to be if you expected to be hired and then keep your job. It was way too much bullshit for me, but we ended up being friends. Hal's a lieutenant now, and I think he'd be willing to research a criminal record or two for us, or maybe he could shed some light on Sean's Mafia legal services."

"I'm ashamed to tell you that I completely forgot to call Greg's lawyer for a referral. I'm making another note right now and I'll call first thing in the morning," I said, taking my pad out of my purse.

"Well, I remembered to call Reverend Andrews and we have a counseling session tomorrow afternoon. I'll try to find out about Christine's scratches, and exactly how well he may have known Grace."

"Please be careful, Stephen. Somebody is already a killer and they don't have much to lose by doing it again," I added, sounding entirely too much like a mother.

"Fear not. I plan to flatter the information out of him. Besides, I hardly think Brunhilda Parker finds me a rival for her spiritual advisor's affections," Stephen said, refilling glasses.

I helped myself to more fondue.

"Now, how am I going to track down Grace's sister Elise Sanderson? Do you think it's possible she didn't come to the memorial service?" I wrote another entry in my little notebook.

"I don't know," Stephen answered, "but as far as I'm concerned the answer can wait for tomorrow. I for one am ready to change the subject."

Chapter Four

The next day I did find Elise Sanderson. No one was more surprised than I was. After calling my husband's corporate attorney, and receiving a referral for a criminal lawyer, I decided to drive to Gilbert Hospital. I had been conscientiously reading the newspapers, and there had been no further information regarding Grace Rogers' actual burial. Surely the body had been released after the autopsy. I had done a stint as a hospital volunteer several years ago. Gilbert was a small hospital, and my hope was to find a vaguely familiar face to tell me who had claimed the body.

On my way to the hospital, I stopped at Carlisle Real Estate. Before leaving the house, I had called the real estate office and asked for Dick Carlisle. He was out of the office until noon, but June was in, which was just what I wanted. I felt I could outwit June more easily if we were alone.

"Hi June. How are you?" I asked after being shown into her office.

"Just fine, Laura. What can I do to help you? Have you finally decided to sell your house?" True to form, June moved right to the dollar sign.

She was dressed expensively in a beige cashmere turtleneck and a patterned wool blend skirt, probably from Talbot's. Over her shoulder a Merino shawl was pinned dramatically. It was a look I could not have carried off, but it worked for June. She had on too much jewelry; large, gold and extremely modern. Her long artificial nails were impeccable and their color matched her extremely dark, raisin colored lipstick. We were about the same age and I did not begrudge her the time and money she spent on facials, manicures, undoubtedly pedicures, Botox injections, and probably Colligen, if it was still legal. My only suggestion was that she should lighten up on the coal black color of her dyed hair. The effect was a little bit like Elvira gone bad.

"Well, maybe," I answered cautiously. "I'm toying with the idea of building on that lot Greg and I had been planning to build on. I have no idea what our home is worth. I guess I need information."

"That's what I'm here for Laura. Let me pull a few comparables for you to consider and that will give us a starting point. It's about time you moved. Who needs all those memories?"

I was not sure how one answered a question like that, but my silence went unnoticed by June.

While she worked her files, I said,

"Wasn't that a beautiful service for poor Grace? Imagine, Bishop O'Malley, and oh, that music! I had no idea Sean was so well-connected."

"He's a philanthropist. Sean has always generously supported the Archdiocese and the arts in Boston."

"I never knew, but I'm really just an acquaintance. Does he know where he's going to bury Grace? She was so young. I'm sure it's nothing they had planned for."

"Sean said Grace's sister is arranging the burial."

"I'm sorry that I didn't meet her at the wake."

"Oh, she wasn't there. Here we are. See if any of these look interesting to you," June said passing me six listings.

"I'll have to read them at home. I'm a little pushed for time this morning, but I'll be in touch, June. Thanks for your help." I escaped before she could say anything.

"I'll call next week. We'll set up an appointment," June called after me.

"Swell," I muttered under my breath.

My next stop was Gilbert Hospital. On my drive there, I wondered if June's knowledge of the burial arrangements and Elise's absence were suspicious. I had no idea she was so chummy with Sean, or maybe June simply had access to more gossip than I did. I parked my car near the hospital's basement entrance. It was convenient to the volunteer office, as well as the morgue. I walked past the volunteer office toward the far end of the corridor. Visitors had to be buzzed into the morgue. In order to be granted entrance, you first had to speak through a glass window in the corridor and convince a clerk of your worthiness. Luckily, I was spared the indignity of my premeditated white lie because seated on a bench next to the window, filling out forms on a clip board, was a woman who looked enough like Grace Rogers to be her sister.

"Elise?" I began.

"Yes," the woman answered, looking up at me.

"I'm Laura English. Your sister and I were friends." This was stretching the truth, but I was on a mission.

"How did you know where to find me?"

"I didn't. I just took a chance. I wanted to meet you at the funeral, but ahhh, suffice it to say, I left sooner than planned. I'm not exactly on your brother-in-law's dance card, but I very much admired your sister, and I was hoping to be able to speak with you before you left town."

I seated myself next to Elise and looked at her. She was lovely. I guessed her to be a few years younger than Grace. Like her sister, Elise was stunning, but her style was more natural and less dramatic. Her auburn hair was shoulder length and she wore less make-up. She was above average height and slim. Her green eyes were both captivating and sad.

"Well, I'm glad to meet you, Laura. I'm feeling a little overwhelmed and I could use some advice, if I wouldn't be imposing."

"Not at all. Whatever I can do." I was struck by my luck of good timing.

"I wasn't at the funeral. I'm not exactly on Sean's A List, either, or maybe I should say he's not on mine." I thought I detected a tone of bitterness in Elise's voice and made a mental note to discover what that was all about. "Would you mind handing this to the keeper of the gate?"

I was closest to the window and Elise had finished her forms. I did as asked, and after checking the form for accuracy, the office worker said everything was in order and she would take care of the rest. This seemed to satisfy Elise.

"Can I take you to lunch?" I asked.

"Actually, could you recommend a hotel? I just flew in this morning and took a taxi right here. I haven't made any arrangements."

"You'll stay with me." I surprised myself with the announcement, but something in Elise's demeanor had touched me. Maybe it was her sorrow.

"Oh, no. That's too much trouble for you. I won't hear of it."

I looked down at her on the bench. "Elise, when there's been a tragedy, everyone wants to help, but there's rarely anything a person can really do. You would be doing me a favor by staying. My husband died last year and I would welcome your company."

"All right. Thank you." Elise paused and I thought she might be reconsidering, but instead she added, "That would be great. How bad can you be if Sean hates you?" Elise smiled a brief, but dazzling smile.

I waited for her to gather her things and stand up to walk with me to my car. That's when I noticed her suitcase in a large metal basket attached to the back of a wheel chair. I was used to seeing wheel chairs in hospital corridors and hadn't noticed that the one next to Elise seemed to be customized and held her suitcase. Elise pulled the chair next to her on the bench, set the brake, and expertly lifted herself up and into the chair.

"I wouldn't want to try that drunk," I said admiring her strength and grace.

"Practice makes perfect," Elise answered as I hurried to catch up with her.

*   *   *   *

While Elise was settling in, I called Stephen and Donald's apartment to leave a message inviting them to dinner. I told them that Elise Sanderson would be joining us. The guestroom in our home had always been on the ground floor, so that overnight company would not have to compete with my kids for their upstairs bathroom. It was the room Stephen had always stayed in. Our home was built in the middle of a gently sloping, one-acre lot. There were eight front steps that led to a small portico at the front door, but the kitchen entrance was on the ground level. Elise had easily followed me inside. After she freshened up, Elise joined me in the kitchen. Our short drive from the hospital had been along the ocean road and all we had discussed were the views.

"Is grilled cheese and tomato all right?" I asked. Stephen and Donald had sent me home the night before with a hefty wedge of their wonderful Vermont cheddar, left over from the fondue. Magnolia boasted a small bakery that specialized in bread. Iggy, the proprietor, usually sold out by noon. I had purchased a warm loaf of my favorite Anadama on my way to see June Carlisle, and the aroma had been driving me crazy all morning. I gently squeezed the Bartlett Farm greenhouse tomatoes, that I had been babying along on my kitchen windowsill. They were plump and perfectly ripe.

"Sounds great to me," Elise answered. "Wow. Where did you find those tomatoes? I haven't eaten one that couldn't pass for a baseball since last October."

"It's from a family farm in the area. They grow a few greenhouses full of hydroponics in the off-season and I indulge myself."

We sat at the kitchen table enjoying our lunch. I had a million questions, but I didn't want to overwhelm my guest, and I was hesitant to reveal to Elise how little I actually knew her sister.

"Are you tired? The shock of it all, and your flight must have left at the crack of dawn."

"It hasn't really hit me yet, Laura. Grace and I were very close, but ever since her marriage, we only saw each other for two weeks a year; usually in Jamaica. This is my first visit to Magnolia. Of course, we talk, talked, I guess I mean, all the time." Elise's voice trailed off.

"You know, I don't think I ever asked your sister how long she'd been married."

"Nine years. Grace was living in New York after she graduated from Sarah Lawrence. Our parents were still paying her rent and she was working part-time as a Kelly Girl, temporary office work, and writing short stories, screenplays, and the odd poem in her spare time. Nothing Pulitzer Prize winning, but she kept trying. Sean was with a Madison Avenue law firm and they needed a temporary receptionist. You know how pretty Grace is, was. It didn't take Sean long to notice her. He was handsome, charming, intelligent. Grace was serious, refined and I imagine quite a contrast to what Sean was used to. She was also lonely and Sean's natural flamboyance swept her off her feet. She had no problem letting him be the center of attention. It was Grace's way, and they were married in a year."

I let Elise control the rest of the conversation. I didn't want to appear nosey. After lunch, Elise asked to use the phone. I told her there was one in her bedroom, if she wanted privacy.

"No need," she answered. "The police want to speak with me. I'm supposed to make an appointment with Detective Miller."

"Why don't you ask him to come here, Elise. It's starting to snow and you've done enough traveling for one day."

"Good idea. I might as well use this damn chair to my advantage."

Elise and Detective Miller made an appointment for three o'clock, giving Elise an hour and a half to nap. I hung up a few things for her and tidied the kitchen, before driving the half mile to Magnolia's fish market for dinner. I left another message suggesting Stephen and Donald telephone before appearing for dinner. It would hardly do to have the boys bump into Sherlock Miller.

*   *   *   *

I eavesdropped the best I could during Elliott Miller's questioning of Elise. At Elise's request, she was seated in a wing chair in my living room when the detective arrived. Her wheelchair was out of sight and my only role was to show him in, before retiring to the kitchen with my notebook. From time to time, I ran the water in the sink and created other sounds of dinner preparation. To give Elliott his due, he was trying very hard to make Elise squirm. Why had she taken so long to arrive in Magnolia? What was her relationship with her sister? Were they jealous of each other? Why was she staying with me? Did she have an alibi? The interview bordered on an interrogation and lasted two hours. When the door closed behind him, I reappeared and announced,

"The bar is open."

"You read my mind. I just hope I don't fall out of this chair before your friends arrive for dinner."

"So what did you think of our detective?" I asked fixing her a vodka, rocks with a splash of soda and two olives.

"Subtle, brilliant, dashing, great sense of humor, and above all, perceptive. He'll get a real kick out of it when he finds out I can't walk."

"Undoubtedly."

I like a person who drinks alcohol that doesn't leave a stain, but I would have liked Elise even if she went for red wine.

The phone rang and it was the boys saying they were on their way.

"You know, the police think my friend Stephen did it. I didn't tell you, but he's the one coming to dinner with his sweetheart Donald. I've known him for over twenty years and it's just not possible that he's guilty."

"Why do the police think he's guilty?"

"Oh, I don't know. Sean blurted out something at the wake about Grace catching Stephen stealing. He's her house cleaner. But that's ridiculous, and no one has claimed that anything is missing."

"I take it Stephen's gay." I nodded my head. "Well, that probably doesn't help his case any with the police. Stereotypes are dangerous. Take it from me. You just watch how Detective Miller acts when he finds out I can't walk. First, he'll be mad at me for making him look like a jerk. Then, if I play innocent, and convince him that I thought he knew, and get a little weepy while explaining how hard it is for me to talk about being a cripple, he'll probably end up hitting on me. Sort of the arrogant 'mercy fuck' mentality. On the other hand, I could simply say, 'what difference does it make?' He'll explain the physical impossibility of me being the murderer. I'll show him otherwise and maybe the detective will learn something about stereotypes."

"Do you have an alibi?"

"Hell, yes. That's why I'll use Plan B."

Elise finished her drink at the same time the doorbell chimed. Stephen and Donald entered, bearing both wine and a tossed salad, accompanied by a cruet of Stephen's homemade Balsamic Vinegrette. I did not have the patience to create a perfect salad, but Stephen did, and it was our tradition that he usually provided one for our shared dinners. He even sauteed his own croutons.

I made the introductions, asked Donald to be the bartender, and retired briefly to my kitchen where I boiled water, melted butter with lemon juice squeezed into it, and put a cookie sheet of my favorite Ore Ida Tator Tots in the oven. Because Elise and I had enjoyed the Anadama with lunch and I knew Stephen would make croutons, I thought family style Tator Tots, with ketchup, would be the perfect accompaniment to our dinner. For my palate, the Tator Tot is to steamed lobster, what the oyster cracker is to clam chowder.

When I returned to the living room everyone was fully engaged.

"I hate to interrupt you, but we'll eat in twenty minutes. I just put the lobsters in to steam. It's a week night. I figured we can eat early and skip hors d'oeuvres." My guests agreed.

"Elise was just telling us why she avoided the funeral," Donald offered.

"Well, Laura, I was saying that I hate Sean. He trapped me in the coat room at his own wedding. My legs worked then, and I had to knee him to get away. I chalked it up to booze, but the next time I saw him was after the accident that killed my parents, and injured me, and the pig tried it again while I was still in the hospital! I had to stick him with my I.V. needle. He is one sick puppy and I refuse to have anything to do with him, including Grace's church service. Grace is less than a year older than me, you know, Irish twins. When our parents died, Grace and I became even closer. We vowed to be buried as a family in Illinois; husbands would be welcomed to join us. Our parents' deaths caused us to talk a lot about burial. There were no other relatives to help us make the plans, and we weren't favorably disposed to the priest's suggestions. Grace and I stood up for our parents, and now I am standing up for Grace. The burial will be her ceremony and not that ostentatious abomination created by Sean."

I thought Elise might cry, but instead she said,

"Stephen, I know you didn't murder my sister. There's no doubt in my mind that Sean is the culprit. I don't know why yet, but I mean to find out."

"Works for me," Stephen agreed.

"And we promise not to hit on you," added Donald. After a short pause, he asked, "Do you mind telling us what did happen to your legs?"

"I don't mind. About eight months after Grace married Shithead," Elise was clearly enjoying her second glass of Toasted Head, "They were living in Chestnut Hill. Sean had left the group he was working for in New York and started his own firm in Boston. A few of the sleaziest clients were from Boston and they set him up in business. I was living in Chicago and working as a low-level marine biologist. The health of the Great Lakes is a big deal in Chicago. It was my mother's birthday and I had gone home to Lake Forest for the weekend. The three of us were on our way home from a great birthday dinner. We were driving down a steep hill, when a huge tractor trailer, filled with bags of cement, overtook us. The driver's brakes had completely failed and apparently his horn was blaring, but he was traveling so fast that we just didn't hear him in time to get out of the way, and besides there was nowhere to go. The hill had traffic coming in the opposite direction and cars parked on both sides of the street. Our car was flattened like an empty beer can, killing my parents and breaking my back. Grace came to Illinois and stayed with me until I could travel to Chestnut Hill. I lived with the two of them for six months, but Sean was unbearable. I never told my sister, but I made sure Sean and I were never alone. Strangely enough, Sean provided me with the desire to regain independence and return to my own life in Chicago. He even sued the trucking company and I was awarded a generous settlement, more than I can ever spend. I insisted he take a hefty commission. I had no intention of being in his debt. Grace and I used to joke that we were lucky the trucking company wasn't owned by one of Sean's clients. Anyhow, I went back to my marine biology. I supervise my own division now, and with the help of a customized van and a specially adapted all-terrain vehicle, I can also supervise most site work. Things could be worse."

Before we could ask another question, the timer on my stove buzzed.

"Go on into the kitchen. It's so much easier to eat lobster near a sink," I said.

Over dinner, we brought Elise up to date on our progress, or lack thereof. One of the benefits of a lobster dinner is that it brings the diners together, more than any other meal I can think of. Inevitably, someone at the table is less experienced with claw cracking, or how to find the sweetest morsel of meat behind the lobster's eyes, and everyone else helps. In my experience, lobster is a most delicious and social meal. I laughed as Donald and Stephen demonstrated the fine art of sucking the delectable meat out of the lobster's legs to Elise.

"Stephen, besides preparing this delicious meal," I teased wiping the lemon butter from my chin, "I also spoke with Greg's attorney and he called me back with the name and number of a criminal lawyer that he unconditionally recommends. His name is Alec McBride and he's expecting your call tomorrow. Greg's attorney assured me of Mr. McBride's competence and enthusiasm."

"Oh, nifty. I do so appreciate a good attitude."

I ignored Stephen's remark and continued,

"I also dropped by to visit June Carlisle and she definitely knows more about Sean Rogers' private life than one would expect."

"Speaking of which, I left a message with the Boston Police Department for Hal to call me, but no word yet," Donald offered.

"Well, I saw my least favorite customer, Genevieve Conlon, Magnolia's most formidable nymphomaniac," Stephen added for Elise's edification, "And found out she's way too fond of Sean Rogers. I also finally gave her my notice, taught two aerobics classes, and ended up canceling my 'counseling' session with Reverend Andrews to do an emergency clean-up for dear Mrs. Hood, my absolute most adorable customer, instead. She had left me a message saying her furnace had suffered an unfortunate blowjob! I think she meant 'blowback.' Soot was everywhere and Lila, her Bassett Hound, was having trouble breathing. She and Lila were going next door for refuge, and it would mean the world to her if I could control the mess before Mr. Hood returned from Boston on the 5:30 train. If I could choose a grandmother, it would be Mrs. Hood."

"If I could count on reincarnation, I would hope to be Mrs. Hood's dog," Donald added.

Our fun was interrupted by the front door chime. I opened the door to find Detective Elliott Miller.

"Do you know the whereabouts of Stephen Macomber?" He asked me brusquely.

Before I could respond, Stephen emerged from the kitchen.

"You better come with me, Mr. Macomber. Margaretta Hood has been found stabbed to death in her rocking chair. I understand you were there late this afternoon, near the time of death."

I decided it was a good time to put Alec McBride's enthusiasm to the test.

Chapter Five

To Alec McBride's credit, he arrived in Magnolia less than an hour after his answering service had paged him. Donald, Elise and I waited in the depressing police department lobby. The sergeant on duty could easily overhear our conversation, so we were keeping quiet. Apparently, Stephen had left a note for Margaretta Hood on her kitchen counter, just before he left the house. It read:

"5:25

Dear Mrs. H.,

I think you and Lila can breathe easy now. Call if you need anything else. We're at Laura English's for dinner. Otherwise, I'll see you Friday.

Kisses to you and Lila,

S."

As usual, Mr. Hood was indeed on the 5:30 train. He had arrived home before quarter of six, and heard Lila baying. Mr. Hood quickly found the distraught dog seated at her dead mistress' feet. He had immediately telephoned for an ambulance, but it was too late.

Eventually the sergeant on duty left his post, presumably for coffee or a bathroom break. When we heard the unmistakable sound of a flushing toilet, and still he did not return, Donald spoke up.

"He's probably on a cot somewhere dreaming of being alone with Stephen."

"Attitude, attitude, Donald," I chided. "Stephen needs positive thoughts."

"You're right, but this is such a buzz kill. Poor Margaretta Hood. Poor Mr. Hood, and poor, poor Lila."

"I think you've just hit on something," Elise interjected. "Lila is a witness to the crime. Sounds like that dog is devoted to her mistress, and she's bred to track."

Something in her tone inspired Donald to ask,

"Tell me about your dog."

"Well, when I returned to Chicago after the accident, I applied for a Handicap Dog and eventually I was given a two-year old sleek Black Lab. Because she was beautiful, brilliant, and fearless, I named her Emma Peel from the Avengers, the sixties British spy series. Emma was trained to fetch items dropped on the floor and otherwise out of my reach, and she protected me. She was even trained to push an emergency transmitter if I fell, became unconscious, or simply gave her the command. But her devotion gave me the courage to live alone. That dog licked my tears when I cried. If we can only figure out some way to let Lila help us, I know she will. We won't be able to stop her."

"I doubt Mr. Hood," Donald paused. "What is his first name by the way, Laura?"

"S. Duffield Hood. People call him Duffy."

"Well, I doubt Duffy will exactly hand the dog over."

"You leave that to me," Elise answered coyly.

Our good thoughts were interrupted by the appearance of Alec McBride. He had used the side entrance and gone immediately to the interview room, without wasting time on us.

"You must be Donald Sebastian," Alec said shaking Donald's hand. "I'm Alec McBride."

I liked that Alec introduced himself to Donald first.

"Pleased to meet you," Donald said shaking his hand. "This is Laura English and Elise Sanderson."

We shook his hand one at a time. His grasp and demeanor were somehow reassuring. Alec McBride was not what I had expected. He was at least six foot five inches tall, big boned and gaunt. His eyes were deep set and so dark they appeared to be black. Alec's eyebrows were shaggy and dark brown, but his thick head of hair was flecked with gray. The overall impression would have been fearsome, if not for the kindness of the laugh lines around his mouth and eyes. He reminded me of a young, clean-shaven Abe Lincoln, a reassuring look for a lawyer. I guessed he was in his early forties. Alec was dressed similarly to Donald, in jeans and a flannel shirt, and I noticed he wore no wedding band.

"Stephen's okay for now. He has to stay the night and be arraigned first thing in the morning. They won't let you see him, but hopefully he'll be out on bail tomorrow. It would be helpful to me if we could all go somewhere and talk. I have a bunch of questions."

"My house is closest," I said thinking of the lobster mess we had left.

Alec followed us home and we used the kitchen door.

"People who know how to live," Alec said when he saw the state of my kitchen.

"Are you hungry?" I asked. "I could make you a lobster, scallion omelet, with Anadama toast, and we still have some of Stephen's salad, but it's a little tired."

"Nirvana. I'll get rid of these lobster shells, while you cook."

Donald made coffee, and Elise put dishes in the washer. We were cleaned up and sitting in front of the rekindled fire in short order.

"These murders were carefully engineered to implicate Stephen. If we can figure out why, maybe we'll know who. All the evidence is circumstantial, so either the killer is a maniac, who implicates Stephen totally by chance, highly unlikely, or this murderer is meticulous, highly motivated, with an extremely personal reason to punish Stephen. In both murders, he has been left without an alibi, making the case for coincidence all the more incredible. I need each of you to focus on the following questions from your personal knowledge.

Do you know of any relationship between the Rogers and the Hoods? Do you know of any relationship, other than professional, between Stephen and Grace, or Stephen and Mrs. Hood?

Except for the occasional maniac and mercy killers, fear, money, hate, rage and jealousy are the only motives I can think of for premeditated murder. It's also my experience that the police often suffer from tunnel vision. Once they get an idea in their heads, they find a way to make clues compatible with their theory. We need to keep open minds. Let the facts lead us to the conclusion and not vice-versa. Excuse me for stating the obvious, but we're dealing with a dangerous sociopath. I don't want us forgetting that. Be suspicious. Take nothing for granted."

We stared at the fire, lost in our own thoughts. My guess was we were all feeling a little sheepish about trying to convict Sean Rogers. Donald spoke first.

"There are plenty of people who think being gay is a crime against God, and reason enough to be persecuted. I suppose being a homosexual could put a person on a homophobe's hate list. Laura, have you ever heard what beliefs the good Reverend holds towards we who lay down with men? Other than that, I can't think of a soul who would want to frame Stephen, unless there's a psycho in one of his aerobic classes that he has unwittingly spurned. Stephen is completely naïve regarding the effect he has on both gay men and straight women, who are ignorant of his sexual persuasion. Then there are heterosexual women who believe they can 'fix' gay men. Remember when that over-sexed Conlon woman sort of stalked him?"

"Really? Let's keep an eye on her," Alec suggested.

"I've never met the Hoods, or heard my sister speak of them. What does Mr. Hood do for a living? Could he know Sean? I hate giving my bastard brother-in-law up as a suspect."

If Alec were surprised by this, he didn't show it. Maybe Sean's reputation preceded him in the halls of justice.

"I'd bet money that the Hoods and the Rogers have never met. Your sister and Sean were new to town and their socializing centered around Boston. The Hoods both grew up in Magnolia. Stephen told me that they were high school sweethearts. He loved Margaretta like a grandmother, and judging from the home-baked goodies she sent home with him on cleaning day, Margaretta felt the same. She knit him a sweater every Christmas, you know. All kinds, cardigan, crew neck, v-neck, boat-neck," Donald smiled, but his eyes were filled with tears. "Great colors. Perfect for Stephen. Damn, I hate that he's alone tonight."

Nobody quite knew what to say, but I careened into the silence, undaunted.

"Duffy works at the New England Aquarium. He used to be in charge of the penguins. I remember Margaretta telling me that he designed their habitat years ago and was responsible for acquiring all the different species. Except for the smell, it's a magnificent exhibit. You should see it, if you haven't. Anyhow, Margaretta was very proud of his work. She used to say Lila and the penguins were their children. When Duffy retired a few years ago, the Aquarium begged him to stay on part-time to train the college interns who maintain the integrity of the tidal pool and feed the penguins. Anyhow, I can't imagine that Duffy and Sean have any reason to know each other. But, to change the subject, I still think we should find out why the Carlisles', our local realtors," I added for Alec's benefit, "seem to know Sean so well."

"I'll nose around," said Alec. "The more leg work we can do for ourselves, the cheaper it will be and in a small town like this, an outside investigator would stick out like the mole on Cindy Crawford's lip. I take it we'll all be at the arraignment?"

We nodded.

"I expect to get Stephen released on bail, but probably not on his own recognizance. Laura, will you volunteer to have Stephen in your custody?"

"You bet."

"And will you also let me spend the night here. Court's at nine. It will save me two hours in the car. I usually travel with a change of clothes."

This amused me and confirmed that Mr. McBride was indeed a bachelor.

"Fine," I answered, yawning. "Top of the stairs, next to the bathroom. My son's old room. I'll see you in the morning."

"I'm leaving," Donald announced. "Good night Laura. Good night Elise. I'm glad you're here Alec. Better days must be ahead."

We embraced and Donald left, but not before Alec cautioned him to keep his wits about him.

I left Alec and Elise by the fire. Before turning in, I placed one of Greg's bathrobes on my son's bed, in case Alec needed it. I felt oddly strange, almost guilty, about loaning Greg's robe to another man.

Chapter Six

The next morning, Stephen was released into my custody. Donald posted the bond and Alec returned to his office, saying he had writs to file.

Elise and I drove in my car, while Stephen left with Donald. After his night in jail, Stephen was anxious to shower and change clothes. Stephen and I frequently teased Donald about his opulent vehicle, the Ferrari, but just like his elegant wardrobe, it was a business perk. Armani wanted the regional managers to present a certain image.

The two men drove in silence until they were calm enough to talk.

"Life is sure full of surprises. Just last week, I was sure I'd go to my grave without ever having the opportunity to post a bond," Donald joked, trying to lighten the moment.

"No need to thank me. I've been put on this earth to expand your horizons, Donald."

They were quiet again.

"So, is jailhouse sex all that it's cracked up to be? Excuse the pun."

"Just the big Swede. The others were nothing special."

Elise and I followed in my black Pathfinder. My car was almost three years old, and I had barely managed seventeen thousand miles. It always starts, and it's good in weather. Unlike the Ferrari, it does not bottom out in pot holes, I can afford the insurance, it has room for my "stuff," and most importantly, it can be driven with one arm, in case the driver needs to hold her ice cream cone with the other.

"So, what do you think of Alec McBride?" I asked Elise.

"I like him. He seems to be a clear thinker and down to earth. He pitched right in with those lobster shells, and he's a good listener. I bet he made your son's bed before he left this morning. He's no prima donna, like another lawyer I could name."

"You're right about the bed. I don't know how he fit in it to sleep, though, but no complaints. Did you two stay up late?"

"Another hour. He asked about Grace, and then my wheel chair. He told me that his father had been killed in a fluke accident, like my parents. His dad was a structural engineer and had been called to San Francisco after their last big quake. Part of the building he was inspecting collapsed onto him; another pointless tragedy."

"You've been through so much, Elise. It's too cruel."

"I've had nine years to come to terms with my parents' deaths. Emma, my dear sweet dog Emma, died from old age last month, though, and it's really thrown me. I don't dare let myself think about Grace yet. I called the mortician yesterday afternoon and her ashes are ready. I just can't face collecting them." Elise started to cry.

"I've been wondering when you were going to do that," I said, pulling off the road and putting my arm around her.

"God damn it! It's all so unfair. We were looking forward to Jamaica. Grace was especially excited. She said there were a thousand things she couldn't wait to tell me. I thought maybe she was pregnant, but Grace denied it. She said I'd just have to wait until we saw each other. I do know that Sean often recorded phone calls; not so much to check up on Grace, but mostly to do with his sleazy clients, and Grace hesitated to speak too freely over the phone." Elise produced a packet of Kleenex from her purse and blew her nose. She seemed to be under control again.

"Don't stop on my account."

"No, I'm finished for now. I'd rather concentrate on helping Stephen than wallowing. There's plenty of time for that when this is over."

We drove in silence to Salem. Donald and Stephen were out front waiting for us, but before we got out of the car I said,

"The ashes will wait for you, but whenever you're ready to collect them, next week or next year, we can go together. I never could have collected Greg's if my children weren't with me. You don't have to take me, but promise not to go alone. It would just be unnecessary bravery. Save it for when there's no choice."

Elise gently patted my knee.

"You've got a deal," she said quietly.

She just had time to blow her nose again before Stephen opened the car door, effortlessly lifting her out of the passenger seat and whisking Elise up the two flights of stairs to the apartment.

"Do you think I should be worried?" Donald asked, offering me his arm. I didn't bother to answer.

While Stephen showered, the rest of us planned the afternoon. Elise and I decided to pay our respects to Duffy Hood. Stephen and Donald were going to reschedule with Reverend Andrews, and check with the health club's manager to see if any of the members had been a bit too curious about Stephen.

Elise and I drove through McDonald's in Salem on our way back to Magnolia. I thought we had earned some comfort food. We parked overlooking the Atlantic Ocean while we ate, nodding our heads in unison to my favorite Four Tops' tape, and singing along with our mouths full.

There were no other cars on the street, so I parked directly in front of the Hood's home. Word of Margaretta's death had not spread, but with the midday television news and the evening papers, that would change. The house was a well maintained, butter colored bungalow, with a friendly front porch and wisteria growing across the overhanging roof and down the stanchions. Margaretta and Duffy had logged a lot of hours in their rocking chairs on that porch. Elise's folding wheel chair was in the back of my car. I retrieved it and we proceeded to the house. The living room was next to the front door and we could see Duffy through the lace curtains. He was slowly swaying in the middle of the room. His eyes were closed and he was holding a short tumbler of whiskey in his right hand. Lila was seated at the foot of her dead mistress' favorite chair; probably where Margaretta had been killed. The dog's chin was resting on the chair's seat. Elise and I could faintly hear music coming from an old hi-fi in the room's corner. We waited for the song to end.

"Whenever I want you in my arms,

Whenever I need you and all your charms,

Whenever I want you, all I have to do is dreeeeam, dream, dream, dream, dreeeeammmm."

Thanks to the Everley Brothers, Duffy and his sweetheart were still dancing cheek to cheek. When the music ended, Lila emitted a half-hearted howl, without even picking up her head. Elise and I looked at each other and would have tried to sneak away if we thought no one would notice. Instead, we gently knocked on the door, and eventually Duffy opened it. He was still holding his whiskey.

"Hi Duffy. How are you doing?" I said embracing him. Duffy and I had known each other for fifteen years, ever since we had co-chaired a town committee to prohibit water skiing (and eventually jet skiing) from Coolidge Cove. It was a very popular spot for harbor seals to breed, and with the ever-increasing popularity of these vessels, an increasing number of injuries were being inflicted on both seals and humans.

"I'm so sad about Margaretta," I heard his tumbler drop onto the front porch behind me, but it didn't break. Elise bent down to retrieve it.

"Sorry," Duffy mumbled.

"No harm done," Elise replied softly.

"Duffy, this is my friend Elise Sanderson. You two have tragedy in common. Elise's sister, Grace Rogers, died here last week." I chose to avoid using the M word.

"Come on in. I'm glad you're here." Duffy's downeast twang was still detectable through a slight alcohol slur. He was country handsome; about six feet tall with broad shoulders and good posture. He looked substantial, but not over fed. His usually twinkling blue eyes were red, but his hands were comfortably warm when he held mine. Duffy was shoeless, and he was wearing light brown, cotton socks. I noticed the right big toe had been neatly darned, undoubtedly Margaretta's loving handiwork. His khaki pants were pressed and he wore a braided brown leather belt with them. Duffy's red plaid flannel shirt had faded to pink and he wore it like an old friend. His full head of slightly curly, beautiful white hair had never been introduced to Brylcream. I wondered if Margaretta had been his barber.

Duffy led the way inside. Lila remained with her eyes closed and her chin resting on Margaretta's chair. Elise rolled herself next to Lila and gently began stroking the dog's head, massaging behind Lila's ears and the furrows above her woeful eyes.

Duffy replenished his drink; two fingers of Wild Turkey, neat.

"Would you ladies care for any?"

"That would be lovely," I replied, "but on the rocks."

"Ditto," answered Elise.

I was glad we had devoured Big Macs and fries for lunch.

"To Margaretta."

"To Margaretta," Elise and I replied in unison.

The hi-fi changed albums, from the Everley Brothers and the overture to the original version of "My Fair Lady" began.

"That was the only Broadway show Maggy and I ever saw. We weren't exactly what you'd call 'city people,' but it was our fifth anniversary and Maggy had sent for tickets way ahead. We took the train from South Station to Pennsylvania Station in New York, and stayed at the Plaza. It was the most money we had ever spent, and it was worth every penny. I guess we looked like a couple of country mice, but we didn't care." Duffy smiled as Julie Andrews sang "Wouldn't It Be Loverly."

"That was forty-five years ago. It doesn't seem possible. This whole thing doesn't seem possible. Why would anybody want to hurt my precious Maggy? One thing I know for sure, Stephen Macomber didn't do it. God, those police can be thick as the make-up on a harlot. More than once I caught Maggy and Stephen having a glass of Sherry and singin' show tunes, after Stephen was finished cleanin'. Probably while he was cleanin' too." I had to smile at that. "I'd always make a joke about how they were carryin' on behind my back."

We were quiet again.

"The police think Stephen killed my sister, too, but I know he didn't. I think these murders are more about Stephen than the victims. Did you know my sister or her husband Sean?"

"No. I never even heard of them until your sister died. I feel like I'm watchin' a movie. Last night was the first time I slept alone in almost fifty years and it's not somethin' I'm goin' to get used to in a hurry."

Duffy looked so sad that I began crying, which prompted Elise to start, and finally Duffy joined us. Lila left her mistress' chair and jumped on the sofa next to him.

"She's gone, Lila. It's not gonna be any fun around here for a long long time."

We were silent, until I noticed Duffy had thankfully dozed off on the sofa with Lila on his lap.

"Well, he's not sleeping alone," Elise noted.

I took our tumblers to the kitchen and returned with a large glass of water and another filled with ginger ale. I placed them on the end table next to Duffy, with the bottle of aspirin I carry in my purse. I went into the Hood's bedroom and returned with a pillow embroidered with daisies, more of Margaretta's handiwork, and a blanket which I placed next to Lila. After making sure the dog had food and water in her bowls on the kitchen floor, we placed a short note under the aspirin bottle and let ourselves out. Rex Harrison's voice followed us to the car.

"I've grown accustomed to her face, the way she makes my day begin.

Her smiles, her frowns, her ups, her downs are second nature to me now,

Like breathing out and breathing in…"

"I'm sure glad we could stop by and cheer him up," I said morosely to Elise as we drove away.

Chapter Seven

Stephen almost decided not to reschedule with Reverend Andrews. He could manage to believe that Christine Parker might kill Grace, in a jealous rage, if the Reverend seemed enamored with her, but it was nearly impossible to conjure any scenario that would link Christine and the Reverend to Margaretta Hood.

"I'm on for ten tomorrow morning," Stephen told Donald on their way to the gym. "I swear I heard Reverend Andrews' hands rubbing together in glee when I told him there had been another death. He seemed happier than Bill Clinton asking Monica if she'd like to know more about cigars."

"Maybe it wasn't his hands that were rubbing together. One thing I do know. Somebody is really pissed off at you, Stephen. What was the Reverend's reaction when you told him about Mrs. Hood?"

"He said, 'Poor, dear Margaretta. Who would ever want to hurt her?'"

"Were the Hoods members of his parish before the good Reverend resigned? Could Margaretta have included any of William Andrews' causes, and I use the word loosely, in her will?"

"Well, I suppose it's possible. But for all we really know right now, the murderer could be one of your vindictive sales reps, pining away for his handsome boss. Maybe with me out of the way, he figures his chances to capture you, and advance his career to boot, are improved."

"Very clever, Stephen. I wonder which one it is? Tonio? Maybe...Lance? Could be...No. No. It's Aristotle. I'm sure of it. That Ari is such a rake! Not to mention his incredible ability to accessorize."

"I'll be sure to tell Detective Miller, the next time we chat."

They parked near the employees' entrance to Stephen's gym, The Work Ethic. The gym had been in business for seven years and was on the south side of Salem. The manager's office was the first door on the right.

"Hi Phoebe. Is the boss in?"

"Sure Stephen. His door's open. Hey, I'm sorry about your friend."

"Thanks." Phoebe was referring to Grace, but Stephen couldn't help wondering what his co-workers and students would think when they heard about Margaretta Hood.

Stephen and Donald tapped on the manager's open door. He looked up from his paperwork and motioned them in.

"How are you doing, Stephen? Sit down. Sit down."

If Chuck Tomley were a contestant on the old "What's My Line," Arlene Francis would have guessed his profession immediately. He looked like a physical fitness guru from his flattop down to his muscled calves.

"You remember my roommate, Donald Sebastion?" The two men shook hands. Stephen had never brought his personal life to work with him, but over the years his boss had guessed that Stephen was gay.

"Good to see you Donald. Jesus, this is a hell of a thing. What can I do to help?"

Chuck was a no-nonsense guy. He worked hard and did not waste time. He left the chit-chat and socializing that goes on in most fitness centers strictly to the customers, and insisted his employees do the same.

"We were hoping you'd let us look at the list of students in the classes I've taught, say for the last two weeks."

Students could reserve space in classes by signing up or phoning in. It was a class by class commitment, and if you weren't on the list, you couldn't attend. The arrangement kept the lessons from being overcrowded. Stephen typically taught the trendiest, and therefore best attended, classes. They were held in the club's largest gym, complete with a stage for the instructor to stand on. That way everyone could see the instructor equally well, not just the students in the first row, and vice-versa. The times of the classes were announced weekly on Monday morning, but not the teacher. However, it was possible to call up and inquire who would be running a particular class, but not too many club members bothered to, because all the instructors were top-notch.

"You bet. I'll have Phoebe make copies of the lists for you."

"Great."

"Go where you need to with this thing, man, but I really hope it's not some psycho club-member. The publicity will kill us." The unfortunate pun escaped Chuck.

"Don't be so glum, Chuck. If it turns out to be a really fit club member, the publicity could bring in business." The attempt at humor passed Chuck by, as well, but Stephen's statement seemed to cheer him up.

"Shallow water makes for easy fishing," Donald told Stephen while they waited in the reception area for Phoebe to photocopy the lists. Stephen simply raised his eyebrows in response.

"Phoebe, have you noticed anyone calling to find out my teaching schedule?"

"Now that you mention it, there's a woman who's been calling and it's kind of odd. She asks when you're teaching. I tell her, and then rather than signing up, she hangs up. I figure she has a secret crush on you, or else," Phoebe smiled as she waited for the photocopy machine to finish, "you make her work too hard and she's trying to avoid your class. Well, here are the lists. I'm sorry they're confusing. Each class has two lists, the telephone list that I keep, and the sign up list from the bulletin board."

"This is fine. I'm sure we can figure them out. Thanks Phoebe."

"Good luck Stephen."

"From her lips to heaven's ear, or however that saying goes," Donald muttered on the way to the parking lot.

The men got into Donald's car, but before they could drive off, Phoebe appeared at the passenger side window.

"Stephen, there was that one other guy who called for you the day before yesterday, I think. It was around 5:30 and I was just leaving for the day. He asked if you were expected soon. Not if you were here, just if you were expected. I told him not tonight and offered to take a message, but he said never mind. I don't think he was a club member. Most of them call me by name, but I don't really know."

"Thanks Phoebe," Stephen said as they drove off. "We didn't have any messages at home, did we?"

"Just Laura inviting us for dinner. Could be nothing. Could be the murderer."

"Could be Citibank offering me a fabulous opportunity to transfer all credit card debt onto a new card for only 4.1 percent the first month, somewhat higher thereafter."

When the boys arrived home, they seated themselves side by side at the kitchen table, and spread the lists out chronologically in front of them. Many of the students were the same from class to class, but one fact jumped out at them as they progressed. The last name on the bulletin board sign-up sheets, in every case, was the same. To ensure payment, someone from the billing department checked off each participant in the class as he or she entered the gym. Without exception, the last one to slide in was Genevieve Conlon.

"Bingo! How could you not have noticed?"

"Well, it's a big class and I'm on the stage. I come down and help anyone who raises their hand, but other than that, I don't look at their faces. I'm studying their bodies."

"Nice, Stephen."

"Well, that's what I do. Damnit, I almost forgot, I'm supposed to clean for her tomorrow afternoon. It's my swan song. What do you suggest?"

"I suggest making the most of the opportunity, but definitely not going alone. She could be one dangerous bitch." Donald thought for a moment. "How about I wait in the car, out of sight with my phone, and you speed dial if I'm needed? I don't know what her agenda is, but she doesn't seem to want to kill you herself. Once she knows anyone's onto her, she might stop, and you'll never be completely cleared. On the other hand, this could always be a coincidence. It's just so easy to believe that Genevieve is dangerously deranged. For my money, she's our best bet so far."

"Is this the way 'Hawaii Five-O' would handle it?"

"No, but Detective Miller isn't exactly Steve McGarrett."

"And you're no Kono."

After stopping at the grocery, Elise and I went home. I checked the answering machine for messages. There was one. I still found myself half-expecting to hear from Greg at this time of the day and I briefly experienced a familiar pang. I wondered if it ever went away. I sorely missed Greg's support, especially at a time like this.

The phone message was from Donald, stating that they had news and to call when we got home. Before we had a chance to call them, my phone rang. I was putting away groceries, so Elise answered. When she didn't call me to the phone, I assumed the call was for her, but after a few minutes she did ask me to pick up the extension in the kitchen. It was Alec McBride. He had us on a conference call with Stephen and Donald. One at a time, we reported our day's activities. Alec had reviewed Detective Miller's evidence and thought it weak.

"Your police are having trouble making a rational case for Stephen's guilt. Their evidence is entirely circumstantial. If we can only give them a more plausible suspect, I think they'd drop Stephen's charges, but law enforcement doesn't change direction easily. We need to hand them reasonable alternatives."

With that said, assignments for Wednesday were discussed. The women were going to visit Duffy again and ask to borrow Lila. If possible, we were also going to inquire if anything in Margaretta's will pertained to Reverend Andrews. Then the three of us, Lila being the third, were going to the Rogers' home so that Elise could sort through her sister's things. All of Grace's personal effects had been left to her sister and there was always the off chance that they contained a clue. Lila and I would accompany her and sniff around for our own evidence.

Stephen was keeping his ten a.m. appointment with Reverend Andrews, ostensibly for counseling, but hell bent on finding two pieces of information; the source of the scratches on Christine's neck, and any link between the Reverend and Margaretta Hood. In the afternoon, Stephen planned to cautiously clean Genevieve's house, with Donald lurking outside. Alec McBride once again cautioned to keep our wits about us. The boys and I hung up, but Alec and Elise continued their conversation another twenty minutes. When it ended, Elise rolled into the kitchen.

"Wine?" I asked.

"Lovely." When she saw my smile, Elise added, "He's a nice man, Laura. I haven't met too many lately."

"Say no more, my dear. I'm defrosting homemade pea soup for supper. If it's not your thing, just tell me."

"My favorite. Would there be any Anadama left?"

We all awoke refreshed and optimistic for our new day. Stephen drove himself to Reverend Andrews' house and was surprised when the minister's wife Dorothy opened the door. Stephen feared that this would make questions about Christine a tad awkward. His concern was misplaced. Dorothy Andrews was on her way to work. She was a grief counselor in the county's Office of Family Services. The Reverend offered Stephen a cup of coffee, and before he had a chance to finish it, Christine Parker breezed in, without knocking.

"Oh, have I missed Dorothy?" Christine asked with disingenuous regret oozing from every pore.

Stephen was disappointed that he was the only one to witness Christine's performance, but he paid close attention, so that he could recapture it for Donald. In Stephen's somewhat limited experience, church ladies seemed to come in two varieties; those who wore too much make-up, and those who wore none. Christine was the former, and Dorothy was the latter. It was also Stephen's belief that one's back was never quite as bloody as when it was leaving church. This notion added a tragic irony to Grace's and Margaretta's murders, if the Reverend and Christine were actually responsible. Stephen had felt for a long time that the out-rageous hypocrisy of church scandal made it especially delicious. He allowed himself to be ushered into the Reverend's office with Christine following so closely, she actually stepped on the heel of Stephen's sneaker. Mrs. Parker was taking no chance of being excluded.

"Before we begin, Stephen, tell me about yourself. Have you always lived in the area? What was your childhood like?"

Stephen had no intention of sharing the intimate details of his painful child-hood with the Reverend and Christine, but he took his time and enjoyed creating a scenario of a doted upon only child, with a beautiful mother and patient dad, who never hesitated to share skills and wisdom with their son. He finished by say-ing what a loving family they were and emphasized his parents' generous accep-tance of his homosexuality.

When Stephen finished his confabulation, Reverend Andrews sighed and said,

"But, how are you bearing up, my son? Really bearing up. There's no need to be brave here."

The Reverend's voice was too sanctimonious for Stephen's taste. Stephen redoubled his efforts to memorize the conversation for Donald, as he again threw himself into his own role.

The minister lived in a modern home surrounded by trees. It had the feel of a ski house to Stephen and looked vaguely out of place in the seaside town. A cross hung on the office door and it had clanged when Bill Andrews opened the door. Stephen noticed there was an inside bolt on the doorway. The room was paneled with formica wood paneling. A degree from Harvard Divinity School was hang-ing on the wall, along with a prerequisite picture of a dewy eyed Jesus. The degree from Harvard surprised Stephen. Bill Andrews might not be as stupid as Stephen had thought. He remembered Alec's caution. The room also contained a televi-sion with a VCR/CD player, and a pullout sofa bed.

All the better to counsel you with, my dear, was the thought crossing Stephen's mind, but what he answered was,

"I don't know, Reverend Andrews. Grace's death was a shock, but I kept thinking it was suicide. We were friendly, but not friends. You know what I mean, but Margaretta was like a grandmother to me. She was so kind and gentle. Who could ever stab her like that? Anyone who knew her must feel the same. Did you two know her?" Stephen was trying to sound emotional and confused. He hoped he wasn't overdoing it.

Christine and Bill exchanged glances. Stephen was not the only actor in the room.

"Well, of course, I knew dear Margaretta. She was a member of my flock for the years I served The Magnolia Congregational, right up to my retirement. She was even a member of the Retirement Committee, as I recall."

"She certainly was," Christine added icily.

Stephen knew full well the scandal surrounding the Reverend's retirement. The terms of his severance were not generous. Maybe Christine blamed Margaretta for the Reverend's financial dependence on his wife. Whether it was true or not, Stephen wouldn't put it past the Reverend to use money, or lack of, as an excuse for staying with Dorothy. Bill Andrews was certainly a man capable of wanting his cake, and eating it too. Unfortunately for Christine, she was under his spell.

"Did you know Grace?" Stephen asked innocently. Again the lovers exchanged glances before answering.

"No. We didn't know her at all," snapped Christine.

"Well, of course that's true for you, my dear, but remember me telling you that Mrs. Rogers came here once for a counseling session? I like to think I was able to help her because she never scheduled a second session." The Reverend settled into what he considered his beatific smile, but it reminded Stephen of the Cheshire Cat.

Stephen was not enjoying himself. There was a barely controlled anger exuding from Christine Parker and it was all too easy for him to imagine what her jealous rage might be like. The minister's office faced east and it was rapidly becoming warmer as the morning sun rose higher in the sky. Instead of her usual mock turtleneck, Christine was wearing a full black turtleneck. She briefly pulled it away from her neck to get some relief from the hot room, before letting it snap back into place, but the gesture provided Stephen a good view of the red marks beneath. A cat had definitely not made those scratches. They appeared to be hickies. He looked down at his lap to hide his amusement. He needed to leave this house. He had what he came for and didn't trust himself to continue the farce much longer, so he closed his eyes and took a composing breath.

"Reverend, I feel so lost, so hopeless. I should be comforting Mr. Hood and instead I'm a pariah. I loved Margaretta and the police think I murdered her. What am I to do?" Stephen prayed his last bit wasn't too melodramatic.

"Put your trust in God, my son. Remember Job. The Lord has a plan for you and you must welcome it. Christine and I will always be here to help. Never hesitate to lean on us. Our strength will be your strength. And above all, don't be a stranger." Stephen found the final sentence odd.

"Thank you. Thank you both. You're right about this being my hour of need. Your support means a lot to me." Stephen stood up to leave. Christine hugged him and the Reverend blessed him. He couldn't get out of there fast enough, and he couldn't help feeling that the Reverend and Mrs. Parker were more anxious to stay in touch with him than vice-versa, but why?

Stephen and Donald had arranged to meet for lunch and then proceed to Genevieve's for the swan song cleaning. Stephen was anxious to relay his discovery linking Christine and the Reverend to both Margaretta and Grace. After this morning's revelations, Christine Parker appeared more dangerous and equally crazy as Genevieve. But, why had Grace gone to Reverend Andrews? He fervently hoped the marks on Christine's neck were truly hickies and not a result of Grace's self-defensive strangle hold, inflicted trying to save her own life. Would this morning's turn of events, in combination with Genevieve's bizarre behavior, give the police two reasonable alternatives to pursue? He wondered if it had occurred to the Reverend that Christine's possessive jealousy might make her capable of murder. Was his ego so oversized that he could justify a murderous act of passion as long as he had inspired it? Was there more to the story of his disgrace at Magnolia's Congregational Church, and did it involve Margaretta?

Elise and I drove to Duffy Hood's mid-morning. I had made three chicken pies the night before, one for Duffy and two large ones for our own dinner tonight. Alec, Stephen, and Donald were joining us and we were planning to compare notes. I have always found homemade chicken pie to be comfort food and the routine of cooking it to be comforting too. Grief saps energy and appetite. Sufferers would rather skip a meal than labor over one. Chicken pie doesn't even require a knife to eat, and the meal was Stephen's boyhood favorite. I still added cream to the gravy and bits of turnip, just the way he liked it.

We recognized Mr. Waterman's black Lincoln parked outside of Duffy's home. He was Magnolia's funeral director of choice and we waited for him to leave before knocking on the front door. We noticed Mr. Waterman was solemnly carrying a dress box from Lord and Taylor. Duffy let us in. Lila was still resting her chin on Margaretta's rocker.

"Hello, ladies. Please come in."

"Thank you, Duffy, we won't stay long, unless there's something we can do for you. I brought a little dinner. It will last days in the refrigerator. The heating directions are taped to the foil; three minutes in the micro, or thirty in the oven. I prefer the oven. It gives me a chance for a civil glass of wine."

"Speaking of which, thanks for puttin' me to bed. Was it only last night? Feels longer."

"Don't give it a thought. How are the arrangements coming? We saw Mr. Waterman leaving."

"Well, the police are releasin' Margaretta's body this afternoon and he's goin' to collect her. I gave him Margaretta's favorite dress. It was new last year. She bought it when I was supposed to retire and the Aquarium threw me that big bash. She loved that dress. It was so unlike Margaretta to splurge on herself, but I insisted. It was pale pink and floaty. She called it her angel dress. Do you think it's silly of me to bury her in it?"

Duffy looked so forlorn, that I didn't trust myself to speak.

"No, I think you're wonderful to think of it. I hope someone makes such a loving choice for me when the time comes," Elise spoke with compassion and quiet authority. Her answer clearly pleased Duffy.

"Thank you. Now, if I can just do as well with the church service. I'm supposed to meet with our minister Reverend Davies in a half hour."

"We're headed to Grace Rogers'. Elise is deciding what to do with her sister's personal effects. How would it be if we took Lila with us? She and I could walk the beach, while Elise works. Lila will be alone here while you're at the rectory and she might enjoy a distraction."

"Good idea. Lila could use some cheerin' up. I don't envy your chore, Elise. I can't even think about Margaretta's things. I went to pieces just huntin' for her dress."

"It's all too much, Duffy. Would you mind if we got together and talked about it next week? We both know Stephen didn't do it and we're trying to help him."

"I'd like to help Laura, and I know Margaretta would want me to."

I put Duffy's chicken pot pie in the refrigerator, found Lila's leash, and we left.

On our drive to Sean Roger's house, Lila curled up on Elise's lap and sighed as Elise gently stroked her.

"I think you have a new friend. Dogs are wonderful judges of character, you know."

Elise smiled. "Lila and I are simpatico, that's all."

"Now there's a sure sign of spring," I said, motioning to a black racing bike on the front porch of a house. "That's Officer Monroe's bike. He's Magnolia's only policeman fit enough for bicycle duty. We call him 'the divorcee's best friend.' And that's Liz Hathaway's house. She was in the second pew of your sister's funeral, hoping to console your brother-in-law. Speaking of whom, have you spoken with Sean? Does he know you're staying with me?"

"I phoned him in his office yesterday, and arranged to be let in today. He said the police were almost finished going through Grace's belongings and Detective Miller would let me in. I told Sean that I had no intention of being alone with him in the house, and I gave him your phone number, when he asked how he could reach me. Hopefully, our paths won't cross today, but I can't avoid him forever."

I parked in the Rogers' driveway, next to a police cruiser, and waited as Lila lazily slid out of the car. Detective Miller was waiting for us, looking out the front window. He walked outside to my car when we pulled into the driveway.

"Mr. Rogers told us to expect you. We're through in the bedroom. I have the insurance list of your sister's jewelry and it's all accounted for, as far as we can tell. If you notice any personal effects missing, we'd appreciate hearing about it. The insurance rider itemizes silver and furs, too. We're still working on that."

"Fine, Detective. I'll start in my sister's bedroom."

While Elise had been speaking to the detective, I removed her wheelchair from the back of the car and brought it around to her side. When Detective Miller saw it, he looked puzzled. I remembered that he hadn't discovered that Elise was paralyzed when he interviewed her in my home. The look on his face was priceless. As Elise gracefully transferred herself into the chair from the car, the detective's face became redder.

"Why didn't you tell me!" he demanded.

"You didn't ask. Does it make a difference?" Elise replied over her shoulder as she briskly wheeled away from him. The detective was left sputtering for an answer.

"Lila and I will be right up, Elise. I just want to walk her around a little first."

I didn't know what I was expecting, but Lila's complete calm when surrounded by Sean Roger's scent put to rest for once and for all that he was the murderer. She did surprise me by emitting a half-hearted growl when we walked through the dining room and persisted in circling the area at the foot of the table. It was the area where Stephen and I had been standing while I spoke to the Reverend and Christine Parker. It was also where we later spoke to the Carlisles. I made a note to discuss my observation over dinner.

"Are you trying to tell me something, Lila?" The house was immaculate and had clearly been well cleaned since the funeral. I remembered the desserts that

Christine could not resist and thought maybe the dog was reacting to the aroma of the recent buffet as much as who might have been standing there. Eventually, Lila followed me up the stairs to Grace's bedroom. Two of the policemen had lifted Elise and her wheelchair to the second floor. She was seated next to the bed with her head in her hands. Her sister's jewelry was arranged on the neatly made bed, but Elise couldn't look at it. The bedroom was spacious with a stunning view of the ocean. It was decorated in pale yellow creams with a soft rose contrast. There was a sitting area and a beautiful Oriental rug, Chinois I would guess. The room inspired tranquility and I hoped Grace had found peace there.

Lila trotted over to Elise and rested her chin on her feet.

"See, we're simpatico."

"You don't have to do this today, you know. Those cops would like nothing better than to show off their brawn by carrying you back downstairs."

"No, I want to get through this. I don't want anything that Sean bought for her. All I want is the sentimental things that were my mother's. They were irreplaceable emotionally and I'm sure Grace didn't have them insured."

Elise rolled herself across the room to her sister's antique, veneer keyhole desk and started going through the drawers and compartments.

"Could you bring me a suitcase from the hall closet?"

After I did as she asked, Elise quickly cleared the desk's contents into it and gathered the heirlooms from the bed.

"The only thing that's missing is my grandmother's hat pin collection. It's probably downstairs in the coat closet. I can come back for it when the police are through."

On our way to return Lila, we passed the remains of a snowman.

"Ten days ago the biggest unsolved crime in this town was the identity of the artist responsible for adding anatomically correct body parts to unsuspecting snowmen. In one instance a bright pink bra was also supplied."

"Bring back the good old days," Elise added.

"Amen."

"Would you like to meet my Dad?" I asked Elise when we were back in the car. "He loves visitors, but I could easily drop you home first if there's something else you need to do."

"No, it would be fun to know your father. Can Lila come?"

"You bet. The nursing home let my parents' old Cairn terrier live with them when they first moved in. Piper was eleven at the time, and very calm. In less than six months, he went from eighteen pounds to thirty. Everyone was feeding him and old Mrs. Stone actually spread Lorna Doones with jam for him at tea time. The unfortunate part was that pills sometimes fall under furniture, or maybe even get tossed there by the residents, and Piper would find them. The dog became addicted to Prozac. He was stoned all the time. We finally had to let him live with us, sort of like the Betty Ford Clinic, but he'd still visit my parents a few times a week until, he died two years ago."

I pulled into Oakwood and parked near the front door. Lila chose to ride on Elise's lap and not walk.

"This place is nice, Laura," Elise said looking around at the wood paneling, eighteen foot ceilings, impressive pipe organ, and crackling blaze in the massive entry hall fireplace.

"It was built as a summer home about ninety years ago and I guess the owners whooped it up pretty good until the crash of '29. Then it was sold to a local schemer who turned it into a brothel. The Magnolia Historical Society claims that the third floor was even used for abortions."

"Not your average old age facility," Elise said while rolling past the original ballroom with its antique grand piano.

"They use that for socializing—birthday parties, Christmas, church services, movies, sing-alongs, wheelchair aerobics. Most of the inmates here are really old and frail. Their days of attending Symphony Hall are over, but their lifestyles remain. This time of day Pop is probably in the solarium having a pre-lunch cat nap."

Elise and Lila followed me past the ballroom and into the solarium, which was filled with huge rubber plants, cactuses, two giant aloe plants, and an extremely robust diefenbachia.

"Hi, Pop."

"Who's that?" he asked opening his eyes.

"It's Laura."

"Who?" he said squinting.

"Your favorite daughter."

"I remember you. Who's with you?"

"This is my friend Elise Sanderson, and Elise, this is my father, Clark Jelliffe."

My dad scrutinized Elise. He clearly liked what he saw. At this stage in his life, he was used to seeing people in wheelchairs and didn't think much about it.

"Did you know I used to be sharp as a tick?" he said smiling and holding out his hand to her.

"And this is Lila," Elise said shaking Pop's hand.

"Glad to meet you Lila. You want to live here with me?" Pop was talking to the dog.

"I'm afraid Lila has a master. We're just keeping her from being lonely this afternoon, but she can visit again if you'd like."

"That would be fine. We could keep each other from being lonely."

Betty Davis had it right. Getting old is not for sissies.

While Elise and I were visiting with Pop, Stephen and Donald had finished lunch and were on their way to Genevieve's condo, to clean for the last time.

"I'll be glad when today's job is over," Stephen told Donald on the way. "It never occurred to me how many sketchy people I know. I hate turning them all into murder suspects."

"Well, these people aren't friends of yours. You found out the hard way that this Conlon woman was fixated on you. She stalked you, for heaven's sake. She is an over-sexed cocaine using flake, if you ask me. And it's a combination that does not foster keen decision-making."

"The trouble is, it's too easy picturing Genevieve tossing Grace off the balcony in a cocaine frenzy. She clearly knows more about Grace's husband than is easily explained. Maybe Genevieve developed a crush on Sean Rogers after realizing that I was definitely spoken for. No wrath like a woman scorned kind of thing. Genevieve could be Joan Crawford in "Hush Hush Sweet Charlotte." Maybe she's trying to make me pay for rejecting her sexual advances, while she clears her path to Sean Rogers at the same time. Two birds with one stone. That bitch is certainly cocaine crazy now, but I bet there's always been hell to pay when she hasn't gotten what she wanted."

"I wouldn't argue that she's a candidate for sociopath of the month, but do you think she'd actually kill Margaretta? Margaretta was hardly her competition."

"Maybe not, but it was no secret how much I adored her. If someone were hell-bent on hurting me, Margaretta would fill the bill. Oh, Lord, if that's the case you and Laura are in danger, too."

"The thought has occurred to me."

They drove the rest of the way in silence. Before Stephen exited the car, he and Donald tested their cell phones' automatic dials.

"Call me when you're finished," Donald shouted through the window, before surreptitiously driving away. They both knew he was parking around the bend, out of Genevieve's sight.

Stephen knocked loudly on the door. He couldn't finish this job fast enough to suit him. No one answered. Stephen decided to try the handle and found it unlocked. If Genevieve was planning a stunt, he wanted to get it over with and leave without cleaning.

"Hello-o-o-o, Mrs. Conlon. It's me," Stephen shouted while thinking maybe she was picking up her mother at the airport or something.

There was still no answer, so Stephen walked in and started cleaning. He followed his usual routine; bathrooms, kitchen, dusting upstairs and down and finally vacuuming his way out. He was relieved not to find any trace of Genevieve. The only room upstairs, besides the master bath, was Genevieve's bedroom. She had a mirrored wall of closets and a ceiling mirror too. There was a night stand on one side of her king-size bed and a sink built into the wall on the other side. Subtle was not a word that sprang to mind when thinking about Genevieve Conlon. From experience, Stephen also knew there would be a hand mirror with lines of cocaine on it under the bed, so he carefully lifted the dust ruffle to avoid vacuuming Genevieve's stash, as he once had. He bent down to avoid the mirror and was met by his employer's unblinking, glazed-over stare. Without thinking, Stephen dragged her body out from under the bed. It was still warm, but there was no mistaking that Genevieve was dead. The garrote was still around her neck. He reached into his pants pocket, removed his phone and pushed the first number on auto-dial to summon Donald.

Chapter Eight

For the second time that week Donald, Elise and I found ourselves in the police station's lobby, waiting for Alec McBride, and hopefully Stephen, to emerge from the interrogation room. Despite my concern for Stephen, I found my stomach was loudly rumbling, a sound it usually reserved for silent meditation in church. It was well past two in the afternoon when Stephen was begrudgingly released, once again into my custody. We were in three different cars and decided to meet at my house. I phoned Magnolia's only restaurant, the House of Pizza, and ordered two large specialty antipastos, which I picked up on my way home.

We gathered around the kitchen table, helping ourselves to food and asking questions while we ate.

"How did it go?" I asked Alec. I assumed Stephen had brought Donald up to date on the ride over.

"Hard to say. Based on the temperature of Genevieve's body, the coroner fixes the time of death between nine and ten thirty this morning, depending upon whether she had just completed a jog, or was about to begin one. She was wearing jogging gear and a fancy sleeve cuff for measuring heart rate, calories burned, distance. You know, the whole nine yards."

Actually I didn't know, but I nodded with great authority. I noticed Stephen raising his eyebrows in my direction while Alec continued.

"Detective Miller kept trying to convince the coroner that it could have been earlier or later, because Reverend Andrews, his wife and Christine Parker can all provide an alibi for Stephen during that time period, as can Donald, but the coroner was steadfast. The good Detective did not seem to be pleased, but I think we made headway convincing him to look further than Stephen. Unfortunately, he now may want to speak to Donald. He hinted that they could be in this together, Genevieve being such a nuisance to both of them."

I looked at Donald.

"Stephen told me on the way over. How did you two make out?"

"Well, we saw Duffy for a minute. No news there, but we succeeded in borrowing Lila and I'm disappointed to say she had no problem tolerating Sean's scent in my sister's house."

"While Stephen was busy charming Reverend Andrews this morning, I did get a call back from old Pal Hal." Stephen rolled his eyes as Donald spoke. "He's more than happy to look into any recent cases handled by Sean Rogers. He'll call me if there's anything that might help us."

Just then my phone rang and I left the room to answer it.

"It was June Carlisle," I said when I reappeared. "She wants to come over tomorrow and appraise the house. The end of a perfect week."

"Well, I'll be here too, Laura, and it could be interesting to see her reaction when she finds out who I am. Didn't you say that she seemed to know a lot about Sean's business associates at the reception after Grace's funeral? I'm sure my sister never mentioned the Carlisles to me, so whatever the connection, it's all to do with Sean. Do the Carlisles have offices other than in Magnolia?"

I nodded my head no.

"Hmmm. Sean's a criminal lawyer and I can't imagine that he handles many real estate closings, especially in this little town."

"We'll simply have to see what tomorrow brings," I said.

"Just promise to be careful." This was sound advice to all of us, but Alec was looking at Elise when he said it.

June Carlisle arrived on the stroke of ten the next morning. She had a clipboard in her hand and appeared to have already jotted several notes before even entering my house.

"Come in, June," I said unnecessarily as she barged past me. "Let me take your coat." It was a sunny, surprisingly mild, late February day, but it had not stopped June from donning a black, shin length Russian sable coat with an oversized hood. She was wearing expensive knee length, pale blue suede boots, that shouted upwards of a thousand dollars, with her perfectly matching cashmere sweater and skirt ensemble. There was a dramatic patterned silk scarf pinned to her shoulder by a large jeweled brooch. She looked briefly alarmed as I tried to shove my bulky and very worn down coat and rain gear out of the way to make room for her fur in the inadequate foyer closet.

"Oh, don't bother Laura. I'll just lay it on the sofa. You don't have pets, do you?"

I smiled and nodded no.

"June, I don't think you know Elise Sanderson." Elise had just rolled into the living room from the kitchen.

"Hello, June. I'm Elise."

"Nice to meet you. Now, I know that name," said June. "Do you live around here?"

"No, I'm here from Chicago."

"That's it! You're Grace Rogers' sister. I didn't know you two knew each other, Laura."

"Actually, we met quite accidentally a few days ago," Elise continued, "and Laura has been kind enough to help me out while I'm here."

"If you decide to stay, I know of a few handicap units that might be available. I don't suppose Sean's home works at all well for you, being on such a steep cliff and all. Try to talk him into selling, Elise. I know three potential buyers."

I averted my gaze to an old red wine stain on the living room rug and inconspicuously tried to put my foot over it, avoiding Elise's amused expression.

"Oh, are you and Sean friends?" Elise asked innocently.

"We've become friendly doing business together."

"I had no idea Sean was involved with real estate, but he's so clever, I suppose there's not much he's not capable of."

"He's not involved with real estate, but we do have other business together, that's all." It was clear June Carlisle had no intention of talking further on that particular subject.

Elise and I now exchanged glances, but didn't ask any more questions, while June got to work invading my beloved home like Atilla the Hun, sadly shaking her head and making tisk tisk noises. June scattered comments like birdseed as she walked from room to room.

"Don't bother to include the drapes when you sell. I can't imagine anyone would be interested."

"You'd be well-advised to remodel that kitchen and all the baths. No one touches a house without granite counters."

That figured. I hated granite counters. They were cold and reminded me of a morgue. The patterns were way too busy and made me nervous. No one should ever be nervous in his own kitchen or bathroom. The first time I saw granite counter tops I was reminded of the pictures of enlarged microscopic bacteria and different cancer cells that were framed and cheerfully adorned the corridors of Gilbert Hospital. I also suspected the famously hard, enduring surfaces would not be kind to my great grandmother's crystal and china. If granite cost less, no one would want it.

"Luckily, this neighborhood is extremely desirable and I suppose a motivated buyer would have to consider knocking down a few walls, creating a great room, and adding a decent master suite."

"Yes, one would hope," I added. June ignored me.

Less than an hour later she was finished.

"I'll write up a report with pricing recommendations, and several other suggestions. Then you can come into the office and we'll discuss it. I'll give you a call."

"Can't wait," I said after closing the door the second time behind June. Somehow I had managed to catch the hem of her sable the first time.

True to her word, June called two days later. I was tempted to tell her that I had changed my mind about selling, but there seemed no other way to probe the Carlisles' relationship with Sean Rogers.

"I know how busy you must be with weekend showings, June. So why don't we make it sometime Tuesday. Dear Margaretta's services are on Monday and I want to be fully available for Duffy all day."

"All right, but could you do me a favor? I don't know the Hoots at all. Would you mind…"

"Hoods," I interrupted.

"What?"

"There name is Hood, not Hoot."

"Are you sure? Anyhow, would you mind giving Mr. Hoot my card? I left a few on your kitchen counter. He'll be much happier starting fresh, and I have several attractive properties in mind. What do you think his price range is?" I had tossed June's cards into the trash days ago.

"I think Mr. Hood cherishes his memories, June." I did not want Duffy exposed to this vulture.

"Nonsense. I pride myself on sensitivity to the client. It will do him a world of good."

"What time is good for you Tuesday?" I asked changing the subject.

"Sometime between noon and three. Tuesday morning is Brokers' Open House and we have a three o'clock in the office."

"How about two fifteen?" I had no intention of being trapped a moment longer than necessary.

"Fine. See you then, and don't forget about giving my card to Mr. Hoot."

"Anything for you, June," but she had already disconnected.

Monday morning dawned sunny, cloudless and slightly above freezing. No menacing wind blew off the ocean and it was easy to believe that the crocus would soon be making an appearance. As we all huddled around Margaretta's grave, I said a silent prayer of thanks for the lovely day. Renewal was in the air.

Stephen and I were attending the ceremony together. The church service had been both simple and extraordinary. There was standing room only in the chapel and the minister clearly knew Margaretta well. He told a sweet story about Margaretta's famous cream puffs, which she created in abundance for the church's bazaars.

"The first year I was here, I noticed Margaretta buying three of her own puffs, which I thought was curious, because they were clearly going to sell out. Then I watched as she gave one to Duffy, one to Lila and ate the third herself. 'You shouldn't pay for those,' I said. 'Everyone tells me that your cream puffs are our biggest draw.' 'Reverend,' she whispered, 'Please don't ask me to take the grace away.' Margaretta, no one could ever take your grace away."

Stephen, Elise and I had spent the weekend cooking for the gathering at the Hood's after the burial. Elise did not attend the church, but set out the food instead, while keeping company with Lila. The only attendees the three of us found the least bit curious were Christine Parker and the Reverend. We knew Christine detested Margaretta and deep down we suspected the Reverend must harbor some ill will.

"They've got cajones. I'll give them that," Stephen said. "You'd think they'd be at least a little embarrassed to be surrounded by the Reverend's old congregation, given the circumstances of his dismissal."

"Given that they hardly knew Margaretta, the best face I can put on their appearance is to say it's out of respect for her."

"Or they're sociopaths and incapable of recognizing their own wrong-doing. They may be here to witness their 'good' triumphing over Margaretta's 'evil'."

"You don't really believe that do you, Stephen?"

"Maybe it's for the food," Elise offered.

Stephen was about to reply, but as though their ears were burning, the Reverend and Christine started making their way through the crowd, heading toward the three of us.

"My, my, and we're not even standing near the buffet," Stephen muttered.

"Hello Stephen. Hello Laura," the Reverend said. "Sad business this."

"Oh, it certainly is," I replied. "I don't think you know Grace Rogers' sister Elise Sanderson."

"No we don't, but there's no denying the family resemblance, is there my dear?" the Reverend said to Christine, while positively preening and taking Elise's hand firmly in both of his.

Stephen gently stepped on my foot as we both noticed Christine's death glare at Elise's outstretched hand, as the unfortunate Elise was forced to wrench it from Reverend Andrews' grasp or endure his unwanted fondling.

"We, I mean the Reverend, was just saying how concerned he was that he hasn't heard from you Stephen, especially with that Conlon woman's murder. You must feel more forsaken than ever."

"Well, bewildered might be a better word."

"Whichever, my son, I am only here to serve. Please allow me to lighten your load. Would you consider another session? We never charge until the third."

"Well, that's very generous, sir." Stephen paused before the word "generous." Now it was my turn to gently step on his foot.

"Fine, fine, my friend. We're on our journey then. There is so much need and never enough time. Nice to meet you Elise. I'm here for you too, in your sadness so far from home."

Christine savagely gripped his forearm and with barely a nod in our direction headed toward the door.

"Whoa," said Elise. "That was interesting."

"And I didn't even have a chance to ask about his wife Dorothy," Stephen added.

"Well, Stephen, you know how it is when there's so much need and never enough time."

"Could they have a tie-in with Genevieve? They certainly knew her last name easily enough, but that probably doesn't mean much."

"Stephen, I only think it's fair that you make one more appointment with the Reverend. After all, Laura is enduring June Carlisle tomorrow, and besides, his rates are so reasonable."

"Thank you for pointing that out, Elise."

I smiled slightly and looked for Duffy. He was surrounded by old friends. Now that Christine and the Reverend had left, there were no interlopers present. I knew how Duffy was feeling. Margaretta's violent death couldn't seem real to him yet. The misery would wash over him in unexpected waves for the rest of his life, hopefully with decreasing frequency, but never with duller pain.

Chapter Nine

Before my appointment with June Carlisle on Tuesday, Elise and I stopped by the Hood's to see how Duffy was faring and finish with the tidying up. We found nothing to do because Stephen had been there earlier that morning.

"You must have been pleased with the service, Duffy."

"To tell you the truth Laura, it's all sort of a blur to me. Stephen and I talked about it this mornin' and I realize that I must have been in a daze, but he remembered every word. I guess my Maggy would have approved and that's all I care about. I do know that your food was real tasty and I'm still enjoyin' the leftovers. You've both been mighty kind."

Duffy suddenly looked so sad that I knew he was being washed anew with a memory. I also knew he would have way too much time to be miserable when Elise and I left, so I chatted on.

"Oh don't mention it Duffy. Have the police had any leads? As far as Stephen knows, he's still the main suspect."

"I reckon that's right enough, but I told them they were dumber than the gum on their shoes if they believe Stephen did it. Imagine some monster doin' that to Maggy. It plum doesn't make sense."

The three of us were quiet with our own thoughts and Lila rested her chin on Elise's lap.

"I was surprised to see Reverend Andrews and Christine Parker here, though. Were they close to Margaretta?"

"Hell, no. I was kinda wonderin' what they were doin' here, too. And I'll tell you somethin' else that strikes me odd, that Genevieve woman. What the devil could she have in common with Maggy that someone would want to murder both of them. And Maggy never even laid eyes on your sister, Elise. I'd bet Lila on it."

"Does that mean she had laid eyes on Genevieve, Duffy?" Elise asked.

"You might say that. She was the woman that Reverend Andrews was carryin' on with when he was fired. Margaretta walked in on them while they were on the floor in the chancellery. Can you imagine that? Maggy was just there to arrange flowers and she got more than she bargained for."

"Oh my. I never knew that Duffy. Of course, I heard that the Reverend was caught in flagrante, but I never knew who was with him, or how it was discovered."

"Well, that's the way Maggy wanted it. She was no gossip and church was important to her. She didn't know Genevieve from Adam, or maybe I should say Eve, but when the good Reverend tried explainin' that his pre-marriage counselin' session had simply gotten out of hand, like there was nothin' really improper about the incident, Maggy would have none of it. She was right, too. Think of all the broken lives those popes coulda' prevented, if they'd been as righteous as Maggy. I'm not sayin' Genevieve wasn't a wild-eyed Susan, but that wasn't Maggy's concern. All she knew was that the Reverend was up to no good, sullyin' the church's reputation, and takin' advantage of someone wishin' to be hitched in the Magnolia Congregational. Who knew what else he mighta done? Even if you are a member of our church, which Genevieve was not, the rules are no gettin' hitched without talkin' with the minister first, so Genevieve had to meet with the guy. The most amazin' part is that the Reverend still ended up marryin' Genevieve, only in that fancy room on the roof of the Hawthorne Hotel and not in a church."

"How did you ever manage to keep all those details quiet in this little town?"

"Maggy just never told anyone except me. She simply told the eldahs that through no fault of her own, she had the misfortune of witnessin' the Reverend breakin' a Commandment and that she was requestin' his quiet resignation, without offer of future employment references. Reverend Andrews was of course welcome to present a defense, but you might say he quit while he was ahead."

"Good for Margaretta. Oh rats, look at the time. I've got a meeting at two fifteen, Duffy. Would Lila like to go for a ride with us?"

"I'm sure she would, ladies. Don't let me make you late, but promise to keep me posted and I'll do the same. There's evil workin' here."

"We'll be back before five, or better yet, come for supper and take Lila home from my house afterwards. How does six thirty sound?"

"It sounds fine. I just feel so damn helpless, Laura. Thanks for…"

"Forget it, Duffy. We'll see you later."

While I was meeting with June, Elise called the three "boys" from her cell phone and invited them for supper and a bombshell. They were intrigued and quick to accept. Lila accompanied Elise inside the grocery store across the street from the real estate office. Lila posed as Elise's Handicap Dog and if anyone doubted the dog's credentials, they wisely kept it to themselves. It took me forty-five minutes to escape from my meeting with June. She went on and on about "comparables" and "market conditions," both of which were apparently against me. I nodded sincerely, hoping to forge a bond between us and keep her talking. She kept shoving contracts in front of me to sign and I kept saying that I'd have to think about it. After three quarters of an hour, June looked past me into the reception area, abruptly stood up, handed me the contracts and walked me to the door. I was surprised to find Sean Rogers and John LoConte being ushered into the Carlisle conference room as I exited. I doubted that they had noticed me, especially since my back was facing them from June's office. Once outside, I spied Elise and Lila putting a bag of groceries into the back seat of my car in the parking lot.

"Well, that was interesting," I said when I joined them.

"Let me guess. She already has a buyer and, considering your outdated curtains, the offer is most generous?"

"Not quite. But your brother-in-law and a thug named John LoConte were just being ushered into the conference room when I was dismissed."

"Well, that explains it."

"Explains what?"

"The bad smell in the air."

Alec McBride arrived for supper nearly two hours early and brought three good-looking bottles of red wine. The lovely day had deteriorated and the darkening sky threatened snow or at least slush. Elise had insisted on being the cook, so I asked Alec to build the fire and keep her company while I settled into my tub. Actually, I didn't have to ask.

I emerged from a luxurious, moisturizing, and faintly honeysuckle-scented tub, feeling totally relaxed; a feeling I had not had since Grace's murder. I decided to don my softest old jeans, cotton socks, and a long sleeve tee shirt from the first Buffett concert Greg and I had ever attended. I decided to forgo shoes.

My house. My friends. I entered the living room and found Elise and Alec comfortably ensconced on the loveseat with Lila sprawled across their laps. The three of them were facing a movie set fire. Alec knew his stuff. Their backs were to me and I smiled at the picture they created.

"I'm a new woman," I announced, not wanting to be caught in the role of voyeur.

"Can I get you a drink, Laura?" Alec said, gently shifting the snoring Lila completely onto Elise's lap and standing up.

"That would be lovely. Toasted Head for me."

One of them had already placed an iced bottle on the sideboard, next to an open bottle of red. Just then a buzzer went off in the kitchen.

"I'll get it Elise. I'm up already."

Alec returned in a minute with an oval plate of sliced baguettes with something heavenly, smelling slightly of curry, melted on top. I sat in one of my fireside wing chairs and basked. As if on cue, the doorbell chimed and Stephen, Donald and Duffy walked in together. Alec and Duffy were introduced to each other and the three most recent arrivals were served drinks. After less than fifteen minutes of cordial chit-chat, the kitchen buzzer sounded again and we adjourned to the dining room for dinner. Elise had created a sumptuous meat loaf, topped with crisped onions. Alec had insisted on making the mashed potatoes himself from his favorite recipe, which I guessed included at least two sticks of butter as well as a healthy dollop of sour cream. Elise had also roasted olive oil coated acorn squash quarters, and then topped them with a generous dusting of brown sugar and cinnamon.

Before anyone could offer a maudlin toast, Alec raised his glass,

"To the business at hand."

"To the business at hand," the rest of us parroted.

"Stephen, the more I think about it, the more I'm convinced that you've been followed. Maybe you still are. Someone has gone to a lot of trouble to implicate you. You need to think about who could hate you that much. This could go way back; something you were practically oblivious to at the time, but it's been festering in somebody's sick mind. It could be before you met Donald. Discuss it with each other, and most importantly, never stop looking over your shoulder. And that goes for everyone here." Once again I noticed Alec's gaze was fixed on Elise.

"We need to find out why Grace met with Reverend Andrews. I can't help but feel he and Mrs. Parker are up to their hickies in this thing. They certainly seem to be the only link that connects the three victims, except for Stephen."

"I guess I'm lost," Duffy said.

"Oh, sorry, Duffy. Shortly before Grace was found dead, she'd met with the Reverend, but we don't know why. However, Christine Parker has made it abundantly clear that she did not appreciate Grace seeking out her paramour for advice. As a matter of fact, I think it's fair to say that Mrs. Parker is downright hostile to even a reference to Elise's sister. Stephen found out how bitter Christine was toward Margaretta for her role in the Reverend's dismissal, and thanks to you Duffy, we now know that Genevieve was part of that too. Mrs. Parker is a large, physically strong, possessive woman, and if I were Dorothy Andrews, I'd be nervous. Reverend Andrews may be a hypocrite, but he's not stupid. To the contrary, I suspect he has a gift for manipulating people, and he's undoubtedly used it on Christine Parker."

"After it probably didn't work on his wife Dorothy," Stephen said, "And, yes, I'll make another appointment with Reverend A, which will no doubt include Lady MacBeth. Hopefully, I can get them talking about Grace. I don't know about the rest of you, but Christine scares me."

"Do you think Dorothy Andrews knows anythin'?" Duffy asked.

"No, I think Dorothy long ago gave in to the sad triumph of experience over hope."

"I think I'm lost again, Laura."

"I just meant that Dorothy might have suspicions, if she even allows herself to think about her husband with Christine, but I don't think she's guilty of anything except silence, or else Dorothy would have been the first one off the cliff. I'm a firm believer that a multitude of women my age spent decades faithfully easing their husbands' paths, and when they repeatedly discover that their husbands are lying scoundrels, there are only two choices that they consider acceptable, and divorce is not one of them. Turn a blind eye, or become a carping bitch. Some end up doing both. You'd have to be a saint or on Prozac not to. Dorothy has long since turned a blind eye. Ironically, the 'carping bitch' existence causes outsiders to excuse the husbands' their transgressions. You know the thinking. 'Who can blame the poor bastard. Look what he has to put up with at home.'"

Apparently, my little speech caught everyone by surprise because the table fell silent. Alec was the first to speak.

"I have one other request for you, Donald. Could you ask your detective friend Hal for a list of real estate closings that Sean and the Carlisles have both been involved with, not necessarily as principals, but also as agent and lawyer? I think the county Registry of Deeds has some way to access that information. If not, we may all have to spend considerable time reviewing the last year or so of real estate transfers in Essex and Suffolk Counties. I don't know what exactly we're looking for, but it bothers me that a lawyer who defends the mob, has business with small-timers like the Carlisles in an unlikely place like Magnolia, which coincidentally is experiencing its first ever rash of murders. I've been working on a few scenarios in my mind. So far the murders don't make much sense with any of them, but I just can't help thinking there could be some connection. More information may shed enough light to pursue or eliminate Sean and his cohorts, at least as murder suspects."

"No problem. Hal's already calling me back about Sean's recent criminal cases. I'll ask him then."

"And I'll see what I can eke out of my brother-in-law. I need to return to his house and retrieve my grandmother's hatpin collection, the one the police wouldn't let me search for last week, but they're finished with the crime scene now. Don't worry, I won't go alone," Elise added, reading Alec's mind.

"He'd smell a rat if anyone here tonight, except Laura, went with you," Alec said. "He knows me from court, and he probably knows I'm representing Stephen. Suggest a meeting in public, maybe a bar or coffee shop. Get Sean to bring the hatpin collection to you. Only offer to go to Salt Hill if he can't find it."

There wasn't much else to say. It was Wednesday night and we were all tired, except apparently for Elise and Alec, who insisted on staying up and doing the dishes. Our mutually decided tasks would take us at least through the weekend. The evening broke up immediately following dinner. Duffy and Lila left together. Duffy looked exhausted and I was hopeful that he'd have no trouble sleeping tonight.

"Thanks for everythin', ladies. I didn't even know how hungry I was. I'm glad to meet you Alec and I appreciate bein' in the loop. We'll get through this, Stephen. I know we will." The two men shook hands and briefly embraced. "Good to finally meet you Donald."

"For me too, Duffy," Donald said extending his hand.

"Good night, darling Lila," Elise called to the Bassett Hound, who turned around and wagged her tail before waddling after Duffy.

I know when my presence is unnecessary, so after saying my good nights, I gladly joined David Letterman in bed. Before turning out my light, I read the yellow post-it note I had placed on my bedside phone. It read "Don't do it" and referred to my habit of calling my grown children, Dave and Abbie, at my bedtime. I started calling them after Greg died. It was my way of knowing they were safe and it helped me sleep. However, after the first month, I sensed that my habit might be turning into an annoyance when Abbie changed her answering machine message to, "Ma, I can't come to the phone right now, but I'm healthy, happy, and, oh yes, alive. Love you. Leave a message after the peep." It was a routine that would have driven me crazy at the same age and I was lucky she refused to let me become pathetic. Live and learn.

Chapter Ten

On my way downstairs the next morning, I tiptoed past my son's old room and tried not to peek inside, but I was unsuccessful. I hadn't heard anyone come upstairs, but then again, I had slept wine soundly and a smoke alarm could have gone unnoticed. The first time Alec spent the night, he had made the bed so perfectly, that no one would have known it had been slept in. The bed was still perfect.

It was eight and I made coffee in the spotless kitchen. I also turned on the radio and listened to Lauren and Wally, my favorite morning radio hosts. When Mr. Coffee finished his job, I dumped a few grounds onto my African violets and threw the rest into the trash. I couldn't help but notice that the last bottle of Alec's red wine had been finished. I removed the English muffins from the refrigerator, popped one in the toaster, and proceeded to the front door to retrieve my newspaper. I was disappointed to notice that Alec's SUV was gone from the driveway. I returned to the kitchen to find Elise dressed and pouring herself a glass of juice.

"Good morning, Laura. Can I pour one for you?"

"Thank you. You're looking especially lovely today, Elise."

"Well, thank you madame. I slept well."

"Did Alec stay late?" I was trying to sound nonchalant.

"Actually, yes. We finished the dishes, he rekindled the fire and we polished off the last bottle of wine. I don't know when I've had a nicer evening. He slept here, but left around six."

I was tempted to ask another question, but resisted.

"Did you find anything else out about his personal life?"

"Well, yes. About two years after his father was killed in that building collapse, his mother remarried an old friend who was also a widower and they seem to be amazingly happy. They do lots of traveling and live in Palm Springs in the winter and Martha's Vineyard in the summer."

"Nice work if you can get it."

"I guess they have a pretty nice life style, but Alec grew up on Martha's Vineyard in the home that his mother still uses. They're locals. He went to public school on the Vineyard and then to U. Mass. Amherst. His father's life insurance put him through Harvard Law."

"It takes a lot more than money to get through Harvard Law."

"Well, yes, but what I'm trying to say is that Alec's not 'to the manor born.' He does lots of pro-bono work. I know because he asked me for a favor."

"Do go on," I said with my mouth full. We had split my English muffin, so I put another in the toaster while Elise talked.

"Once Stephen is no longer under suspicion, Alec asked if I would visit a nine year-old girl with him. She was paralyzed a year ago in a car accident that killed her parents. She lives as a ward of the state in a private residential childcare facility, especially for the so-called handicapped. The state reimburses the agency for her care. Alec is their corporate attorney, and he donates his fees back. Anyhow, you can imagine all the legal issues involved with any kind of childcare and Alec is at the agency at least once a week. This child was only placed there three weeks ago, when she was finally released from the hospital, and she's made a lot of trouble. The children there have all kinds of handicaps, mental and physical, and I'm sure it's overwhelming to wake up and find yourself in the middle of a world you didn't know existed. She is not transitioning at all well and she'll have to be moved to a more restrictive, that would be 'jail-like,' setting if she doesn't shape up, for the safety of the other kids and staff, not to mention her own. Alec thinks I could help her. It's worth a try. I don't think I can make things worse, at any rate."

"Where is this place?"

"It's in Amherst. Alec was a volunteer during his college years. How far away is Amherst?"

"Two and a half hours. First you drive south on Route 128 and then west on Route 2. There are lots of country inns along the way. Maybe you'll get a romantic dinner out of it."

"Suits me," Elise said smiling.

We were interrupted by a phone call from Donald.

"Laura, I'm in the car headed to Boston. I can't avoid work another day. If my phone cuts out, I'll call you when I'm in the office. Anyhow, Hal called and Sean's been involved in a Federal money laundering case. It's been going on over a year, but the I.R.S. can't find the money or prove the sources of income. Sean's clients have been before two Grand Juries, but the prosecution can't produce enough hard facts, just lots of reasonable speculation, to indict. Maybe that's what Grace wanted to tell her sister. Ask Elise what she thinks. Would you mind passing the info along to Alec for me?"

"Of course not. Did you have a chance to ask Hal about real estate transactions Sean might be involved with on the North Shore?"

"I did and he got pretty excited. Said he'd look into it and mention it to the Feds, too. He'll be in touch as soon as he knows anything."

"That's great. I'll tell Elise. Donald? Hello? Oops! Donald? Rats. We were cut off," I said to Elise.

"Tell Elise what?" she replied.

"Donald heard from his friend Hal and found out that Sean Rogers has clients who have spent the last year avoiding indictment for money laundering. When Donald mentioned that I had seen Sean and John LoConte at the Carlisles' office here in Magnolia, Hal was certainly interested. Do you think Grace might have accidentally discovered something about hiding cash? Do you think that's what she wanted to tell you?"

"Well, I suppose it's possible, but Grace and Sean never discussed his clients. It's just something Grace had no interest in and Sean had no interest in telling her. No, whatever Grace wanted to tell me made her happy. That's why I thought she might be pregnant."

"Oh, Donald asked if we would call Alec and tell him what Hal had to say. Would you mind doing that while I get dressed?"

"Not a bit."

Stephen took a deep breath before ringing the Andrews' doorbell.

"Here goes nothing," he muttered to himself.

His mission this morning was to discover, once and for all, why Grace had met with Reverend Andrews. They were such an odd combination. From what Stephen had gleaned from Elise, Grace was no churchgoer, although she was devout in her beliefs. Maybe that was it. Maybe something spiritual was troubling Grace and she chose Reverend Andrews to confide in. He no longer had a parish and was hardly in a position to pass judgement. Also, meeting him at his home and not in a church office, where a curious, officious and probably possessive secretary was bound to be hovering, had to be a plus from Grace's viewpoint. Most parishes had a constant stream of nosy church ladies to avoid. Even phoning to make an appointment could start the rumor mill. Stephen felt this explained why Grace had chosen Reverend Andrews as a confidant, but not what they had discussed. Stephen did not wish to arouse Christine's suspicions, so this would be his last attempt to unearth the topic. From his observations, Christine's temper was frightening. He had even dreamt about her sporting a maniac's grin, stabbing Grace and then flinging her over the balcony.

His nightmare's leading lady responded to the doorbell.

"Good morning, Stephen. You're certainly prompt today. The Reverend is waiting for us."

Stephen followed Christine to the office. Dorothy Andrews must have already left for work.

"Good morning, Reverend,"

"Aah. Hello, Stephen. I wish you would call me Bill. I feel as if these trying days have brought us together."

"All right, um Bill. I feel the same way."

"Stephen and I are already on a first name basis, from my days as Laura's neighbor, Bill."

Stephen wasn't quite sure this was true, but he just smiled in agreement.

"Well, my son, how goes the battle?" Stephen was learning how fond his new friend was of that phrase.

"I'm not sure. I still seem to be the only suspect, but so far the police can't come up with a motive, just circumstantial stuff. I keep thinking, if I only knew a little more about Mrs. Rogers, I wouldn't feel so helpless." Stephen took a deep breath. He had practiced the next part of this charade repeatedly in his head and fervently hoped Christine took the bait.

"All I knew was that Mrs. Rogers was lovely, beautiful really. She had exquisite taste, real style. She was refined and totally devoted to Sean, from what I could tell. You knew her. What can you tell me?"

As Stephen was dwelling on Grace's virtues, he noticed the veins on Christine's neck start to throb and her jaw clench. Her hickies had faded and she was wearing an open collared blouse. Her complexion flushed even redder beneath her bountifully applied make-up.

"Stephen, perhaps you are a tad too generous in your praise of Grace. Far be it from me to be critical, especially of the departed, but her beauty, as you call it, is not uncommon among young women who live in the lap of luxury, with unending time and money to spend on themselves. As for her adoration of Sean, would it surprise you to hear that Grace Rogers came to us because she was considering a divorce?" Stephen noted that Christine Parker had managed to stop just short of adding "fuck you Grace."

"That's all quite true, my dear, but we must remember how torn and troubled poor Grace was, and we certainly wouldn't want any of this to go further than my office. Sean Rogers has been through enough."

"Then he didn't know Grace was considering a divorce?"

"No. Grace sought us out, so she could discuss it at all. She was absolutely clear in her desire that no one else know what she was considering. She hadn't made up her mind and too often well-meaning friends repeat confidences, making delicate situations worse." The Reverend had his feet on the desk and his hands folded in a prayer-like fashion across his belly. He was slowly nodding his head, which held an expression reminiscent of a politician pretending to listen.

"Isn't that right Christine?"

His paramour remained silent, nodding affirmatively. Stephen noticed a furtive, uneasy expression on her face, as if she'd been caught in a lie, or maybe Christine had simply had too many prunes for breakfast. The Reverend continued,

"She died the next day, without even having a chance to make another appointment. Tragic. Tragic."

Again, Christine said nothing, but the clench of her jaw and continued throbbing of the veins in her neck sent an unwanted chill down Stephen's spine.

At Alec's suggestion, Elise called her brother-in-law and arranged to meet him at Magnolia's upscale coffee shop, The Daily Grind, at five that afternoon.

"He was so nice over the phone, Laura. I thought I had the wrong number. Sean said he had personal business in Magnolia this afternoon and it would be nice to see a friendly face afterwards. I almost told him that I was no friend of his, but bit my tongue instead. He even thanked me for calling."

"Then he found your grand-mother's hat pin collection?"

"It was in the coat closet, like I thought."

"How about I leave you at the coffee shop a little before five and then I'll drop in at the realtors to sign the contract that June keeps pushing at me. Maybe Sean's personal business is with the Carlisles and I can get June to let something slip. You can try the same thing on Sean and we'll compare notes afterward."

"Very clever, Mrs. English, but you don't really want to sell your home, do you?"

"Heaven's no, but I've decided to put a whopping fat price on it. June will tell me I'm looking at my property with sentimental blinders, and I'll agree but hold firm. I have another clever idea, Elise. How about we invite Stephen, Donald, and Alec, if he can, for dinner after our busy day? Maybe there's more news from Hal, and you and I are bound to have learned something. I know it's a bit of a haul for Alec, and he was just here last night, so do what you think best."

Elise smiled.

"Alec's already coming for dinner. We were going to take you out."

"How about we order Thai? Donald and Stephen can pick it up. They have a favorite spot in Salem."

"Perfect."

Elise and I parked in the back of the lot across the street from the real estate office. Next door was the grocery and on the far side of that was the coffee shop. Elise rolled toward her meeting with Sean and I crossed Main Street to the Carlisles'. I spent several minutes pretending to be window shopping in the antique store next to the realtors and was gratified when I saw Sean Rogers and John LoConte exit without noticing me. They crossed Main and walked toward Sean's big Mercedes, which was parked along the curb. They spoke briefly and John LoConte climbed into a gold Cadillac parked behind the Mercedes. He immediately started talking on his cell phone and slid down comfortably in the driver's seat. He appeared to be waiting for Sean to finish the meeting with Elise. I watched Sean enter The Daily Grind before I set foot in the realtors' office. June Carlisle was just exiting the conference room and noticed me come in.

"Hello Laura. What can I do for you?"

"Well, I've decided to sign your contract and put my house on the market, but I have a few questions to ask first."

June wasted no time escorting me into her office. On the way there I said,

"Did I notice Sean Rogers leaving just now? Is he selling his house?"

My question momentarily flustered June.

"No, but Mr. LoConte is considering buying another house here."

"Another? I had no idea he lived in Magnolia." I couldn't help but remember what John LoConte had told me after Grace's funeral and it didn't add up.

"Oh, I didn't mean John was buying another house. I meant he was buying a house other than Sean's."

"I see. Where is it?"

"Um, I'd rather not talk about it until the papers are passed, but you came here to put your house on the market. Here is the contract. What did you want to ask me?" June seemed anxious to change the subject.

"What is your commission?"

"Six percent. That's very fair and standard for the industry."

"So you want me to spend time and money updating my home and pay you six percent commission?"

"Laura, in return we'll advertise the house. I assume we'll be exclusive, which guarantees no strange brokers will view the property without a representative from this office accompanying them."

"That's comforting, June," I said thinking of last year's scandal when two brokers from the Carlisle office were caught by an angry husband trying out the springs in the master bedroom's kingsize mattress.

"Now, what about the price?"

"Considering how outdated your home is, I would suggest four hundred ninety eight thousand. You'll get a lot more action by keeping it under five. Once the decision to sell is made, it's much better for the client to move forward. You don't want to drag this out, Laura, believe me."

"I'm sure you're right June, but humor me. We'll price it at eight seventy five."

June actually gasped. "You're making a big mistake, Laura. You've come to me as a real estate professional and now you're not listening. That price will attract inappropriate buyers. You'll be stuck in that house forever. Believe me."

"Call me crazy, June, but I'm firm with my price. I totally understand if you don't want me as a client. Maybe I'll have to try selling it on my own." I was starting to enjoy myself.

"Now Laura, that's really crazy. We'll try eight seventy five if you insist, but don't blame me if the property lingers."

I was feeling strangely empowered when I left June. I walked toward my car where Elise and I had agreed to meet, but in the parking lot I discovered Duffy, who was carrying a bag of groceries to his car.

"Hello Duffy. How are you faring?"

"Hi Laura. Good to see you. I'm a little discombobulated, to tell the truth. Maggy did the grocery shoppin', you know, and I'm feelin' like a fish out of water. I woulda' skipped this trip if Lila wasn't out of kibble."

We continued walking toward Duffy's car. I knew how he felt. Taking over your loved one's responsibilities was a painful reminder of your loss, and going out in public left you way too vulnerable to unwanted encounters.

"Duffy, can you and Lila come for dinner? The boys are bringing Thai food, and Alec and Elise will be there. We might even have a few new developments to talk about."

"I can't tell you how much we'd both like that Laura. And hey, I've never had Thai food."

Just then I noticed Elise and Sean entering the parking lot.

"Here comes Elise with her brother-in-law, Duffy. Don't mention dinner," I added hastily, while they were still out of earshot.

As Elise approached Duffy's car, Lila suddenly appeared at the car's passenger side window, wiggling with joy and yipping.

"Hi Duffy. How are you and Lila doing?" Elise asked.

"Well, Lila's a lot better for seein' you. There's nothin' wrong with her nose, that's for sure. She must have smelled you comin'."

"I'll take that as a compliment, Duffy. Do you know my brother-in-law Sean Rogers?" The two men exchanged pleasantries and shook hands. Sean excused himself, claiming to have another appointment.

"Yesterday I would have said the 'other appointment' probably wore perfume and three inch heels, but just now the man was gracious, charming and teetering on the brink of being kind. A side of him I've never seen. Why is it that I hate thinking I've misjudged him?"

"We can talk about it tonight, Elise. Duffy and Lila are coming for dinner, too."

"I have to go home first and put these groceries away," Duffy said while Lila continued her happy dance in the front seat.

"Would you mind if Lila came with us now?" Elise asked.

"Not a bit. I'll be along in three quarters of an hour or so. Does that suit you?"

"You bet, Duffy."

He unlocked the car and delivered Lila to us. Elise and I proceeded to my car. It took a minute to stow Elise's wheelchair, and then we drove home, stopping only for wine. I pulled into my drive, retrieved the chair and pushed Elise, with Lila following, toward the kitchen door.

"I thought I left lights on," I said as we approached the kitchen.

Suddenly Lila started barking ferociously and snarling, too.

"There must be a raccoon around," I said unlocking the kitchen door.

Lila hurdled past us into the house and seemed to lunge at something in the dark kitchen. We both heard a whooshing sound and the dear dog collapsed onto the kitchen floor briefly squealing in agony and then lying deathly mute. In an instant, I felt what I assumed was a gun with a silencer poke into the small of my back.

"Shut up and do what I tell ya', unless ya' want to end up like duh dog."

John LoConte managed to throw Elise over his shoulder, while keeping the gun against my back. I guessed he must have done this kind of thing before.

"I been wantin' to kill dat flea bag since it bit me at the old lady's house, but I had a knife and it kept runnin' in circles."

Elise was doing her best to struggle and she bit him in the neck.

"You bitch," he roared and slammed her head into the door frame, all without moving the gun from my back. Elise was silent and I guessed she was unconscious, slung over his apelike shoulder, as he forced me to walk ahead of them across my back yard. He had parked on the wooded street behind my home. It was a dead end cul-de-sac with no houses, a feature I had always considered an asset until now. Elise was unceremoniously dumped into the trunk of the gold Cadillac de Ville, which had been left open; a detail not everyone would anticipate. I climbed in at gun point and Big John slammed the lid. I had only a few thoughts as I heard the car's motor start and felt us drive away; I now knew the true meaning of "pitch black," and it was true what they said about the size of a Cadillac's trunk. I did my best to cradle Elise's head and she seemed to be breathing regularly, but I didn't trust myself to think about Lila.

Chapter Eleven

In the movies, clever kidnap victims keep track of their location by carefully estimating the time between turns and guessing at speeds, unless of course they are unconscious. They listen for sounds; rushing water, train whistles, airplanes overhead, the ever famous fog horn, church bells. Basically, this is a crock. While spacious, the trunk of a Cadillac de Ville is noisy. There is no soundproofing or heat, and the nonstop noise of twigs, small pebbles and other road debris being constantly crushed by the tires and bouncing off the car's undercarriage pretty much obscures the other clues. All the roads in Magnolia curve, so Elise and I were frequently sliding from one side of the trunk to the other. We did go over what I guessed were railroad tracks once, which meant we were heading west, maybe northwest, maybe southwest. The car never came to a full stop, so probably we were running traffic lights and stop signs.

After about fifteen minutes we accelerated and seemed to be going in a straight line. I figured we were probably on Route 128, but which direction? If we were headed south, there was practically nowhere in the United States that we couldn't get to. If we were headed north we would soon be at the rotary near Gloucester. The size of Cadillacs' gas tanks is legendary and I prayed John LoConte had forgotten to fill his. Then I had a terrifying thought. What if we were in a high speed chase and the car crashed? All that fuel could ignite. Where was the fuel tank exactly? Probably next to the trunk someplace. Auto mechanics were not my strong suit. If we weren't in a high speed chase, we'd probably be shot like dear Lila and become part of the foundation for the final phase of Boston's Big Dig.

I told myself to stop these negative thoughts and calmly assess our options. On the bright side, there had not been time to tie or gag us. If we stopped, or even slowed down, I would start screaming and kicking the trunk's hood. Hopefully, the plan was not to roll the car off a cliff into the ocean. Damn, more negative thoughts. Eventually, John would have to open the trunk, wouldn't he? And when he did I would lunge out flailing. That would catch him by surprise. I'd show the big lug he couldn't get away with shooting Lila.

While I was holding onto that thought, Elise moaned.

"Elise, are you okay?"

"I can't tell. Where are we? What happened?"

"We're in the trunk of Mr. LoConte's car."

"Oh, I remember. The bastard shot Lila. Where do you think we are?"

"I'm pretty sure we're on 128, but I can't tell if it's north or south."

"Have you tried getting into the back seat?"

"What do you mean?"

"If you pull away the carpeting from the rear of the trunk, you might be able to push the rear seat forward enough to hear him. Maybe there's someone else in the car, or he's on his cell phone, and you can eavesdrop."

"How do you know that?"

"Everyone knows that, Laura. I'll try fiddling with the lock. New models can all be opened from the inside. It's a government mandated safety measure to prevent children from locking themselves in during hide and seek, or something. Let's just hope our host is as dumb as he looks and hasn't modified this lock."

I did as Elise suggested and with difficulty, due to the confines of being locked in the trunk, I managed to pull back the rug and felt the back of the seat. I pushed the rear seat as hard as I could on the driver's side with both feet, bracing myself against Elise, who was shoved against the front of the trunk. I felt the back seat give slightly and a small amount of light filtered into our pitch black prison.

"Laura, I can open this lock. If we slow down at all, help push me out and jump out yourself. It can't be any worse than what he has in store for us. If you can find the trunk light, break it. He may not slow down at all and darkness might give us just a few more seconds. I'll pretend to be unconscious while you try to push your way into the back seat. He might leave the keys in the ignition and while he chases you, I'll crawl up front and start the engine, or vice versa."

"Of course, he might shoot us both."

"He's planning on doing that already. Nothing to lose for us."

"Can't we just raise the lid a foot or so and start waving for help?"

"We could, but it would set off the trunk alarm and he'd probably shoot us through the seat before anyone noticed us, pull onto the shoulder, re-slam the hood and act like nothing was wrong."

So much for lunging and flailing. In no time at all Elise had become the general, and I was a grateful private.

While we waited for the speeding car to slow down, I did my best to listen through the crack in the seat. Our captor was alone in the car and using his cell phone.

"Nah. Dey don't know nothin' about no money. I went ovah dere with duh bug, but dey walked in on me and I shot duh witness. Yeah, I know what to do, Boss. I'll meet ya' afta."

When it was clear that John LoConte had disconnected, I whispered to Elise, "You were right. He knew Lila could recognize him. I'm sure he was watching when Lila smelled you coming in the parking lot. I wonder why he didn't kill us too."

"He needs time to implicate Stephen. Then he'll kill us. What just happened was unplanned. I'd bet money that Sean's the Boss he was talking to."

Before we could say more, the Cadillac's breaks squealed and John LoConte shouted,

"You cocksucka!"

"Now!" Elise commanded releasing the trunk. The car had slowed, but was easily traveling at twenty miles an hour. She adroitly pulled herself over the rear fender and I flipped her onto the highway, tumbling out afterwards. Cars veered around us blowing their horns. I madly started waving my arms in the air and noticed we were at the rotary in Gloucester, undoubtedly headed to the Blackburn Industrial Park, which provides dozens of acres full of warehouses and manufacturing facilities. Apparently, Mr. LoConte had failed to keep abreast of a recently amended Massachusetts' traffic law. The old law required vehicles already on the rotary to yield to entering traffic, a regulation that contradicted the rest of the country and caused thousands of accidents every year. Thankfully, John LoConte must have taken it as his due to barrel onto the rotary, forcing him to slam on his brakes when no one yielded.

I could hardly drag Elise across the busy road, so I kept waving my arms like a deranged metronome. After a minute that seemed like an hour, a State Trooper with sirens blaring and lights flashing sped onto the rotary and rescued us. Two other State cars arrived moments later. The first car to see us flee the trunk had phoned *77, the State Police emergency line. The gold Cadillac had disappeared. Four roads flowed into the rotary and the other cruisers proceeded down two of them. The troopers in the first cruiser whisked us into their vehicle and with sirens still blaring, we proceeded south on 128. Strangely, I found myself thinking of the time I won my elementary school spelling bee and was allowed to ride on the fire engine, with its bells and whistles sounding, as we led the Memorial Day Parade, forty-seven years earlier.

"Look for a new gold Cadillac de Ville. The driver's name is John LoConte and I think he works for my brother-in-law Sean Rogers. Sean lives at Ten Salt Hill in Magnolia. You need to arrest him before the thug in the gold Cadillac tips him off, if it's not too late already," Elise shouted over the whine of the siren from the back seat.

The trooper in the passenger seat immediately spoke into his transmitter instructing police to proceed with caution to Ten Salt Hill and detain Sean Rogers.

"You also need to send an ambulance to Twenty-Seven Cradleskid Road in Magnolia. That creep shot a Bassett Hound before he abducted us," I added.

"I'm not sure about that Ma'am. Dogs are a little out of our purview."

"Do it! She's your best witness to another murder and if she's dead, the bullet in her is evidence."

He immediately picked up the transmitter. My tone of voice probably foreshadowed hysteria and he wisely decided to comply. Elise gave me a thumbs up.

"Don't worry ladies. Every trooper south of the rotary is on the lookout for the Caddy. We're headed for the hospital. You gals may not have noticed, but you're both bleeding and who knows what else. Flopping out of that trunk may not have been the brightest thing to do, but it sure was gutsy and probably saved your lives."

Elise and I looked at each other in the back seat. She had the beginnings of a real shiner from where her head had been slammed against the door frame. My knees, palms, and forehead were bleeding. I must have landed on them when I exited the trunk. Luckily we still had our winter coats and boots on or we would have been in worse shape. The back seat of the cruiser was too dark for me to see much more of Elise than her face.

We arrived at the Gilbert Hospital emergency room and were each placed on a gurney and rolled inside. This was Elise's second visit to this hospital.

"At least it's not the morgue," I said reading her mind.

From my supine position I had a clear view of the water stains on the ceiling and a large clock, which had been placed high on the wall enabling patients and visitors to know exactly how long they had been kept waiting. In my case, I was struck by the fact that barely one hour had elapsed since Elise, Lila and I had unsuspectingly entered my kitchen. I prayed Lila was alive and medical help had arrived.

The troopers remained by our sides. They had many questions for us and we were anxious to tell them what we knew, but hospital bureaucracy came first. My primary care physician's office was in one wing of Gilbert Hospital, so with my permission, they simply down-loaded my file. I recommend being brought to the emergency room by state troopers. They insisted Elise go immediately to X-ray and fill out paperwork later. After all, she had been knocked unconscious and complications involving her paralysis could be serious. The troopers and I were provided with a vacant room where we could talk.

"Before I say anything, I need to make a phone call."

Trooper Ed Kleven, according to the pin on his uniform, requested an outside line and handed me the wall phone's receiver. I dialed my own number and Stephen answered.

"Oh, Laura. Thank God! Where are you? What happened here. We found Lila in a pool of blood on your kitchen floor."

"Is she alive?"

"She was alive when she left here a few minutes ago. Officer Miller and Duffy just took her to the vet's. I guess the state police called the locals."

"Elise and I are at Gilbert Hospital. John LoConte kidnapped us, but we escaped. I'll tell you about it when you get here. Is Donald with you?"

"Yes, and Alec's on his way."

"Call Alec and have him meet us here."

"You bet. We're out the door."

I handed the receiver to Trooper Kleven. Now that my heart wasn't racing, I noticed that my head was beginning to ache.

"My friends will be here soon. How about I tell you what I know, which isn't much, and then you ask me what you want?"

"Works for me," the trooper said, seating himself at a table with his pen and pad. His partner had gone with Elise to x-ray. It occurred to me for the first time that we needed police protection, and so did Lila.

"You know the three murdered women from Magnolia? Well, my friend Stephen Macomber seems to be the only person they have in common. He's a house cleaner and barely knew the first and third victims, but he discovered their bodies while cleaning their homes. He was very close to Mrs. Hood, the second victim, and had been alone in her home shortly before she returned and was murdered. No one who knows Stephen could think for a minute that he had anything to do with these deaths. The first victim was Elise Sanderson's sister and the dog who was shot belonged to Mrs. Hood and witnessed her murder. Lila is a Bassett Hound and I believe she recognized John LoConte's scent earlier at my house. She attacked him and he shot her. I overheard part of a phone conversation while we were in his trunk. He was talking to 'duh boss' and referred to Lila as 'duh witness.' He even mentioned being bitten by Lila when he murdered Mrs. Hood, but he didn't even know the Hoods. Elise and I think Sean Rogers could be the boss, but maybe not. He's a criminal lawyer for some very unsavory mafia types, who are being unsuccessfully prosecuted for money laundering. I just can't imagine any motive Sean would have to order these women murdered, including his own wife. None of it makes any sense to me."

I wouldn't have blamed Officer Kleven if my disjointed, rambling account of our abduction caused him to dismiss me as an incompetent, but he continued jotting down notes, and occasionally looked up at me with an encouraging, kind expression.

We were interrupted by Elise being rolled into the room, accompanied by the other state trooper and Alec.

"How'd you do?" I asked her. She had an ice pack over her black eye.

"Concussion, but no breaks. Bumps and bruises."

"Wait until you wake up tomorrow and feel how stiff you're going to be," Alec said.

"At least I'm going to wake up tomorrow. I wouldn't have bet on that an hour ago."

"What about you, Laura?"

"Elise got the worst of it. I was too scared to fight him."

"Why don't you let me decide that, Mrs. English," the emergency room doctor said as he rolled me toward x-ray with Trooper Ed in tow.

By the time I was finished, the boys had arrived. Alec had somehow managed to convince the doctors that Elise need not be admitted for observation. He told them he had considerable experience with concussions and would be vigilant overseeing her care through the night. My injuries looked worse than they were. My forehead and palms had nasty scrapes, which the doctor had meticulously dressed and wrapped in a few miles of gauze. No concussion. No broken bones. After an uplifting speech on recognizing the symptoms of internal bleeding, the doctor released us from the hospital. While I was being treated, Trooper Ed had arranged for security at my house.

Elise and I chose to travel home in Alec's S.U.V. and spare ourselves the Ferrari's hard ride. I also doubted that I'd be able to climb back out of the race car once I settled in. The troopers followed us home and canvassed the immediate neighborhood and house while we waited for the security detail to arrive. Among the five of us, we had managed to answer the troopers' questions. Finally, they believed that Stephen had nothing to do with Margaretta Hood's murder, but the tenacious Magnolia police force was astoundingly disinclined to dismiss Stephen as their suspect in the murders of Grace Rogers and Genevieve Conlon. My head hurt too much to think about it.

The smell of Thai food greeted us when we opened the door. My trepidation was replaced by hunger, but first Elise and I craved baths. Because of the bandages on my hands, I couldn't undress or turn the water on and off, so Stephen did it for me, with his eyes averted. He helped me on with my robe and we waited for the tub to fill.

"What should we do to help Elise?" I asked Stephen. "I can't lift her in or out of her tub."

"Laura, I'd worry about something else if I were you."

"Oh, right. I forgot about Alec."

Stephen undoubtedly would have rolled his eyes at my naivete, but I guessed he had no desire to risk viewing me in my birthday suit.

"I left a message for Duffy asking him to call us when he could. Holler if you need anything, Laura," he said leaving the bathroom.

"Oh, Lordy, Stephen, what if Lila dies? It's all my fault for involving her."

"Let's not get ahead of ourselves, Laura."

The phone rang while I was soaking. When I walked into the living room after my bath, everyone was all smiles.

"Lila's going to be all right. The bullet went through her waddle," Elise said.

"Through her what?" I asked.

"You know the loose skin under her jaw. She lost a lot of blood, but she's all patched up and on intravenous through tomorrow."

I looked at Elise and we both burst into tears.

Chapter Twelve

After dinner, Elise and I went to bed. Alec left the boys in charge while he visited the Magnolia Police. The officer in charge looked to be about twenty-two. He was talking on the phone, tipped backwards in his desk chair with his eyes closed and didn't notice Alec walk in.

"Oh, I wish you were on my lap, too, baby…uh, gotta go. Some dude just walked in," he finished in a whisper, nearly falling out of his chair in an effort to sit up quickly and look competent.

"I'm Alec McBride. I'm here to find out if you're questioning Sean Rogers regarding the kidnapping of Laura English and Elise Sanderson."

"Well, we sure did question him at his house, Mr. McBride, but he didn't have nothin' to do with it."

"Why didn't you bring him here for questioning?"

"Because his time was accounted for. We had no reason to bring him in. He was watching the Bruins on TV and eating a pizza. He hadn't heard from or seen John LoConte since leaving Mrs. Rogers' sister at the Daily Grind. We checked with the phone company and there are no records of any calls to or from his home that would be incriminating. And besides, the guy was wicked upset to hear about the abduction. Well, more than that, more like shocked. He promised to call us the minute he heard from Mr. LoConte, but he wasn't expecting to. He gave us LoConte's phone number and address too. We didn't have to ask even. Cripes, he's a criminal lawyer. What else could we do? He coulda' thrown the book at us."

Alec looked at the name sign on the desk in front of him.

"You might have that wrong, Officer Coffin. I think the police could have thrown the book at him. He is a possible accessory in a kidnapping. You didn't feel searching his house might have been a good idea? You didn't consider the possibility that he keeps a cell phone registered to someone else?"

"We didn't have a warrant and since he offered to let us search, we figured we didn't need to."

"He offered to let you search and you didn't? Two women were kidnapped and would have been murdered, if they hadn't escaped."

"Well, he asked us if we wanted to come in, not exactly search specifically, but that's the same thing. Besides, you don't know LoConte was going to murder the women."

Alec McBride looked at the ceiling, counted to ten, and took a deep breath.

"Surely, you no longer consider Stephen Macomber a murder suspect?"

Officer Coffin looked decidedly squeamish.

"I couldn't say. You'd have to ask Detective Miller, but he's off duty."

"I'm asking you, Officer, unless of course you're not trusted with the information." Alec knew there were four full-time policemen in Magnolia and he doubted that there were any secrets among them.

"You're his lawyer. I suppose I can tell you. They still like your client for the first and the third victims, but he's off the hook for Mrs. Hood."

"Splendid. I don't suppose you could offer any theories as to motive, that might support these suspicions."

"Oh, I couldn't say. You'll have to ask Detective Miller, but like I said, he's off duty."

"May I leave a message for Detective Miller?"

"Well, if you want to, but tomorrow's his day off and I couldn't say exactly when he might get it."

"Thank you, Officer. It's been a pleasure." Alec McBride knew not to waste anymore time on Officer Coffin.

The young man nodded, redialed his girl friend, and was just putting his feet back on the desk as Alec left.

"Sorry for the interruption, babe…yeah, wicked busy."

By morning, we were both feeling the worse for our narrow escape. Stephen and Donald had gone to their respective jobs and Alec was working from my house. I didn't bother to peek into my son's room when I hobbled past. My knees hurt, my shoulders and arms ached, and my face had scabbed over. My forehead looked as painful as it felt. I couldn't even raise my eyebrows, but the cruellest blow of all was the perfectly round scab that had formed dead center on the end of my nose. I felt like Wiley Coyote after he fell off the cliff chasing Roadrunner.

"Good morning," Elise said as I limped into the room.

Her eye looked horrific; blood red where it wasn't swollen shut, and completely surrounded by black and eggplant colored bruising. She was on the sofa, propped up with pillows. We were both wearing our bathrobes. Bending my knees and pulling on slacks was out of my realm of possibilities. I headed toward the BarcoLounger and Alec gently helped me into it. Elise and I looked at each other aghast.

"Lucky for us, that beauty pageant isn't until next week."

"Oh, Laura, don't make me laugh. It hurts too much."

"Has anyone had a chance to call Duffy?" I asked.

"Alec did and Lila's being released this afternoon."

"But they won't be safe, will they?"

"Alec thinks they will. He's hired a security firm that he trusts to guard them and us, too. Two men are outside now, but the chance of LoConte being reckless enough to try finishing the job are slim, assuming he even knows the dog is alive."

Alec had gone into the kitchen to fix me breakfast.

"That's very kind, not to mention generous, of him."

"I know," Elise said smiling painfully.

Alec brought me tea and toast on a tray.

"Any sign of John LoConte?" I asked, slowly stirring milk into the hot tea.

"Not a trace, and Magnolia's finest don't think Sean had anything to do with it either. On the bright side, they do believe LoConte murdered Mrs. Hood, but Stephen is still under suspicion for the other two."

"Jesus! How can they be such perfect idiots?" Elise shouted.

"Well, from what I can tell, they've been practicing a long time. In their defense, the public hates to hear that the police don't have a suspect, so maybe they're using Stephen more to keep a monkey off their back than seeing him as a serious suspect. Otherwise, they seem to be operating on the premise that Magnolia, a town that has never experienced a murder, now has two psychos on the prowl," Alec answered.

"How reassuring. What should we be doing?" I asked.

"You should be resting. Oh, there's something you need to hear," Alec said, walking over to my answering machine. "In all the excitement last night, we didn't notice the light blinking."

He pushed the button and the message began.

"Thursday, January First, eight seventeen p.m.," the machine announced. I had never figured out how to program the date on my answering machine, so it was perpetually New Year's Day, but the time was right.

"Hello, Elise. This is Sean. The police were just here. I can't believe what happened to you. Are you all right? I have no idea what John LoConte is up to. I know you think I'm a jerk and I'm sorry about all that, but I'm as upset as you are. Call me when you get this message and I pray to God you're okay."

"Well, he got 'the jerk' part right," Elise said.

"He sounded sincere to me, Elise."

"I know, but the guy is such a creep, Laura. There's way too much water over my dam for me to trust him."

"He offered to let the police search his house last night, without a warrant. Unfortunately, they declined," Alec added.

"I hate letting the sleaze off the hook."

"I'm not saying that we should, Elise, but tell me what you think of this little idea. You could return his call, being sure to appear vulnerable and frightened."

"That should be easy enough," Elise said wryly.

"Then invite him to visit you here. Get him talking about Grace and mention the separation. I'm curious to know how he'll react. If Sean already knew Grace might leave him, it could be motive for murder. Grace might have told him after all. See if he knows who Reverend Andrews is. We want to catch him off guard. Bring up the Carlisles and ask how they know LoConte. Maybe his answer won't jibe with what June told Laura."

"You're a sly devil, Alec. I don't think I'd enjoy being cross-examined by you. Just give me a little time to plan the attack."

"Do you want to hear what I think?" No one answered, but I forged ahead anyhow. "LoConte was here to plant a listening device, not kill Lila or kidnap us. He said as much to his boss over the phone. We were unlucky enough to surprise him. Elise and I think Sean is the boss, but we can't prove it. If LoConte were bugging our phone, our house, whatever, he and his boss think we might know something. Anyhow, the only reason we weren't shot right here, like Lila, was because John LoConte wanted to frame Stephen. But why?"

"Damned if I know, but if Sean is the boss, he'll be trying to get information from Elise, too. Let's see what he asks."

Around eleven, Elise called Sean in his office. Alec and I acted as monitors. His receptionist paused and then said he could not be disturbed. I could picture Sean's secretary writing "Elise" on a sheet of paper and showing it to her boss, while he hovered over her desk. Predictably, before Elise had time to leave her return number, the receptionist announced that Mr. Rogers' meeting had just broken up.

"Hello, Elise. How are you? Where are you?" a convincingly earnest Sean inquired.

"I'm pretty banged up, but nothing that won't heal. I'm still at Laura English's."

"Are you sure you shouldn't be in a hospital?"

"I've had enough of hospitals for a lifetime. I can rest better here, Sean, but to tell you the truth, I'm scared. None of this makes any sense to me. First, Grace. Now, Laura and me. What's happening?" Elise had managed a panicky edge to her voice and I gave her a painful thumbs up.

"To be perfectly honest, I have no idea what's happening, and believe me, I'd like to know every bit as much as you. Maybe we can compare notes. Are you fit for company?"

"Not today, but maybe tomorrow. What's your schedule like?"

"Does late afternoon work for you? Say four o'clock?"

"That should be okay. I'll call your office if I'm not feeling up to it."

"Fine," Sean paused and added, "Honestly, Elise, I can't tell you how miserable I feel about all this, but thank God you'll be okay. Can I bring you anything? Please let me do something for you."

"If I think of anything, I'll sing out," Elise said, rolling her good eye at us. "See you tomorrow."

"I hope so, Elise, and you need to promise me you'll be careful, too."

"Promise. I'll see you tomorrow, then."

"Tomorrow."

I'm no shrink, but in my experience phrases like "to tell the truth," "honestly," "believe me," and "to be perfectly honest" are most often used when someone is lying. Elise was purposefully being insincere when she used one of the phrases on Sean and I'd bet Sean was lying when he used the others on her.

"That was shameful," Elise said after hanging up.

"You were great. With any luck we'll be able to eliminate, or zero in on your brother-in-law after his visit to our lion's den."

"I'm not so sure we haven't just invited the leader of the pride," Elise said.

Stephen and Donald came over for dinner, bringing the groceries and doing the cooking. Stephen donned a nurse's hat and firmly refused all help. We ate on trays in the living room. Alec built his trademark fire and the security detail joined us. Except for the way Elise and I looked and felt, the memory of a mere twenty-four hours earlier seemed surreal.

"Hal is FedEx-ing copies of real estate transactions involving Sean, John LoConte, and any other of your brother-in-law's infamous defendants. The FBI has looked at them, but nothing suspicious, so far," Donald said.

"Let's not leave them lying around for dear Sean to see. Which reminds me, I think I left the hat pin collection in Laura's car."

"I'll go check," Alec said. He returned with a small parcel.

"That's it," Elise announced. Alec handed it to her and she carefully opened the lid.

"My grandmother must have had a hundred hats. Grace and I used to play dress-up when we visited. Most of these pins were her mother's and some were my great-great-grandmother's. I'm so glad to have them," she said looking inside.

"Would you mind if I looked at them tomorrow, Elise? I'm beat. Thank you all for everything you did for me today."

"I'll help you upstairs, Laura," Stephen said. I would have refused, but my legs felt like rubber and the room started spinning as soon as I attempted to stand.

"Thank you, Stephen."

I was surprised how much stiffer I was tonight than even this morning and Stephen's strong arm was a comfort.

"I hate to ask you for anything more, but would you mind running a tub for me?"

"I was just about to suggest the same thing, Laura. It will do you a world of good."

Stephen ran my bath and helped me off with my terry cloth robe. He kept his eyes on the rug and held up an over-sized bath towel to shield me.

"You're a brave man, Stephen. Not many guys would risk a glimpse of me in the buff. Do you think Elise and Alec have the same system?"

"I sincerely hope not," he said averting his eyes while easing me into the tub. Stephen had laced my bath with the heavenly frangipani oil he had given me for Christmas. "I'll be in your room watching TV. Call if you need anything."

I don't know how people live without bathtubs. My soak felt so good that I almost shed tears of joy. Stephen came in twice to run hot water and only when facing terminal prunification did I exit the tub, with Stephen's help. He wrapped me in my robe and then instructed me to lie on my stomach.

"I'm sorry Stephen, I'm just not up for sex tonight."

"Now you tell me," he said easing my robe off of my shoulders, but leaving my backside covered. Next he took my giant sized Lubriderm for Sensitive Skin into his hands and squirted a generous glop onto his palm, warming it before gently rubbing my aching shoulders, back, arms and legs. He had found my oldest, softest flannel nightie while I was luxuriating in the bath and helped me into it, once again averting his eyes. He turned back my sheets, plumped my pillows, gently assisted me into bed and tenderly kissed the ridiculous scab on the end of my nose.

"You are a prince among men," was all I could manage. I was asleep before he turned out my light.

Donald had washed the dishes while Stephen was tending to me and they left when Stephen came downstairs. Donald fired up the Ferrari.

"Would you mind handing me my gloves?" he asked Stephen, who popped open the glove compartment and reached inside.

"Ow! What else do you have in here?"

"Nothing that should hurt," Donald said, stopping the car at the end of the drive and turning on the interior light. Underneath Donald's leather gloves were three bejeweled hat pins and a pair of thong panties.

"Shit," Stephen said. "I've seen panties like those in Genevieve's bathroom."

Donald put the car in reverse and returned to the house.

Chapter Thirteen

I heard about the planted evidence the next morning over breakfast. Alec was heartened by its discovery. Clearly, we were making someone nervous enough to take a big chance.

While Elise and I slept, the three men shared the discovery with the security guards. Alec took the evidence with full intention of turning it over to the authorities in the morning. He had no desire for a late night séance with the Magnolia Police and decided to use Detective Miller's failure to return his message from the previous night as an excuse.

Elise and I awoke feeling marginally better than the night before. We even managed to change out of our night clothes and into sweat suits before breakfast.

"What do you make of it all?" I asked Alec.

"A lot is happening here. My gut tells me that John LoConte planted the evidence in the Ferrari, but when? Or did he have an accomplice, but who? And was he working for himself or someone else? Until two nights ago, everyone assumed the three murders were committed by the same person, but the evidence reflects the police's brand new theory that Margaretta was killed by a paid killer, John LoConte, while Grace and Genevieve were murdered by Stephen. All for reasons unknown. It's absurd. Donald is convinced that it happened during the day, when the Ferrari was garaged near his office."

"And I never lock my car when I'm at home. The hatpin collection has been sitting on the seat for a day and a half."

"And I'm not sure those three hat pins were in it when Sean gave it to me. I never opened the box until last night, but Genevieve's thong, if it really is hers, took a lot of premeditation. She's been dead for ten days."

"Is that all? It feels longer," I said.

"Hal's FedEx arrived first thing this morning. You two were still in bed. Do you feel like looking at it? Maybe you'll notice something I'm missing."

Elise and I nodded and Alec continued,

"There are only six real estate closings over the last two years that the FBI could discover. None involve Sean directly, but they all use a real estate specialist in his office. John LoConte has bought and sold one piece of property over a two year period, and his cohorts from the Grand Jury investigation have each done the same. The two year period makes sense because if the property is considered a primary home, then no capital gains attach to the sale, but in these transactions, everyone took a small loss, which is unusual in the real estate market around here over the last two years."

The three of us sat around my dining room table shuffling pages.

"How much does a guy like LoConte earn?" I asked.

"He reports under forty thou' a year," Alec answered.

"Well, the house he purchased was ten times that. Isn't that kind of steep for him?"

"Yes and no. The guy is single and except for his car, this property is pretty much his only asset. He could always be hiding income, but he seems to be living within his means, on paper anyway. He didn't pay cash. He had a mortgage." Alec paused to shuffle through another pile of papers. "It appears they all had mortgages with the same outfit."

"Let me guess, Sharky's Bank and Trust," Elise said.

"No, some outfit named Town and Country Mortgage. I've never heard of them, but there are a ton of mortgage companies. Maybe Hal will look into it for us."

Sean arrived promptly at four. Alec's car was hidden in my garage and Alec was listening from the guest room. I hobbled to the front door in response to Sean's knock and opened it with difficulty, due to the bandages on my hands. As soon as Sean saw my scraped face and bandaged hands, he grimaced and insisted on helping me to the BarcoLounger, which the pillow and blanket clearly identified as my nesting place. Elise was still surrounded by pillows on the sofa. Sean hung his parka and scarf on the back of the rocking chair and sat in it.

"You weren't kidding about being banged up," he said looking at both of us with disbelief. "You shouldn't be here alone. Can I get you anything? I'm useless in a kitchen, but I can manage tea or ginger ale."

"Stephen and Donald will be here soon, and the security men outside check in on us, but thank you," I said trying to sound civil. I had never seen Sean Rogers without a designer Italian suit, and his worn brown corduroys, topped by a pale cream cashmere crew neck, patched at one elbow, surprised and disarmed me.

"Elise, your eye looks awful. I can't believe John LoConte did that! What was he up to?"

"That's the question we've been asking," Elise answered. "We were hoping you might be able to tell us."

"Me? I have no idea. The last time I saw John was at the Carlisles' office, before I met with you. He's buying another house. I haven't been spending much time in my office since Grace died and I left early that day and saved our real estate specialist a trip to Magnolia. It's a straight forward deal. The deed's in order and the land is registered. He's supposed to close next week. Do you mind telling me exactly what happened?"

Elise spoke up, "There's not much to tell. Laura and I drove here after the *Daily Grind* and discovered him planting a bug. The Hood's dog Lila was with us and he shot her. She recognized him from Margaretta's murder."

"Are you sure of that?"

"I heard him say as much on his cell phone, but I don't know who he was talking to," I answered.

"I can't imagine he knew the Hoods. I don't even know the Hoods. Why would he kill Mrs. Hood?" The three of us looked at each other before Sean continued, "Did you hear him say anything else? Anything at all?"

"Nothing."

"How is Mr. Hood doing? First his wife. Now his dog." Sean sounded genuinely distressed to me.

Elise and I resisted looking at each other and chose not to correct Sean's assumption that Lila was dead. Instead Elise spoke up,

"How are you doing, Sean?"

"To tell you the truth, Elise, I'm rattled. You must know that I've never defended choir boys, but nothing like this has ever come close to me. How could anyone kill Grace? She was so good, so beautiful. I don't get it. She didn't want to know anything about my clients and I kept it that way. The worst part of all for me is that I'd been neglecting Grace the last few months. I was really tied up with the Grand Jury and under a lot of pressure. I snapped at her more than once and she didn't deserve it," he paused and hung his handsome head. "You know when I heard she had been found dead on the rocks, the first thing I thought was suicide. I felt like such a selfish prick. I was relieved to find out it was murder. Imagine? I'm only starting to realize that I'll never find anyone like her again. She was always there for me and didn't ask a thing."

That was all Elise needed to hear.

"So you didn't know she wanted a divorce?"

Sean's head snapped straight up. His eyes were wide and unblinking. His mouth was open and Elise and I watched the color drain from his face.

"That can't be true. She never said a word to me. Did she tell you?"

"No, but she did talk to someone. Do you know Reverend Andrews, Bill Andrews?"

"I never heard of him. Oh, yes I have. He was at Grace's service. He and his wife came to the house afterwards, didn't they? Is he from Magnolia? How did Grace know him?"

We didn't bother to correct his assumption that Christine Parker was the Reverend's wife.

"I don't know how Grace knew him, but Magnolia's a small town. He mentioned it to me. I've known him for years," I lied, but there was no need to involve Stephen.

"How discreet of him," Sean mumbled and was quiet again. I studied Sean as discreetly as I could. The guy looked in shock to me.

"How does John LoConte know the Carlisles?" Elise asked, changing the subject.

"I introduced them. Strictly business. John thought he might want to leave the North End. The big lug still lives with his mother. Grace and I bought our house through Carlisle, so I put them together."

Sean sounded and looked like a devastated husband. He reminded me of the way I felt when I heard that Greg had died, and that was a heart attack, not murder. He slowly stood up and reached for his coat.

"Don't take this wrong, ladies, but you two look like hell. I'm leaving so that you can rest. Thanks for letting me come. I feel dreadful about all this, and can't help but think I'm somehow to blame. I just have no idea why. I'm glad you've hired guards. Something dangerous is afoot…Do you think your cleaner friend knows John LoConte?" he asked, as an after thought.

"No, I don't Sean, and there's no way Stephen had anything to do with this."

"You're probably right. We're all missing something. Call if you think of anything. I'll do the same. Please don't get up." Sean put on his jacket, kissed Elise on the top of her head and let himself out. He was in such a daze that he left his scarf behind.

Alec entered the room, noticed the scarf and put his finger to his lips. He picked the scarf from the rocker and inspected it.

"No bugs," he announced, then added, "I don't think I'd like to be cross-examined by you either, Elise. You really caught him off guard. I couldn't see him, but he sounded sincere to me." Elise and I nodded in agreement.

"I think he's as confused as we are," Alec continued. "He's right. There's a missing part to this puzzle. We're not making any progress tying Sean to the murders. Maybe it's time to look at the situation from a different perspective."

"What do you suggest?" I asked.

"How about the Reverend and Christine? They knew all three victims, didn't they?"

"Stephen will be pleased. I know Christine Parker gives him terminal heebee jeebees."

"I don't think we should ignore the Carlisles, either. They're the ones doing business with John LoConte and we know he killed Margaretta Hood," Elise said, gingerly touching her damaged eye.

That night, across two large pizzas, the five of us discussed alternative theories. For the time being, we decided to concentrate on Reverend Andrews and the jealous Mrs. Parker. After an exhausting discussion, Stephen and Donald drove home.

"I never thought such a grisly discussion could give me hope," Stephen began. "In my opinion, it's just a matter of time until they arrest Christine Parker and my name is cleared. I can't wait."

"There's no doubt that Christine appears to have jealousy issues," Donald said wryly. "But who would guess she would actually kill two women just because the Reverend was attracted to them?"

"And what about poor Margaretta? All she was guilty of was getting the Reverend fired."

"Yeah, but in Christine's sick mind, losing that job is what makes him financially dependant on his wife. She blames Margaretta for keeping Dorothy and the Reverend together."

"The scariest part of all to me is that Christine must have enjoyed killing Grace and Genevieve. At least she had to hire John LoConte to murder Mrs. Hood. She wasn't jealous of her, just furious. Mad in both senses of the word. But how did she know to contact LoConte?"

"Grace might have said something when she met with them. Laura and I saw the three of them talking at Sean Rogers' after Grace's memorial service." Stephen paused. "Do you think the Reverend knew?"

"Who knows? Do you think Christine will plead insanity?"

"I don't care. I just can't wait to be off the hook. The sooner I can put this behind me, the better. Are you as exhausted as me? When was the last time we had a good night's sleep?"

"The night before Christine murdered Grace."

Stephen turned up the radio and they drove the rest of the way home without further conversation. Donald glanced at his partner and noticed the downcast tilt of Stephen's handsome head. He could see the uncharacteristic dark circles under Stephen's eyes in the street lights. Donald took his right hand off the steering wheel just long enough to cover Stephen's hand with his own.

"What would I do without you, Stephen?"

"For one thing, you'd get more sleep."

John LoConte sat smiling only a few miles from Laura English's house. He had heard every word of the conversation inside the Ferrari. There was no reason he could think of to tell the boss about this turn of events. The fewer people who knew, the better for John. Barely more than forty-eight hours had passed since the botched abduction, and less than twenty-four since he planted the evidence and bug in the Ferrari for the boss. John LoConte was growing tired of taking the big risks for other people. He should have stayed with kneecaps and broken arms. The pay wasn't as good as hits, but John's tastes were not extravagant. He bought his mother's apartment for her when the old Prince Spaghetti factory had gone condo and he had always earned enough to gamble and get laid. He didn't like traveling, except in his Cadillac, and he never understood why anyone would go to a restaurant, if their mother could cook. He loved his mother's cooking, as much as he enjoyed eating in his underwear. Try doing that at a restaurant.

He wished his mother was cooking for him now. Ever since Monday night, John had been holed up in Gloucester. When he realized those crazy broads had jumped out of his trunk, he sped around the rotary and south on Route 128. He drove his car into the salt marshes barely an eighth of a mile from the rotary and watched as it sank out of sight in the newly dredged inlet where a marina was planned. From there it was barely a two mile walk to a spare set of wheels he had stashed in Blackburn Industrial Park. Gloucester had a large Portuguese and Italian population with hundreds of fishermen who are laid off during the winter. John just had to don a yellow slicker and a black knitted cap to fit in. Months ago, under an assumed name, he had rented a watchman's apartment in a small fish factory that was closed for the winter. John knew to always have a place to hide.

But what he just heard made him happy. If he could only get rid of that priest, or whatever the fuck he called himself, and that big broad, the heat would die down. The trick was to make it look like suicide. Let the police think they had solved the crime. He could start again someplace else, maybe Chicago. John knew guys there. But first he was going to take his time and think this through real good. That's what Ma would tell him to do. He remembered standing next to the big broad at Sean's. They were at the food table and she was loading up with cream puffs.

John wondered if the boss knew what Sean was up to, and he wondered if Sean knew what the boss was doing. As John mulled over his predicament, he began realizing that he was in a pickle.

"I'm fucked," he said out loud. The police knew he had murdered that old lady. They had the reason wrong, but he wasn't going to get out of this one if they caught him. John also realized that he knew too much for Sean and the boss to let him be arrested. Sean and the boss must be looking for him too. He wondered who they would hire to kill him. Maybe those guys in Chicago. He had never gotten into trouble on his own. His mother was always quick to point that out to him.

"Think for yourself, Johnny," she would say. "Don't let those other boys talk you into trouble. Make them do their own dirty work."

But somehow, John always did get talked into trouble. He loved how the other boys let him hang out with them and told him he was a stand-up guy after he stole a key, or hid a gun. He never killed nobody for them until he was sixteen and had dropped out of high school. It just sort of seemed a natural progression. John had never been to jail. Sure he'd been brought in for questioning lots of times and arrested five times, but never convicted. He knew those boys had been smarter than him, and now they were men and still talking him into trouble.

Yes, it was time for John to think for himself. It was time to commit a crime on his own and start again someplace else. Eventually, the police might even stop looking for him. John needed a plan. He was used to other people telling him the plan. He hadn't planned to kidnap those women and that's what got him in trouble, but he was going to do these murders perfect, without anybody's help. These murders would be the balls.

That night John walked to the strip mall where the Super Stop and Shop was located. He went to the bank of phone booths inside and looked up William

Andrews' address. The only listing in Magnolia was for William and Dorothy. John remembered what he had heard the fags say in the Ferrari. The big broad Christine was the guy's girlfriend, not his wife. Dorothy was the wife.

"Oh yeah, different last names," he said to himself and he knew he should have noticed that before. John wished he could talk to Sean or the boss. They'd know what he should do, but then again they probably wanted him dead. Maybe John could talk to Sean after he got rid of Andrews and the big broad. Sean was always nice to him. He'd been to Sean's house four or five times. The boss had never asked John to his house even once. Yeah, that's what he'd do. John would figure out these hits and then Sean would help him. He wrote down the Andrews' address, ripped the map from the phone book and grinned all the way back to the fish factory.

In the morning, the owner of the fish factory was on the dock checking the lines on his two trawlers and replacing a bent propeller. John offered him five hundred dollars to use his dory for the week. If the old captain thought this was odd, he didn't say anything. He just pocketed the cash. Fishermen did what they had to during the cold off-season. They refitted their vessels and fished the rocky coast when it was too rough for ocean fishing. They weren't beyond transporting a friendly haul of marijuana that had been left in a lobster trap not too far from shore. One thing they did not do was ask questions. Between the environmental police, the I.R.S., and both state and federal regulators, entirely too many people were interfering with a fisherman's God given right to earn a living. The old captain didn't want to know John's plans. He just wished him good luck fishing.

John LoConte settled into the dory, awkwardly started the old engine on the third try and cast off, nearly falling overboard with the line. His experience with the ocean was limited to Revere Beach, just north of Logan Airport. He preferred cruising the Revere Beach Parkway, looking at the high school girls in their bikini tops and cut-offs, the ones who would gather in front of Kelly's Roast Beef, watching the bikers and snapping their gum.

"Hey, Johnny," one might shout, leaning forward and doing a slow shimmy, "How about you buy us a Junior with sauce?"

"Dream on, cunt," he'd always answer, gunning his engine and speeding further down the boardwalk.

But this was not July, and the Gloucester waterfront in February was no day at the beach. According to his map, the Andrews' road abutted Halibut Point, a state park along Gloucester's rocky coastline. The wind picked up as soon as he left Gloucester Harbor and he had to head right into it to get to Halibut Point.

He took a few waves over the bow, getting drenched by the thirty-eight degree water.

"Fuckin' fishermen. Fuckin' stoop-it boat," John LoConte muttered as he continued pounding into the wind for the fifteen minutes it took to reach his destination.

He maneuvered into one of many coves along the park's coastline. There were too many rocks to beach the dory, so John was forced to set an anchor. He sloshed ashore in the rubber waders he had found in the apartment, and struggled up the steep climb from the beach. A rustic sign at the top of the cliff read *Lover's Leap*. John LoConte noticed it and grinned. Things were finally going his way. He didn't need no stinkin' Boss tellin' him what to do. Ma was right. John was just gonna think for himself.

He walked inland following one of four worn paths, where another sign pointed in the direction of the parking lot. John avoided the grassy open areas that meandered along the coastline, where his bright yellow sou' wester would cause him to stick out like a bumblebee on steroids. The day was raw and overcast. John hadn't noticed any other vessels on the water. He was carrying a fishing rod and had a thirty-eight in his shoulder holster. It took him ten minutes to reach the parking lot at the park's entrance. The split rail gate was closed, but not locked, and a sign announcing that the park would re-open in April was posted.

He swung the gate wide and crossed the road. The houses on this road were too low and far from the ocean to have a water view, so most of their owners had chosen to keep the lots wooded for privacy from the street, which was jammed with sightseers when the state park was open. John kept his eyes peeled for cars and began looking for number Thirty-Seven Halibut Point Road.

He found the driveway about a hundred yards down the road. Before reaching it, he had a momentary scare when a navy sedan drove toward him, but it turned into the driveway without passing John. Through the trees, he watched as Christine emerged from the driver's seat and entered the minister's home without bothering to knock. While he waited, trying to figure out who might be inside, the minister and Christine emerged from the house and climbed into the car. The Reverend sat in the passenger seat.

"Pussy wimp," John muttered. He hated when broads insisted on driving.

LoConte hurried down the road and intercepted the car just as it was turning out of the driveway. He waved his arms and the Reverend rolled down the window. John was wearing the hood of his slicker up with his black knitted cap beneath. Christine and the Reverend showed no sign of recognizing him.

"Could you give me a ride? I was fishin' the rocks at Halibut Point and my boat ran out of gas."

"Sure we could," the Reverend answered. "Say, don't we know you from somewhere?"

"Uh, I don't think so, Mister, but I'm glad you came along. This is the first car I saw. I left the gas can in my boat. That climb up from the cove was too steep for me to carry it and my fishing rod. Would you mind driving me to pick it up?" John said climbing into the back seat.

"We're in no hurry, are we my dear?" The Reverend asked Christine.

"No there's always time to help a friend in need," she answered smiling.

"Just drive on through. I left duh gate open. Duh boat's under *Lover's Leap*. It might take me twenty minutes to get there and back. Can ya' wait?" John had reached under his slicker and his hand was on the gun.

"No need," Christine announced, "I'll drive you out to the cliff. The ground's frozen. This time of year, nobody's around to stop us, and the Reverend and I are rather fond of Lover's Leap."

"Tanks, Lady."

Christine Parker had a momentary memory, but she couldn't pin it down. She felt sure that she had met this fisherman before.

When the car came to a halt at *Lover's Leap*, John pulled out his gun.

"Get outta the car!" he said pointing the gun at them.

They did as he asked, staring in disbelief at the weapon, and holding onto each other. John LoConte was no conversationalist and he did not waste any time talking now. Instead, he ran at the terrified couple like a rabid charging bull elephant during mating season, savagely muscling them over the cliff's edge. Christine Parker's final thought came too late to save her life, but it was of Grace Rogers.

If the couple had screamed, John didn't hear them in the stiff northwest wind. He looked over the rocky ledge and saw the two bodies splattered below. They had landed face down and John could tell by the amount of blood flowing from their shattered heads that they were dead. He climbed down the steep path as quickly as he dared and slogged back to the dory. He realized the tide must be coming in because the water was deeper than when he arrived, something John LoConte had not considered previously. He struggled to climb into the boat, and it nearly capsized under his whale-like weight on the gunwale. The anchor was wedged firmly on the rocky bottom, and he had a hell of a time disengaging it. Despite being soaked by the frigid water, John LoConte was lathered in sweat by the time he managed to fire up the old engine. Christine's car would be found,

and John LoConte was counting on the police to conclude it was a double suicide. Shit. Lover's Leap. How lucky could he get? Maybe he'd even try some fishing on the way home.

Chapter Fourteen

Dorothy Andrews began to worry on Friday morning. Her husband had been out all night. This was not like Bill. During twenty-eight years of marriage, he had never failed to produce a meticulously conceived confabulation in advance of his amorous absences. Bill considered this a kindness on his part, just a gentle story to keep his wife from fretting. Dorothy saw these lies for what they were. She was stoic, not stupid, and at this stage in her life, Dorothy Andrews had suffered enough scandal at the hands of her husband. She contented herself with her profession of grief counselor and hospice worker. The job was fulfilling and she was good at it. But now Bill was missing and only the machine had answered Christine Parker's phone. With some misgiving, Dorothy called the police.

"Police. Officer Coffin speaking."

"Good morning. Is the chief in?"

"Well, um, yes. Can I tell him who's calling?"

"It's Dorothy from the county Hospice and Grief Counseling Center."

Dorothy regularly interacted with the police in many towns, and she had no intention of telling the young officer her last name. Chief Doliber would know who she was.

"Hello, Dorothy. What can I do you for?"

"Skip, can we keep this between us?"

"I assume you're not confessing a crime?"

"That's right, but Bill didn't come home last night. Have there been any accidents reported? He could be in Christine Parker's car. It's a blue Maxima four door sedan. Maybe two years old. His car is here in the garage."

"I haven't heard of any problems, but what's the best number to reach you?"

"My cell. Six one seven, five four oh, two six six seven."

"Does anything else seem out of place."

"No, the house is just how I left it when I went to work yesterday. I'm sure there's an explanation."

"So am I, Dorothy. Give me a call, will you, if you hear anything?"

"Sure I will, Skip."

"Don't worry, my friend. He'll turn up." Skip hung up before adding, "That bastard."

In the Chief's experience, more havoc and misery were created by the institution of marriage than any other cause, but being a lifetime bachelor, he was hardly qualified as an expert. Dorothy and the Reverend had been married a long time. Dorothy's only mistake was to believe that phony when she was too young to know better. Now, she was spending the rest of her life paying for her naivete. Skip thought the world of Dorothy. He didn't know how he could have coped with his own dear mother's tortuous final months of life without her. Dorothy had eased his mother's pain and arranged for around the clock help. She had been a constant, compassionate presence during that hellish time and Skip was not going to add to Dorothy's burden by telling anyone that Bill Andrews was missing. Instead, he looked up Christine Parker's address in the local phone book and called young Officer Coffin into his office.

"Larry, can you drive by Seventeen Leominster Road and tell me if a blue Maxima is in the drive? If you don't see it, check the garage. Knock on the door if you have to."

"Sure Chief. What's up?"

"Nothing. Some good citizen found a license and car registration. Mrs. Parker, the owner probably doesn't even know she lost it. Just ask her to give me a call. And Larry, for heaven's sake, don't use the siren."

"Okay, Chief," Officer Coffin said, clearly disappointed about the siren.

The phone rang while Larry Coffin was on assignment and the Chief answered it.

"Magnolia Police Department. Chief Doliber speaking."

"Skip, it's Ned. I'm at the lighthouse. I think you better get out here."

"Sure Ned. What's up?"

"Some dead lady washed ashore on the west side of the Point."

"Be right there."

Ned Martin was the lighthouse keeper on Gloucester's Eastern Point. He and the Chief had known each other their whole lives and been co-captains of the high school hockey team thirty years earlier. There was no one you'd rather have on your side in a fight or your team for a breakaway. Over the years, lots of things had washed up on Eastern Point. The current from the harbor and the mainland flowed around the point, depositing more than a dozen bodies ashore over the last three decades. The dead tended to be inebriated summer vacationers who were cruising the spectacular New England coastline and fell overboard, unnoticed during the night. Occasionally, a lone lobsterman, repairing his traps would become tangled in his lines. At this time of year the ocean temperature was in the mid-thirties and anyone unfortunate enough to fall in would be dead from hypothermia in no time. Skip Doliber didn't need to tell Ned what to do about the body. Ned would know.

The last thing the Chief wanted was a high mass on Eastern Point, so he radioed Officer Coffin, instructing him to return to the office ASAP after checking for the Maxima.

"Roger that Chief. My E.T.A. is two minutes and counting. There was no car and no one home, by the way. Request permission to use my siren."

"Permission denied. Over and out." Skip telephoned the Coroner and left his office.

He found Ned seated on a rock near the body.

"Any thoughts, Ned?" The Chief asked circling the body.

"Not many. Her face is bashed in, which will make her hard to identify. She ain't bloated, so I reckon she was dead before she went in the drink. The body ain't deteriorated, so I make death less than a day ago. High tide was two thirty this mornin' and judgin' from the position of the body, that's when she washed up. She's wearin' three crosses around her neck and she's dressed in black. This is one big woman. My size I'd say. Maybe five ten and a hundred and sixty."

"I don't know why I bother with the coroner, Ned. Anything else you'd like to say?"

"Nah, you can say it."

That was just like Ned. Both men knew it was Christine Parker, but Ned was a team player. Skip was reminded of the many times Ned had passed the puck instead of taking the score for himself. Poor Dorothy. The chief couldn't keep this news quiet forever and with Reverend Andrews among the missing, tongues were bound to wag. The best Skip could hope for was to delay positive identification. He doubted that the coroner knew Christine Parker, and with the Reverend's whereabouts unknown, who would report her missing? He was curious to hear the coroner's report, but more anxious to find Bill Andrews.

The coroner arrived and the body was eventually removed. Skip called Dorothy and arranged to meet her at home. She had not heard from the Reverend and Skip wanted to tell her what had happened. After being shown in, he got right to the point.

"Dorothy, I've got bad news. I've just come from Eastern Point and Christine Parker's body washed ashore. Nobody knows who the corpse is except Ned and me for the time being, but we've got to find Bill. I don't think you should be alone here when he returns. Do you have anyone you can stay with?"

"Was she murdered?"

"Hard to tell. I'm waiting to hear what the coroner thinks."

Dorothy was calm, but she was used to bad news and death. Skip wouldn't have expected anything else from her.

"I can stay at the hospice house. I often do. I'll just leave a note for Bill."

"Would you like a lift?"

"Oh, no. I'm fine, really."

"There could always be a reasonable explanation." Dorothy just raised her eyebrows and smiled sadly.

Skip returned to the police station and began filling out his report. He would be lucky to hear from the coroner by tomorrow morning. Just before four that afternoon Ned Martin telephoned him.

"What can I do for you, Ned?" he asked when he was sure young Coffin wasn't eavesdropping.

"Skip, you ain't gonna believe this, but another body washed up on the afternoon tide. It's the Reverend."

Officer Coffin discovered Christine Parker's car on his way home from work. While driving by the entrance to Halibut Point he noticed the open gate. It was barely dusk, too early for kids to be necking and too raw for surf casting, so Larry Coffin drove in to investigate. He noticed the car right away because the doors were open and the inside light was on. He also noticed the keys in the ignition and when he couldn't locate the driver, Larry radioed the Chief. Skip was already on Eastern Point with Ned, once again waiting for the coroner. He instructed the young officer not to disturb any possible evidence, and to wait for Detective Miller at the park's gate.

Chapter Fifteen

Chief Skip Doliber was not completely satisfied with Detective Miller's conclusions. Reverend Andrews was hardly the profile for a double-suicide. He was intelligent, and liked himself entirely too much to be talked into such a demise. Skip believed it more likely that Christine Parker had snapped. Maybe the Reverend had become wary of her possessive, jealous nature and made the mistake of ending their affair. No threatening weapon had been found, but that didn't mean Christine was not wielding one when she drove the short distance to *Lover's Leap*, and then the tide washed it away. Skip would order scuba divers and dredging before signing off on the detective's findings. The Chief thought about the similarity between this incident and Grace Rogers' death, two deadly plunges onto the rocky coast. They'd probably never know if the latest involved a weapon, and unless the Reverend had a life insurance policy, the point was legally moot. Suicide or murder, Christine was the likely perpetrator and she was dead. He couldn't help but think about Dorothy. The question of life insurance aside, either determination would heap more scandal unfairly upon her.

After the news of the bodies washing ashore was released, Alec McBride met with the Chief at the police station. They discussed evidence and exchanged theories. The two men shared common sense, and by the conversation's conclusion, charges against Stephen Macomber were dropped. The Chief was glad to have these murders solved, or at least mostly solved. Finding John LoConte and somehow connecting him to the Reverend or Christine Parker seemed increasingly remote. Until such an occurrence, Skip would have to content himself with the knowledge that the guilty had been identified and the crimes would stop. What an appalling chain of events these murders had been. Skip Doliber was glad to have this nasty business behind him.

We were relieved to have Stephen vindicated, but the experience had been so painfully abominable that there was no celebrating. Ironically, on the day Stephen's charges were dropped, Donald's old pal Hal called Alec with an intriguing discovery. Only a week had elapsed since the arrival of Hal's FedEx chronicling the real estate activity of John LoConte and two of his partners in crime. During the week, my time had been spent recuperating, reeling from the discoveries of Christine and the Reverend's bodies, waiting for the coroner's findings, and finally seeing Stephen vindicated. At the same time, Hal had been following up on Town and Country Mortgage. It was a duly recorded, three year old Tennessee corporation, licensed to do business in fourteen states, all of which he said was unremarkable. But after further digging, Hal discovered that the incorporation had been executed by Sean's old firm in New York City. The President and CEO of Town and Country Mortgage was Meredith C. Raymond and the Treasurer was none other than Richard Carlisle.

"Why Meredith! That's Dick's sister. Carlisle Real Estate was started by their father and I've always understood that she's a silent partner or something," I said.

"That's what Hal found out," Alec replied.

"I had no idea Carlisle Real Estate was profitable enough to have its own mortgage company."

"It's not," Alec said. "And Hal's other discovery is equally fascinating. In three years, the only mortgages written have been the three to Mr. LoConte and his two pals. However, consider this. Say the three properties in question were really purchased for cash, but a friendly mortgage company recorded the transactions otherwise. Then imagine that two years later the property is sold for a small profit or loss, nothing that would attract attention, and the fake mortgage was paid off, on paper anyway. A lot of dirty money would become clean. Next, consider that there are maybe a dozen small mortgage companies doing business in different states, all writing only a few mortgages, none of them attracting much scrutiny."

"I take it that's what Hal thinks," Elise asked.

"Yes, and more importantly, the Feds think so, too. They don't plan on tipping their hand to the Carlisles, just keeping the operation under surveillance and hoping it leads somewhere. At least they know what they're looking for."

The five of us were gathered in my living room. A week had made a huge difference in the way Elise and I were feeling. The blood had disappeared from Elise's eyeball and the swelling was gone. Her bruising had turned from eggplant and black, to an impressive rainbow of pinks, yellows and greens. My most visible lingering injury was the raised dime shaped scab perched on the end of my nose like a big lazy housefly. I occasionally found myself looking at it cross-eyed. Alec had dismissed the security guards. The police were looking for John LoConte and he knew it, giving him every reason to stay away. Elise was returning to Chicago the next day with the intention of giving her six-week notice at work. She felt she owed them that. Her plan was to sublet her condominium and then move east. Elise knew she was welcome at my house, but I suspected other arrangements were being considered.

I had spent the day paying bills and marinating a butterflied leg of lamb in red wine, olive oil, onions, garlic, fresh rosemary and sour cream. I had two jars of Smuckers' Apple Mint Jelly. Stephen was in charge of grilling the meat outside. Each time he opened the kitchen door to check the progress, a celestial aroma wafted into the living room. March was here and tonight's weather was considerably kinder than February. Our collective mood was optimistic. I raised my Toasted Head and said,

"Here's to Elise and Alec, the silver lining in this dark cloud."

Stephen, Donald and I were grateful not to be losing our new friends, who graciously toasted us in return.

"Laura, take your house off the market tomorrow. Use 'seller's remorse' as an excuse. Knowing what you do, you don't want either Carlisle around. It would be impossible to act nonchalant and we don't want to tip them off. I suspect the reason LoConte was here planting that bug in the first place was because of who you saw in the Carlisle office. They couldn't take a chance that we were onto them in any way."

"Nothing would suit me better. Do you think June is part of this? She just doesn't strike me as clever enough to keep her mouth shut."

"From what I've heard, probably not, but luckily we don't have to figure that out."

"And what about Sean?" Elise asked. "I was just starting to feel sorry for him."

"Another tough call. Hal told me they're trying like the devil to connect him with the money laundering, but so far, no success."

"And can you believe that we figured out the scenario with Christine and the Reverend? It took us long enough, but Christine Parker was scarier every time I met with them. Even the Reverend was nervous enough to make the mistake of trying to dump her. Too bad for him," Clearly, Stephen would never believe the double suicide theory.

"I can believe Christine went crazy. I've known a few jealous types in my life, but what are the chances of something like that happening in this little town at the same time as the Mafia is laundering money with the local realtor?" Donald added.

"Oh, Donald, I don't know how you can be so naive. Haven't you ever heard of Cabot Cove?" Stephen said on his way to check the lamb.

After dinner, the boys left and I went upstairs. Alec and Elise volunteered for the dishes and time alone. Elise's flight was shortly before noon the next day and we planned to leave for the airport no later than nine-thirty. Alec wanted to drive her, but he had a court hearing that had already been rescheduled twice.

"Can you believe that the Carlisles are money launderers?" Stephen asked Donald on the way home in the Ferrari.

"It's not like I know them or anything, but even so, how incredible is that? Another example of truth being stranger than fiction."

"Amen to that."

A few miles away, in his fish factory apartment, John LoConte was listening. He was not tempted to tell the Boss what he had just heard. Fuck Richard Carlisle. That pompous ass had hung John out to dry. No, John decided he would tell Sean and then blow this burg. He knew not to trust phones, so he planned to drive to Sean's first thing in the morning. Sean would have cash and he'd know what to do. He'd appreciate knowing that the Feds were wise to the mortgage company. Yeah, that's what he'd do. He could trust Sean. Sean had invited him over lots of times.

John grinned thinking about the night Sean had driven him to Wal Mart. Eight of them had gone out to dinner after a long day in front of the Grand Jury and Sean offered to drop John in the North End, on his way home. When John said he had to go to Wal Mart to buy a house dress for Ma's birthday, Sean said that was no problem. Sean had never even been inside a Wal Mart and he wanted to see what everybody was talking about. So, while John stood in the checkout line with two flowered house dresses, Sean walked around, sneaking packets of condoms, which he had removed from the store's drug department, into the carts of other shoppers. It was funny as hell when the unsuspecting shoppers got to the checkout. Sean wasn't like the boss. That prick avoided him like an overflowing toilet at the bus station. Yeah, he'd tell Sean. Double fuck the boss.

Elise, Alec and I were up early. I was happy to discover that the scab had fallen off my nose during the night. Alec left by eight. I spied through the kitchen window, anxious to see their parting kiss. As I watched them, tears welled up unexpectedly in my eyes and my heart beat faster, a combination of happiness for the two of them and self-pity.

Elise and I were ready to leave by nine. On our way out of the house, I noticed Sean's scarf, which had been lingering on the rocking chair for over a week.

"Mind if we drop this off on the way to the airport? I'll tie it on the door handle, if he's not home."

"And I'll leave him a good-bye note. I suppose I should have phoned, but I just didn't feel like talking to him. I don't know what to make of my brother-in-law."

Ten minutes later we were at Sean's house on Salt Hill. There was a beat-up green pick-up truck parked in the driveway. Elise handed me the note she had written after I pulled on the emergency brake with my right arm. I put the car in park, leaving the engine running, and walked to the front door. I was just about to use the brass knocker, when the door opened. I found myself face to face with John LoConte. He appeared to be leaving with a large briefcase. I'm not sure which one of us was more startled, but I wasted no time leaping off the front steps, screaming for help. The big lug grabbed me around the neck before my feet even reached the walk. What started as a high pitched scream for help, instantly turned into a sputtering gargle. He dragged me kicking into the house, while Sean rushed past us, headed toward my car. Elise saw what happened. With her left hand she immediately pushed the automatic door lock on the center console, released the emergency break and put the car in reverse, while simultaneously hitting auto-dial on her cell phone with her right thumb. She held the phone to her right ear and attempted to steer down the steep driveway with her left arm, from the passenger seat. She knew Alec was in court and his phone would immediately go to message mode without even ringing.

"Alec, LoConte has Laura and Sean's chasing me. I love you, my darling."

Elise dropped the phone. Sean had reached the driver's door and was attempting to shatter the window, but my Pathfinder gained enough momentum to out pace him, while plunging in reverse down the steep drive, forcing Sean to let go or be dragged. When Elise reached the bottom of the driveway, she shifted into drive and prayed the car's idle would keep her ahead of Sean. She had no way to reach the pedals on the driver's side, so with both arms clutching the closest side of the steering wheel, Elise feverishly attempted to turn the car down the winding Salt Hill. Again Sean appeared at the driver's window, only now he had a rock in his hand.

"Come on, Baby," she willed the car. "Go go go go!"

Sean was pounding the driver's window with his rock. Out of the corner of her eye, Elise noticed a crack in the safety glass. She leaned on the car's horn as the vehicle's speed increased with the Pathfinder's descent. Sean's face disappeared from the window. Elise hoped he had slipped under the car and been run over, but she was now hurtling too quickly down the sharply curving hill to risk taking her eyes from the road. Elise down-shifted to four wheel low, kept her hand on the horn and prayed. Salt Hill's intersection with busy Atlantic Avenue was in sight. She turned the wheel sharply to the right and the car spun onto Atlantic where it was rear-ended by none other than Larry Coffin, crashing the Pathfinder into a large maple tree and knocking Elise unconscious. He hadn't heard the blaring horn because he was late for work and had decided to use his siren.

Chapter Sixteen

By the time Sean returned to the house, John LoConte had me tied up with duct tape. Hit men must travel with a supply of it the way grandmother's always have Kleenex. Where was Elise? As though reading my mind, Sean said bitterly,

"My cunt sister-in-law got away. Whether she's dead at the bottom of the hill, or not, the police are bound to be here soon. Our only chance is to leave right now. You take my Mercedes in the garage. The windows are tinted and we can't risk somebody seeing the body." I didn't like the sound of that. "Drive to Canada and stay there. Dump our friend here along the way, the sooner the better. I'll take the pick-up and leave it at Logan."

As he spoke, Sean removed a pack of bills from his wall safe and slid them into his wallet, which he placed in the breast pocket of his sport's coat. Despite everything, he looked remarkably calm and even well groomed. He tossed the car keys to LoConte, who caught them with one hand.

"Mine are in duh truck," he said.

"All right then, my friend. Cover her up with the coats in the closet, like you're taking them to the cleaners. Good luck." They actually took the time to embrace. A regular Kodak moment. Sean sprinted out the front door and John threw me over his shoulder cave man style. When he leaned over to lift me up, I caught a glimpse of his shoulder holster beneath his open parka. I would have wriggled, but I remembered all too clearly where that had gotten Elise ten days earlier. We stopped at the coat closet on the way to the garage. I was hanging over

LoConte's shoulder like a big rump of beef and envisioning a cascade of grisly deaths, each one more unpleasant than the last.

"You forgot your briefcase," I said, hoping to endear myself to him.

"Oh, yeah. Tanks, lady."

"Laura, my name's Laura."

He didn't say anything. All he did was open the car's passenger door and deposit me on the floor in front of the seat. I was riding shotgun, in a manner of speaking. The car was Mercedes' largest, most luxurious model. LoConte had taped me into the shape of an S and the floor provided me with plenty of space. Next, he covered me with coats. Apparently, I had lost trunk privileges. He got in the driver's side, and locked the doors before starting the car.

"If duh police are at duh bottom of duh hill, dey'll havta shoot you to get to me. Got it?"

"Yes, sir." Through the pile of coats it sounded like "humph humph."

We were at the bottom of the hill in less than a minute. I was praying for a miracle, maybe a cloak of invisibility or the temporary ability to fly.

"Yo. We're in luck. Your car got hit by a police cruiser and went into a tree. Dat's funny, huh? What's duh chances of hittin' a cruiser anyways? Duh road's blocked off and it looks like your friend's dead. We gotta turn left, dat's all."

Not exactly what I was hoping to hear. My captor's sense of humor left me cold. I willed myself to stay calm. I could hear sirens in the background, probably police and an ambulance. Would they send an ambulance if Elise were dead? I poked my head out from the coats. My captor raised his tree trunk arm to back-hand me, but dropped it when I made no effort to sit up, as if I could have from my taped fetal position. I needed to get LoConte talking.

"Don't get no ideas, lady."

"Oh, no. It was hard to breathe, that's all," I paused a moment, desperately thinking of something to say, but panic had caused my mind to become a blank. If I could somehow get John LoConte to like me just a little, maybe he would leave me somewhere to starve instead of murdering me outright. My inexperience with the subject of hit man bonding was proving a liability.

"How does this car handle, John? It certainly has a comfortable ride, but it's no Cadillac." I had no idea what to say. In my terrified state that was the best I could muster. I was hardly in a position to ask the questions I really wanted to, but comparing the relative merits of the Mercedes 500 Class to the Coupe de Ville? Really. If I lived to tell the tale, Stephen and I could have a good laugh about this.

"You mockin' me, lady?"

"No, no. I'm interested, that's all," I replied quickly, staring up at him from under the dashboard with what I hoped were admiring eyes and a coquettish tilt of my head.

"Well, I think dese foreign jobs are over rated. Yeah, it's built like a tank and its got a big engine, but it ain't no Caddy. If it cost less, half duh people wouldn't want it."

"I've often thought the same thing," I said truthfully. "But I've never even driven a Cadillac or a Mercedes. Now I know. Thank you."

"Don't look like you'll ever get to drive one neither." LoConte actually slapped his knee laughing over his remark.

More hit man humor. I wondered if John LoConte had grown up talking that way, or if he learned to after he chose his career path. I decided to laugh, too. People love it when you laugh at their jokes.

"Do you like your job, John?" I asked after our merriment had subsided.

John LoConte stared down at me from behind the wheel with an expression of blank amazement.

"What duh fuck you talkin' about lady?"

"Well, a strong young man like you could do lots of things. I'm sure your job isn't easy. You take risks for other people and you've got to have nerves of steel." I decided to omit the brain-dead requirement.

John's expression changed to his version of deep thought. No one had ever asked if he liked his job before, and a man in his business didn't survive long by talking, but this broad had seen her last sunset. He decided to answer her question.

"Yeah, I like my job. Some whacks are better dan others. I used to whack for any of duh bosses who asked me, but not any more. Only duh guys I like."

"What do you mean?"

"I hated stabbin' dat old lady, but Sean asked me. I did it real quick and she never even knew I was dere. You got it wrong about duh priest and dat big broad. I'd never whack for dem."

"Sean? Why did he want Margaretta dead?" I was stunned. There was no doubt that John LoConte was going to kill me. After all, that lovable rascal Sean had asked him to. I started feeling numb. Maybe it was the fetal position I was confined to. I futilely tried moving my bound wrists and ankles.

"To cover up for his wife. Sean's real smart like that. Duh big broad called him and said Grace wanted to get a divorce and Sean should keep his wife away from duh priest. You know how much money Sean got salted away? And it ain't what you might call declared income neither. Some divorce lawyer starts lookin' at his finances, and Sean's screwed. He was gettin' real tired of Grace anyhow. Sean said after all duh stuff he gave her, she was an ungrateful slut. So it was really her fault. Duh police already suspected your cleanin' buddy, so I tailed him a coupla days and whacked the old lady, to make him look more guilty."

"Good for you. It worked, too." He didn't notice my lack of enthusiasm.

"Yeah, I know," he said grinning proudly. "It was my idea to whack that big broad and duh priest, too. It gets me off duh hook for most of it. Dey can't prove I stabbed duh old lady. It's just what dey call speculation. Police are dumb fucks. Duh only thing dey got me for is snatchin' you and duh gimp sister week before last and we didn't go over no state lines or nothin'. It ain't even a Fed wrap."

I was having trouble breathing. None of this would have happened if Christine and the Reverend had kept their conversation with Grace confidential.

"What about Genevieve?" I asked, not sure that I really wanted to know.

"Oh, that crazy bitch. She was Sean's idea. Duh priest told her about Grace wantin' to take a walk and when Grace got iced, she sort of figured it out. It didn't bother her or nothin'. She went over to Sean's, pretendin' to give condolences. She told him what she knew and got it on with him to prove that she didn't blame him. He said she was a real good lay, too. Very athaletic, he said. Then she said maybe dey should start seein' each other in secret and get hitched when it all blew over. Sort of like blackmail, ya' know. Well, Sean pretended to go along with it and saw her a coupla times and I guess she mentioned how your fag friend was cleanin' before her old lady came to visit. So Sean paid me to whack her. I never whacked nobody like her. She was all coked up, dancin' naked when I snuck in. She saw me as soon as I got to her bedroom because of all duh mirrors. 'Well, hello,' she says, 'Do you like what you see?' Her eyes were real glassy and she was touchin' herself all over. It was disgustin'. Then she lay down on duh bed and said, 'Let's have some fun, big guy' like I was a freak or somethin'. So I walked over to the bed and strangled her. She thought it was a game. Stoop-it bitch."

By now, we were headed south on Route 128. I figured we would soon exit north onto Route 93, toward New Hampshire and Canada. He'd have to kill me before the border. I could just see the fuel gauge from my nest beneath the dashboard. Half a tank. He surely wouldn't risk refueling with me in the car. I was pretty sure that Mercedes had huge tanks, but I also thought they were gas guzzlers. I'd be in heaven for lunch. I started praying. I prayed to God to save me. I asked him to watch over my beloved Abbie and Dave and I thought about Greg. It would be nice to see him again, but I wouldn't mind waiting a few years. I prayed that Stephen and Donald would always know the joy they had brought me. I prayed that Elise was alive and that she and Alec would live happily ever after. I started to cry and my nose ran. I wiped it on the sleeve of Sean's cashmere Armani coat. I wondered if Donald had sold it to him. I could feel the car slowing down. We were probably at the interchange with 93. If I could only open the passenger door, this would be the place to throw myself out. If I survived today, I might consider a career as a stunt woman.

Once again I struggled futilely with the duct tape. My wrists were taped behind my back and my ankles were bound together. LoConte had bent my legs at the knees and used more tape to attach my feet to my hands. I wasn't going anywhere. The only body parts I could really move, besides my head, were my fingers. I quietly started walking them through the nest of coats, trying to locate pockets. I found one and explored the recess. It held a handkerchief. John LoConte could wave it when I talked him into surrendering. My fingers continued searching. They eventually found another pocket crammed with something. I slowly started pulling a silk, fringed scarf from the pocket. The scarf must have been four feet long. I could tell its fine quality from the texture, probably three hundred dollars at Armani's. Maybe LoConte would strangle me with it.

Just as I pulled the last of the scarf from the pocket, something solid slid into my hand. I held the object in my palm. It felt familiar and in a heart pounding rush, I knew it was a Swiss Army knife. Greg carried one and the corkscrew had saved the day more than once. I carefully tried releasing the blade and succeeded in cutting my thumb when it slipped from my awkward grip and powerfully snapped back into its sheath. God bless the precision of the Swiss. The blade was razor sharp and the jack knife's hinge recoiled like a sling shot. I gritted my teeth and shut my eyes with the unexpected pain, but once I succeeded in opening the knife, it easily sliced through the tape below my shins, separating my ankles and freeing my feet from my hands. My wrists were still bound behind my back. I strained to position the blade in a manner that would slice the tape. My palms were sweating and my wrists were wrapped so tightly that my fingers were asleep. I paused to rest my aching hands and thought about all the actors I had seen free themselves from similar situations. What would MacGyver do?

My captor seemed oblivious to my efforts and I meant to keep him that way. He had placed the car on cruise control and we were traveling at an unobtrusive sixty-three miles per hour. Traffic was passing us on both sides, but the tinted windows prevented voyeur truck drivers from noticing me on the floor of the Mercedes. Some of the passing motorists must have admired the car because once John LoConte shouted,

"What duh fuck you lookin' at, cunt?"

We had been traveling for forty-five minutes and had crossed into New Hampshire. The border is marked by Route 93's only toll. Unfortunately for me, Sean had the Fast Lane Pass and he didn't even take the car out of cruise control as we drove through. I was momentarily heartened by the thought that if Elise had survived, Sean's car might be part of an Amber Alert, and his use of the Fast Lane Pass would tip the authorities. I wished I could remember if New Hampshire participated in the Amber Alert System. They'd probably nail LoConte at the Canadian border, too late to help me. I'd already be practicing the under water stare.

I knew this road from a decade of driving to Canada with the kids' youth hockey teams. The countryside would not become truly wooded and rural until north of Concord when we entered the Lakes District, another hour and a half. I guessed that would be John LoConte's choice location to murder me and dump my body into a lake. The White Mountains had a plethora of lakes and unmarked, winding, dirt roads. He would probably weight my body with rocks. After all, New Hampshire is the Granite State. Then he'd knock a hole in the ice and dump my body into it. The hole would refreeze and I wouldn't be found for weeks, if ever.

I glanced at the gas gauge again. It was an eighth lower than my last look. I guessed that a car like this might have an emergency tank, too. There was a distinct possibility that I had witnessed my last fill up, in this world, anyway. I started wishing that Route 93 were a toll road. With such few vehicles on the road, a traffic jam was unlikely, and delays due to roadwork wouldn't occur until the frost was out of the ground. The day was clear and dry, so I didn't hold out much hope for a traffic accident, unless I caused it. I prayed that for once the dire roadside warning signs about falling rocks and deer crossing would come true.

While reviewing my options, I continued the battle to free my wrists. I tried placing the dull side of the blade perpendicular to my spine with the handle below, allowing the cutting edge to press against the tape. This was not an easy position to achieve and when I finally did, the manner in which my wrists were bound prevented me from exerting any pressure on the tape. I was so intent with my struggle that I inadvertently swore out loud. LoConte glanced at me, but said nothing. Instead, he turned on the car's radio. After trying all the buttons twice, he switched to the AM band, selecting a country western station. At least it wasn't hip hop.

I remembered the force of the blade when it snapped close on my thumb and decided to approach my problem from a literally different direction. If I couldn't press the tape against the blade, maybe I could press the blade against the tape.

Lying on my back was out of the question. I didn't dare do anything that would stimulate Cro-Magnon man's curiosity, or risk moving the coats in a manner that would expose my liberated ankles. First, I made sure that the duct tape was aligned with the blade. My palms were facing each other and I held my left hand out of the way the best that I could. Carefully, I lifted the handle toward the blade with the fingers on my right hand, hoping the hinge would swing into action and the force of the knife folding shut would cut the tape. The trouble with my plan was the weight of the handle. Despite my best efforts, I just couldn't bring the handle close enough to the blade for the hinge to engage.

I was sweating from my exertion, but refusing to give up, when unexpected help arrived. The Mercedes hit a pothole. The jolt caused by the heavy vehicle's descent into and out of the crater snapped the knife shut, blessedly freeing my hands. I found myself smiling and was surprised to look up and see John LoConte doing the same.

"Ain't my fuckin' car," he said.

With my hands free, the time to plan my escape had arrived. The element of surprise was on my side. I took inventory of what I knew:

He had a gun.

I really didn't want to throw myself out of a car traveling at sixty-three miles per hour.

LoConte would probably kill me within ninety minutes, when we reached the desolate Lakes Region.

With this information in mind, I decided that grabbing the wheel and causing a car accident might be my best bet. The next time the Mercedes slowed down, we would probably be in the Lakes Region. I felt the odds of surviving a highway crash would be higher than outrunning John's bullets. Either way, I was in no hurry to die, and I took my time deciding when to grab the wheel. I became a clock watcher. Just south of Concord, the highway splits and Route 93 bears to the left toward the Lakes Region. After negotiating the split, LoConte surprised me by immediately pulling onto the highway's left side soft shoulder, which, unlike the previous section of Route 93, was shielded from oncoming traffic by thick woods on the median. Surely, he wasn't planning to kill me here with so much traffic whizzing past.

"I've hadda take a leak for duh last half hour. My eyeballs are floatin'," he said, turning off the car engine and stepping out. I wondered if those might be the last words I'd ever hear.

He left the driver's door open as a shield from passing traffic and stood in front of it, facing into the car and watching me through the windshield. Who said hit men have no social graces? Presumably, John was peeing onto the Mercedes' door. Thinking I was still tightly wrapped in duct tape, he had left the keys in the ignition. I gave him a few seconds for his stream to get started, and when I saw the look of relief on his face, I sped my left hand to the ignition and my right hand onto the transmission. The engine instantly turned over and I moved my left hand to the gas pedal, while my right put the car in gear. I couldn't see a thing, but the Mercedes responded by racing down the soft shoulder, throwing a shower of gravel behind it. The open car door knocked LoConte flat on his back before he could even draw his gun. I climbed over the center console, slammed the driver's door and never looked back.

Chapter Seventeen

Alec had spent the morning in the Middlesex County Courthouse trying to settle a complicated custody issue for the childcare agency in Amherst. One of the resident's fathers was about to be released from jail after serving a term for drug possession and he wanted his son back, in no uncertain terms. The mother had died two years earlier from an overdose. The father had fulfilled his debt to society and Alec knew full well that parental rights trumped just about everything else in the state of Massachusetts. Over the years, he had learned that no matter how dreadful a child's life had been, there was something about human nature that made most children yearn to be with family. Children were not meant to grow up in institutions.

The child in this case was no different. He was counting the days until he could once again live with his father. All the parties involved were working together to create a successful discharge plan. The agency was helping the dad with job placement and housing. He had agreed to live and work near Amherst, so the agency could continue to provide support systems like after school supervision, transportation services, respite care, and meals, if needed. The goal was not to set the father and son up for failure, but it was a balancing act that Alec found exhausting.

The court took its lunch break at one o'clock. Alec bought a hot dog with mustard and sauerkraut from the vendor in front of the courthouse. He was seated on a sunny bench with his mouth open, about to take the first delicious bite, when he noticed Elise's cell phone number on his phone's digital readout.

Smiling, Alec pushed the button, anticipating a tender message from her, prior to boarding the flight. Instead, Elise's panicked voice emerged from the phone. The hot dog fell to the sidewalk as Alec sprinted toward the parking lot. He managed to call Chief Doliber as he ran.

"Magnolia Police Department. Officer Coffin speaking."

"Chief Doliber."

"Who's calling, please?"

"Alec McBride. It's an emergency!"

"He isn't here right now. Can I help you, Mr. McBride? Oh, yeah, Mr. McBride. Now, the Chief gave me a message for you. I wrote it down here somewhere. Can you hold please?"

The irksome policeman didn't wait for a reply and Alec found himself on hold. He reached his car, climbed inside and started driving toward Magnolia, while still waiting. He was just considering hanging up and calling back when the annoying young officer came back on the line.

"Hello, Mr. McBride?"

"Yes," he answered, doing a slow burn.

"Man, you're lucky I found it. Somehow, it ended up in the wastebasket. Some woman made me crash her car this morning and…"

"Just give me the goddamn message!"

"Hey, don't get an attitude with me, Mister. I've had a long day."

"Excuse me, officer. May I please have my message now?"

"All right. The Chief wants you to call him on his cell phone."

Alec couldn't believe that this idiot couldn't have remembered that message, but he controlled himself.

"You wouldn't have the number, would you Officer Coffin?"

"Umm. It's here somewhere. I'll just put you on hold."

Again, Alec was forced to wait. He wondered if this guy was born an imbecile, or if Larry Coffin had perfected the behavior over time.

"Hello, Mr. McBride? You still there?"

"Yes."

"That's good. Sometimes people get cut off. I hate when that happens. Now, what can I do for you?"

"The number. The Chief's cell phone number! You were going to give it to me."

"Oh, yeah. That's right. We been real busy today and like I told you, some lady made me crash into her on my way to work and I'm here alone and all."

Alec took a deep breath. "I'm sure it's been a very trying day Officer Coffin. If you could just give me Chief Doliber's number, I'll be out of your hair."

"Okay. I got a lot of other things I should be doing instead of talking to you, you know. The number is ONE, six, one, seven, seven, eight, nine, three, three, oh, one. Got that? ONE, six, one, seven, seven, eight, nine, three, three, oh, two."

"Is it two or one?"

"Two or one what?"

"The last number. What's the last number?"

"Like I said, 'two,' but don't forget the ONE."

Alec disconnected from the phone call from hell and reached Skip Doliber.

"Chief Doliber."

"Chief, it's Alec McBride."

"Alec, I've got bad news. I don't know who else to call. Grace Rogers' sister, you know the crippled one? Was in a car accident. She must have been leaving her brother-in-law's house shortly after nine this morning, but he's not home or in his office. We've been trying to…"

"Is Elise alive?" Alec interrupted.

"Barely. She's unconscious. Fractured skull."

"Where is she?"

"Gilbert Hospital. I'm there now. She was alone on the passenger side. We're…"

"I'll be there in a half hour. John LoConte has kidnapped Laura English and Sean Rogers is involved, too. That's all I know."

"See you when you get here."

Skip Doliber disconnected, feeling badly for the lawyer. Over the years, the Chief had learned to detect the emotions within a voice. Alec McBride was in love with this woman, or the Chief would eat a hockey puck.

Chapter Eighteen

I sped north on Route 93, distancing myself from LoConte. I needed a phone. I passed an emergency call box, but visions of John hijacking a good Samaritan's car kept me from stopping to use it. A sign for gasoline and a MacDonald's ten miles down the road answered my prayer. The ten miles felt like a thousand. The enormity of the last two hours hit me. My hands started shaking and the trembling spread up my arms and throughout my body, until even my head was quivering like a ridiculous bobble doll. I clutched the steering wheel, trying to steady myself and began singing *sotto voce* with the country western station.

"Stand by your man, blah blah blah blah blah blah blah, give him all that you can, blah blah blah blah blah blah blah, even though your heart is broken, blah blah blah blah…stand by your man! Sorry, about not knowing the lyrics, Tammy," I apologized out loud when our duet was finished.

"Well, I beg your pardon. I never promised you a rose garden," I added to keep the conversation going, which struck me as exceedingly clever. I suspected I was teetering on the brink of hysteria. I recalled a television interview years ago with Burt Reynolds and Dinah Shore. They were an item at the time, but somehow Burt mentioned what a great lady Tammy Wynette was and Dinah agreed. I thought that was nice all the way around. Both those women were dead now. I was telling myself not to think about dead women, when my thoughts were interrupted by another song.

"He stood six foot six. He weighed two forty five…" Jimmy Dean was singing. The roaring sound in my ears kept me from hearing the next words. I willed myself not to faint. Breathe in. Breathe out. Keep breathing. MacDonald's loomed ahead. I continued to breathe and focused on the sign. Golden arches had never looked so good. I drove the Mercedes onto the sidewalk and stopped inches from the front windows, facing into the restaurant. The song was just ending as I fled the car.

"And everybody knew you didn't give no lip to Big Joohhn, Big Bad John."

MacDonald's had just changed to its lunch menu and a small group of diners were present. My arrival must have looked like I was planning to crash through the front plate glass. Two men, who I took to be truck drivers, intercepted me at the door. It's possible they had been in the window booth inches from the Mercedes' resting spot. They probably thought I was drunk or deranged and they were half right.

"I've been kidnapped. Please help me." The roar came back into my ears and I fainted. I came to in the manager's office, which had a cot with a blanket. Maybe I wasn't the first traveler to collapse, or maybe the manager sometimes napped. The truck drivers had locked my car and were waiting for me to regain consciousness. I had only been out three minutes and the State Troopers had been notified and were expected shortly. I sat up with no ill effects and asked to use the phone. I called Alec's cell phone and left a message.

"Would you like a drink?" the manager asked.

"Ginger ale would be lovely. Thank you."

"Listen, lady. I got somethin' more potent in my rig. You're welcome to it," the larger of the truck drivers offered.

"Thank you, no. I need to be clear-headed."

Everyone was staring at my right thumb, which was bleeding impressively where the knife had sliced it.

"Let me wrap that up for you. First aid training is a job requirement and I've just passed the mandatory refresher course. You'll need stitches, but this will help until you get to an emergency room."

My luck seemed to be changing. I sat gratefully on the cot and let everyone tend to me. The ginger ale was the most delicious I had ever sipped. We introduced ourselves and talked about the weather, as though it was important. No one asked me what had happened. They just let me calm down, while we waited for the authorities. I have always found kindness to be the best restorative.

The State Troopers arrived. They were all business. We heard them approaching before we saw them. They were walking in cadence. The larger of the truckers smiled, raised his eyebrows, made a fist with his right hand and moved it back and forth, stopping just before the troopers entered the office. The room could not accommodate the six of us.

"I guess it's time for Gary and me to get back on the road. Good luck, Laura. You're one gutsy lady," Bobby, the smaller of the truckers said. He turned to the troopers as he passed them and added under his breath, "She's the victim. Don't go thinking anything else."

"Thanks for catching me," I said, not feeling a bit gutsy, but appreciating the kindness.

"I'll be at the grill," Pat, the manager, said.

"I'm Trooper Salvucci and this is Trooper Long."

"I'm Laura English," I said taking them in. Salvucci was stocky and about five foot nine. I had the feeling he might be bald beneath his tan trooper's hat. I guessed he was forty. Long was three inches taller and probably five years younger. I found myself wondering if Troopers liked their uniforms. They were designed to flatter and intimidate, which was an asset, but those uniforms looked like a lot of work to me. Heavy, tall leather boots with a matching leather strap diagonally across the chest, encircling the waist. Always wearing a hat must get old. These troopers' hats were sort of modified cowboy style with a rope around the brim. Live free or die. Yippee ky ay. And what about that chain underneath the nametag, leading to the buttonhole? The pair did not sit down, but chose an "at ease" position to question me. I was forced to tilt my face up at them, or stare at their crotches. They do that on purpose. That way they're in the power position.

"All right, Laura, what happened?"

More power. I was old enough to be their mother, but I was "Laura." According to their nametags, their first names were both "Trooper." I was coming out of shock and feeling grumpy. A sure sign of life. I hoped their uniforms were hot in the summer.

"John LoConte kidnapped me. He stopped to urinate on the left hand shoulder at the split of 93. He didn't realize I had cut the tape, so I was able to knock him over with the passenger door and get away. But he has a gun. I don't know what kind. Anyhow, it fits in a shoulder holster. He did the same thing two weeks ago. His boss, Sean McBride owns the Mercedes out front. He drove a banged up green pick-up truck to Logan Airport. My guess is an international destination. I have no idea of the make or model, but it was a full size with one row of seats, no double cab. There's a suitcase full of money in the Mercedes. Chief Doliber from Magnolia, Massachusetts, can give you more details. It's all to do with the murders in that town." I was trying to give them the most important facts first, but clearly I was babbling. The troopers just stared at me, so I continued.

"They tried to abduct my friend Elise Sanderson, too, and she ended up in a car crash at the intersection of Atlantic Avenue and Salt Hill in Magnolia, shortly after nine this morning. I'm very worried about her and I'd be most grateful if you could find out her condition."

"We'll get in touch with Chief Doliber. You'll have to come with us and file a complaint. Then, if everything checks out, you'll be free to go." I didn't think I liked the sound of that. Salvucci and Long showed no reaction to my story, probably a ploy to keep me babbling.

"Shouldn't you tell somebody to be on the lookout for John LoConte?" I snapped at them while getting to my feet. The blanket had hidden my hands and legs. When I stood up, they noticed the duct tape attached to my wrists and ankles for the first time, along with the bandage. Blood was already soaking through Pat's bandages.

"What happened? You need to get to a hospital," Trooper Long announced.

"I'll get medical attention later. I just want to file charges, make a phone call and get home. Can you try contacting Chief Doliber? Or the Massachusetts State Police? They know about my last abduction."

"That will speed the process along. I'll stay with the vehicle until the tow arrives. Trooper Long will drive you to headquarters." Long was probably the low man on this totem pole. I bet Salvucci tried to scam a freebee from Pat as soon as Trooper Long and I left. Probably a Big Mac, large Coke, and fries.

John LoConte's arrest warrant was in the New Hampshire system from two weeks earlier, which considerably shortened the time I had to spend at headquarters. Even so, the paperwork was tedious. A female officer wearing rubber gloves carefully removed the duct tape. She placed it in a plastic bag, and wrote the time, date, and case number in a white rectangle on the outside. I called Stephen and asked him to pick me up. He made the drive and still had to wait nearly an hour for me. I could see him through the glass partition of the room where I was seated. He looked so worried, that I was afraid I might cry, but when Trooper Long wasn't looking, I made cross-eyes at him instead. I hate crying. Once you start, it's so hard to stop.

It was two o'clock by the time I was free to go. The State Police Headquarters had a first aid room and a medic, who re-bandaged my hand, but he was forbidden to give civilians stitches. Apparently, he was also forbidden to have a sense of humor.

Stephen and I bear-hugged in the parking lot and he wouldn't even allow me to fasten the seatbelt by myself.

"Have you heard from Alec?" I asked as soon as we were in the car.

"No, should I have?"

I realized Stephen didn't know any of this. Why would he?

"Let me use your cell phone. Mine was in a car crash."

Chapter Nineteen

We arrived at Gilbert Hospital before three thirty. Alec met us there. En route, I had called Alec and filled him in, while Stephen listened. Alec then relayed the events to Chief Doliber, who returned to the police station to file a report. The Chief told Alec that he would bring the report to me and I could make any changes that were needed before signing it. He would also retrieve my handbag and Elise's luggage from my crashed Pathfinder. Skip said I had been through enough. Elise was still unconscious and in Intensive Care. She was not allowed visitors. While waiting for Stephen and me, Alec had filled out my paperwork for the emergency room. No flies on Alec.

The two men hovered outside my curtained cubicle. I could see their feet pacing back and forth like expectant fathers from an era gone by, Stephen's Nike cross-trainers and Alec's rubber soled brown tassel Cole Haans.

"Didn't feel a thing," I told the young doctor.

"Oh, you will when the novocaine wears off," he said happily.

He gave me a tetanus shot, a prescription for an anti-biotic, told me to keep the wound dry, call with any questions, and return in a week.

"Fourteen," I announced proudly opening the curtain.

"Thank heaven for that knife, Laura," Alec said.

"Amen," I answered.

"I called the security firm and arranged for them to work the next couple of nights."

"Oh, Alec, surely that's unnecessary."

"You're probably right, but I'll sleep better. Humor me."

"Well, in that case, thank you."

"Any news on Elise?"

"Just what I already told you. Her skull is fractured, but so far there's no brain swelling or any inter-cranial bleeding. If nothing develops in the first twelve hours, there is reason to be cautiously optimistic. They said I could sit with her after nine tonight, if all goes well."

"How does this sound," Stephen said. "It's four thirty now. No offense Laura, but you're looking kind of pale. I'll take you home for cookies and Toasted Head before those nasty anti-biotics are in your system. While you're collecting yourself, I'll get the prescription filled and pick-up some 'to go.' Alec, you'll need a wash-up and a bite if you intend to be any use to Elise later. Go to Laura's any time after six. We'll feed you and send you right back here a new clean man. Donald and I will tuck Laura in and you can return later for some shut-eye, or not."

It's so nice to have a take-charge person when you need one.

"It's a plan," Alec said.

Donald was already at my house when we got there and so was the security. Stephen must have called Donald from the hospital and he left work early. He had my pillows and favorite blanket on the Barco-Lounger. A bottle of Toasted Head was in the ice bucket. I could hear my bath water running. Donald was holding a plastic wine glass in his hand.

"For your bath, Madam. Fourteen stitches are enough for one day."

Stephen must have told him. Now it was safe to cry.

I came downstairs after my bath wearing a robe and slippers. I was carrying my hairbrush because left handed hair dressing was one of many skills I had never mastered. Donald French-braided my hair. I was amazed.

"My first boyfriend was a hair dresser," he told me.

Stephen returned with two bags of food from my absolute favorite restaurant a few miles away in Gloucester, Sugar Magnolia's. Their motto was "Sugar Mag's, cuz it tastes so good."

"Oh, Stephen, you angel!" I said, realizing I was famished.

"In honor of Elise, I decided to go with 'brain food.' Hope you feel like fish. We have roasted corn chowder with a salmon fillet and fish tacos."

Both were my favorite favorites. I had begged the restaurant's owners, Missy and Pete, to tell me their secret recipes, besides the obvious wriggling fresh fish, but they always smiled and refused. Sugar Magnolia's actually had customers who ordered the same thing each time they came, because they couldn't believe any other item on the menu could be as good. For me it was this chowder and fish tacos.

I was nestled in the Barco-Lounger when Alec arrived.

"She's still holding her own," he said in response to our anxious expressions. "I'll just wash up, eat and get back to the hospital, if that's not trouble for you."

"Your wish is my command," Stephen said from the kitchen.

Alec was back at the hospital before eight.

"Oh, Mr. McBride, I was just about to phone you. Dr. Hodgeson wants to talk to you," the charge nurse said motioning to the far side of the nurse's station. "Doctor, Mr. McBride's here."

Dr. Hodgeson looked up from the chart he was filling out. Alec's heart skipped a beat.

"Mr. McBride, Ms. Sanderson seems to be agitated. She is experiencing what we call 'REM,' or rapid eye movements. She is also turning her head from side to side and moaning. This can be a sign that she's descending into coma, or it may indicate that she's trying to regain consciousness. It could be helpful if you would sit with her and talk about anything that might be meaningful."

Dr. Hodgeson escorted Alec to Elise's bed in Intensive Care. When the doctor left, Alec held Elise's right hand between the two of his and started talking.

"Elise, it's Alec. I need you to wake up. We've learned so much since this morning, but we, make that I, need you to put everything together and nail that bastard Sean. Laura got away from John LoConte. She cut her hand, but otherwise she's fine. LoConte murdered everyone, on orders from Sean. You were right. That S.O.B brother-in-law of yours masterminded the whole thing, except for the Reverend and Christine Parker. LoConte donated his services for them."

Alec paused just a moment, wondering for the first time how John LoConte had known about their theory regarding the Reverend and Christine. He'd think about it later, after Elise was awake. First things first.

"Grace was murdered because Christine Parker told Sean about the divorce. That pious prat thought..." Alec continued, chronicling the reason for Genevieve's demise, when Elise opened her eyes, saw him and smiled.

Chapter Twenty

John LoConte lay motionless on the soft shoulder of Route 93. The back of his head hurt. What the fuck happened? He had been taking a whiz and looking right at the prisoner, when the cunt drove off. How the hell did she get free? Son of a bitch! He better get out of sight before some frickin' do-gooder stopped to help, or even worse, phoned the incident in to the State Police. John rolled down the embankment into the wooded median strip and out of sight. He better get moving. Slowly he tried to stand, but was momentarily overcome with dizziness. Like a bull waiting to gore the matador, John rested on all fours with his head hung low. He'd felt a lot worse than this. Being hit by a lead pipe was much worse than this. Being shot by a twenty-two wasn't so bad, but anything over a thirty-eight was brutal. His dizziness passed and John began trudging through the forest to the other side of the median. If the bitch U-turned and headed home, he might get a shot at her when she drove past.

John assessed his situation. He had a gun and a pocketful of bullets, which was good. He had stashed two packets of cash from Sean's briefcase into his parka, so he had twenty thou', also good. The rest was in the Mercedes, not so good. Worst of all, that ball-busting bitch would turn it over to the cops. He felt a cold breeze on his loins and realized his fly was still down. John LoConte zipped it up thinking how much he would enjoy shooting this cunt.

John LoConte had been in trouble often enough to know he had to keep moving. He could steel a car, but that was risky. He'd have to grab one at a highway fast food joint and there'd be lots of witnesses and the theft would get reported pretty quick. Hitch-hiking was always dicey. People really studied hikers, even if they didn't stop, because hikers were a suspicious type, unless they were in uniform and he didn't have no fuckin' uniform. No, John had better get off this median, where it was too easy to get trapped. He better cross to the south side of Route 93, walk to the first rest stop and find some trucker who'd give him a lift.

Crossing the highway was a breeze. Mid-week, and late morning traffic was light. Beyond the soft shoulder, the terrain dropped steeply into the low-lying woods. In New Hampshire, the month of March is referred to as mud season. The snow melt from the White Mountains had formed an impressive brook running between the embankment and the woods. John needed to slosh through it if he wanted the woods to shield him from a state trooper's prying eyes. He did his best to jump over the stream, but he landed squarely in the mud on the far side, sinking up to his calves and falling backwards into the brook. The entire rear of his pants was soaked and he struggled to stand up.

"Fucking mud. Fucking cunt," John muttered as he tried to right himself. The mud was thick and pervasively cold. His foot came out of one of his boots when he tried to pull his leg from the dark muck. John had to reach over from the wooded side of the stream to retrieve it. The boot was so firmly embedded in the gunk that John had to get on all fours to create enough leverage to free it.

"Fucking cunt. Fucking mud," he reiterated before beginning his trudge south.

Each step was an effort and produced a kersloshing sound. He knew there was a rest area just ahead, or John would have walked through the woods and risked breaking into the first empty looking house he encountered. Christ, he hated this shit. He could bench press three hundred, no sweat, but aerobic had never been his thing. After twenty agonizing minutes, John saw the rest area. He kersloshed around behind the Burger King and used the rear entrance to access the men's room, which was just inside the door. It was the lull between breakfast and lunch, and for the time being, John was the only one in the bathroom. He removed his mud soaked pants and socks, rinsing them in hot water. He used his murderer's hands to squeeze them dry and then held his clothes underneath the electric hand dryer. Two scraggly men in their early twenties entered the bathroom, dressed in sneakers, jeans and parkas.

"I slipped in duh fuckin' mud. Don't worry, I ain't no pervert," he said.

"Bummer, dude," one answered. "Ya' want some help?"

"Uh, ya' don't mind?"

"Nah, just let me take a leak and I'll hold the legs on those pants. Jack can dangle the socks for you."

"Tanks. Dat would be very much appreciated."

John only dared linger another five minutes. He wiped the mud from inside his boots with paper towels. At least his socks were dry. His pants were damp, but warm for now. He got dressed and went out the door he came in and proceeded to the truckers' parking lot. No State Troopers had passed him on the highway. Maybe the broad couldn't find any. She didn't have no phone or nothin'. John decided to approach the first driver he saw returning to his rig, when he noticed a gray semi with big red letters on the side "Airport Express. Cargo for All Major Carriers." John smiled.

He sat on the passenger side running board, hoping the driver would soon emerge from the Burger King. He didn't have long to wait. John stood up when the driver arrived.

"Hey, pally, you goin' to Logan? Could ya' gimme a ride? My freekin' car broke down up duh road. My stoop-id old lady can't drive a stick worth shit and the thing just died. I got bagged for DWI for duh second time and ain't got no license, so I havta depend on that moron to get me to work. If I'm late again, they'll can me. It would really help me out. I could give ya' a sawbuck."

"Hey, keep your money. Climb aboard."

"Tanks. I wouldn't ask, but I'm up shit creek without a noseplug."

"Jeez, I hate being the passenger when my wife drives. How long did you lose your license for?" the trucker asked, pulling onto the highway.

"A frickin' year. I couldn't bahlieve it."

"You got a lousy commute, too."

"Yeah. My old lady wanted a house. Said the kids was gettin' a bad influence in Revere. I can't afford no goddamn Mass.taxes. So now I'm in duh Live Free or Die state without no license and I'm thinkin' maybe I'd be better off dead, cuz I sure ain't livin' free. Dere ain't no jobs in this frickin' state, unless you work one of those ski joints, but that's iffy cuz of no snow and only good in duh winter, anyways. And besides, I ain't no snow bunny. Ya' know what I mean Pally?"

"Yeah. It's a helluva thing, for sure."

The trucker dropped John at the East Boston Park and Fly. One of the big bosses owned it. No tickets, no surveillance, and the boss' pals got a ride with one of the guys to his terminal and picked up when he returned. The public had to take the frickin' bus. John knew that's where Sean had left the truck.

"Gimme duh keys, Antny," John said to the kid on duty. Even if they knew LoConte was in hot water, they'd keep their traps shut.

John figured if he could just make it back to Gloucester, he'd be okay. Nobody knew about his hideout and he could still listen to the fags in their Ferrari. He filled the tank to just over half before he left the Park and Fly."

Logan wasn't as easy as it used to be. John had grown up in East Boston and he knew the airport like he knew Angie deNucci had a third tit. Cripes, the scams they used to run out of Logan. It used to be that more cargo walked out of the storage areas than got delivered, but 9/11 and the Big Dig had changed all that. Now, instead of one circular road through the airport, there seemed to be twenty. Overpasses, under passes, loop de loos and the roads were different every time he went. And the frickin' troopers always yellin',

"Don't stop. Keep movin'."

He had sent Ma to Sicily in the fall and when he picked her up, the troopers wouldn't let him stop. On his third trip by, John got out of his car anyways and gave the trooper the finger.

"Whaddaya want from me? She's an old lady. She can't run that fast. She's got bags." At least the guy had laughed.

Nowadays you had to be a fuckin' brain surgeon just to make a U turn at Logan.

It was only two in the afternoon and there hadn't been any reports on the trucker's radio about him, but there would be soon. That Laura broad must have blabbed by now, but what did she know, really? She had seen the truck and knew Sean was driving it to Logan. Big deal. The cops would start checking the terminal parking first and by the time they got to the Park and Fly, they wouldn't find anything. All John had to do was get back to Gloucester and lay low. If he didn't get picked up in the next hour or so, he had it made. John took back roads through East Boston and then paralleled old Route One the rest of the way. He was back at the fish factory by three thirty and parked the truck inside the closed fish processing facility. John pulled his black knit cap low over his forehead and walked down the street for a big bowl of steamed mussels and linguica in a spicy tomato sauce, with plenty of Portuguese bread for dipping. Man, was he hungry. He could listen to the bug in the fag's car later.

Chapter Twenty One

Sean heard the Pathfinder crash before re-entering his house. The sounds of metal on metal, a siren, and shattering glass traveled up Salt Hill on the breeze. He hoped Elise had collided with an ambulance because its weight and speed would likely have killed her and Sean wanted Elise dead. Every minute became crucial now. Anyone in Sean's position needed contingency plans, even John LoConte. Sean had scrupulously covered his own tracks for years. If Elise were dead, and if LoConte successfully eliminated that friend of hers, Laura Whatshername, Sean had no reason to run. No one could prove that he had hired John LoConte. He could say Elise must have stopped in to say good-bye on her way to the airport, not knowing that Sean had made a spur of the moment plan to revisit Europe, where he and Grace had honeymooned a decade earlier. He would claim to have just missed the two women.

Elise hadn't told Sean that she was returning to Chicago. The police would hypothesize that a desperate LoConte must have surprised them, while looking for cash to make his getaway. He must have stolen Sean's Mercedes. But Sean could not afford to risk all of the ifs right now.

Finding someone to say he had driven Sean to the airport was not a problem, but had a neighbor seen him chasing the car with Elise in it? No, Sean needed to disappear. He could always return innocently, when and if the circumstances allowed. No one would fault him for needing time alone to mourn. Or, if need be, Sean could stay away forever.

Over the years, he had salted away millions. Most of the money was in numbered Swiss accounts. Sean had worked hard, making sure his clients trusted him. He had taken calculated risks on their behalves and they had paid off. What Sean's clients didn't know was that only he could access the accounts. Sean had convinced these thugs that they were better off not knowing the details of the banking arrangements. That way the money could never be traded for a get out of jail free card, if one of them were arrested. Contrary to the cliché, Sean knew there was rarely honor among thieves.

He had never been forced to disappear before, but Sean was experienced in helping others do it. He was well prepared for this adventure. He went inside his house and stayed just long enough to collect the carefully packed suitcase and briefcase from the hidden compartment in his study's wall. He had already given one briefcase to LoConte, but Sean took time to embrace the hit man, and relay a few instructions before he was out the door.

He understood John LoConte. John had spent his life being ridiculed because he was so stupid. Cruel teasing takes a toll. When the person being humiliated can't tolerate it any more, there is hell to pay. Sammy the Bull didn't bring down the mob because he feared jail. Sammy had spent half of his life in jail. Unlike on the streets, he was respected in jail. No, Sammy had reached his humiliation limit and he had retaliated. Sean knew of one goodfella who Sammy had carefully protected. It was the guy who was kind to Sammy, the guy who befriended him, seemingly with no ulterior motive. If John was captured, Sean was going to be that guy.

His suitcase was packed with the clothes and toiletries anyone would take on vacation, except cash was stitched into the linings of sports jackets and the bag itself. His briefcase contained innocent reading material, travel documents, and a brand new laptop. The lining held more cash and false documentation. He would turn into the other identities, only if necessary. If need be, Sean intended to establish his alibi by revisiting the destinations of his honeymoon, which included Geneva. He was allowed to travel with ten thousand dollars, which was in plain view in his briefcase. Sean had never understood why the government didn't weave aluminum or nickel fragments into paper currency. The metals were cheap, lightweight and flexible, and would make detecting smuggled bills much easier. Sean was not about to look a gift horse in the mouth, however.

There was no reason that a trip this morning should arouse suspicion, but tomorrow might be a different story. He planned to leave on the first available flight to Europe. He would monitor newspaper stories on the internet and return in a few weeks, if the coast remained clear. Otherwise, Sean would disappear forever.

He left the truck at the Park and Fly and was inside the International Terminal shortly before ten thirty. A flight for London was on the airport departure screen flashing Boarding. Sean proceeded immediately to the Virgin Air counter and was dismayed by the length of the line, when an efficient, middle-aged, female Virgin Air supervisor appeared.

"Any passengers for London, please proceed to the head of the line at this time. Passengers for London, please."

Sean had always enjoyed listening to a British accent, but never more than today.

"Yes, I'm hoping to catch that plane," he said, smiling his well-practiced, most disarming, trial lawyer smile. "I'm afraid I'm unticketed. There's been a bit of a family emergency and my car suffered a flat on my way to the airport. Not my lucky day, you might say."

"We'll do our best to change that, Mr. Rogers," she said glancing at his passport.

"I can't tell you how much your help would mean. Mother's on a tour with her garden club, and I'm afraid she's had a fall and broken her hip. She's scheduled for surgery in the morning and I want to be there for her. You know, the tour must go on and she's quite alone."

"Consider it my pleasure, Mr. Rogers." She detached her walky-talky from the waistband of her sensible navy blue skirt and spoke into it, requesting immediate transportation services at the Virgin Air ticket counter. She alerted the gate that another passenger would be arriving momentarily. A motorized golf cart arrived and they proceeded to the head of the security line.

"Special circumstances, Jack. Sorry," she announced to the security officer.

Sean and his luggage passed muster and they drove to the gate, with the golf cart beeping fellow travelers out of its way. His ticket was waiting for him when they got there and his over-sized bag was given dispensation to be carried on board because the luggage compartment door had already been secured.

"Thank you, Elizabeth," Sean said reading the supervisor's nametag. "May I know your last name? I will be writing a letter of commendation."

"Oh, no, that's not necessary, Mr. Rogers," the no-nonsense Elizabeth replied. Sean noticed a very British flush emerge from beneath the buttoned collar of her white blouse. He watched as it traveled up her neck, crossed her cheeks and turned her ears bright red.

"Yes it is, Elizabeth. You've made all the difference in what could have been a dreadful situation."

"It's Angell. Elizabeth Angell. Two L's. I'm pleased I could be of assistance."

"The perfect name for you. Thank you Elizabeth Angell." Sean shook her hand, turned, and walked on to the plane.

Once on board, he settled into his First Class seat. The plane was only half-filled, which had probably contributed to the airline's willingness to accept a last minute First Class passenger. The airliner immediately pushed back from the gate and was airborne before eleven. The pilot's voice announced a significant tailwind and estimated a five-hour flight. Sean couldn't believe his luck. When it was permitted, he reclined his seat and looked out the window. He had lived with the knowledge that one day he might have to go on the lam and his emotions were not as mixed as he had anticipated. After all, what was he really leaving behind?

He thought about Grace. Sean had always prided himself on being an astute judge of people, but he had misjudged Grace. Originally, her beauty and style attracted him. She exuded good breeding, which was an asset a young lawyer could use. She was undemanding and easy to be with. Sean's mistake came when he mistook Grace's shyness and quiet serenity as a sign of not being too bright. He wanted a wife who would not ask questions, but more than that, not even think of questions to ask. He wanted a wife without dreams or personal aspirations beyond his own. When Grace became unhappy, she became dangerous to Sean. When the Parker woman had phoned him, Sean had a harsh awakening. A divorce would cause his life to unravel, not emotionally, but economically. There was even an outside chance that discoveries unearthed by a good divorce lawyer would send him to jail and Sean Rogers wasn't about to be held hostage by anyone, let alone his own wife. Grace had suffered the consequences for not living her life on his terms.

*   *   *   *

The flight touched down five hours later at Heathrow. The local time was just past nine. It would be four in the afternoon at home. Sean made a mental note not to think of Boston as home any more. He had been prevented from using his laptop during the jet's forty-five minute descent into London, but as of an hour ago there were no postings on Boston's local news websites about him. Sean would have been surprised to find any so soon, but hopefully it meant no one from New Scotland Yard would be awaiting him in the terminal. He checked his laptop one more time before proceeding to Customs.

The next twelve hours would be the riskiest part of Sean's scheme. In the best case scenario, Sean would get away with everything, in which case he could return to America. Hopefully, Elise and Laura were dead by now. John LoConte successfully getting lost would be icing on the cake, but Sean was not worried about John betraying him. Surely if a neighbor had seen Sean chasing Elise in the runaway car, Sean would have been stopped at Logan, or even en route. The authorities could easily discover that he had flown to England, but in the likelihood that Sean emerged rose-scented from all of this, he wanted to leave a trail to support his story. If nothing went wrong, he would call his office on Monday, innocently letting them know where he was, and be shell-shocked with distress to learn about his sister-in-law's demise. He might even return to make funeral arrangements, after all, Elise didn't have anyone else, did she?

Sean dallied on his way to the Customs line. He exchanged two thousand dollars for pound notes. He resented money changers and their greedy commissions. His fellow passengers were waiting for their baggage and Sean didn't want to encourage a lengthy questioning period from the Customs officer, simply because no one else had queued up yet. On the other hand, Sean was anxious to leave the airport and disappear into London. If he were still in the clear tomorrow, Sean would be home free, so to speak.

He heard his fellow passengers behind him in the corridor, racing one another to Customs, without wishing to appear to be doing so. Sean increased his leisurely pace and secured the fifth place in line.

"Are you here on business or pleasure, Mr. Rogers?" the officer inquired, scrutinizing Sean's passport photo.

"Pleasure."

"How long do you intend to stay in the country?"

"A few weeks."

"Are you traveling alone?" he asked arching his eyebrows and peering over his half glasses.

"I'm meeting my mother."

"Really? Does she live in England?"

"No, she's traveling with her garden club and she's had a fall. She's having surgery in the morning."

"Very sorry to hear that, Mr. Rogers. Which hospital?"

"Prince Albert." Sean had been prepared for this question.

"Just like the Queen Mum. I wish her a speedy recovery. Thank you Mr. Rogers. I hope you can take in the theatre and at least have a bit of fun while you're here."

The officer efficiently stamped Sean's passport and motioned to the next in line.

"That's a good idea, Officer. Thank you."

Before exiting the terminal, Sean pulled the generous collar of his Burberry high. He entered the first dimly lit bar with a view of the runway, looking at the ground, as though stooped by the weight of his luggage. Sean wanted to be shielded from the myriad of surveillance cameras that he knew covered every inch of Heathrow. He seated himself in the darkest corner and ordered Tanqueray on the rocks, a drink he had never tried. After the cocktail arrived, Sean subtly poured it onto the rug, a swallow at a time. He carefully extracted the collapsed Burberry hat from his coat's inside pocket and placed it on his head, along with a pair of thick dark framed eyeglasses. The hat had a fringe of softly curling gray hair that had been carefully stitched into the headband and the simple disguise remarkably altered his appearance. He left cash on the table and walked out of the bar with the stooped gait of a much older man. His collar remained high as he exited the terminal and proceeded to the Hertz bus stop. Sean had secured a rental car from his laptop en route. He waited fully ten minutes for the rental agency's bus to appear and a small crowd was huddled beneath the kiosk by the time it did. As if ordered by central casting, there was a light fog and a fine mist of drizzle. Sean graciously invited the weary passengers to climb on board the overheated bus before he got on, allowing him to stand and be the first to disembark.

There were no customers waiting in line at the Hertz counter, and three agents were on duty. Sean strode to the young man in the middle, who was yawning and seemingly suffering from a cold. His eyes were watering, his nose was red, and a wet looking handkerchief protruded from his shirt pocket.

"I have a reservation for a four door mid-size. Here's the confirmation number."

"Last nabe, please," the sorry fellow asked.

"Cushman."

"Ah, yes, 'ere it is Mr. Cu, excuse me," the agent turned his head and sneezed violently into his handkerchief, "Cushman."

"Bless you," Sean said. "You've got a nasty one there."

"I'm off duty at ten. You'll be my last tonight," he said filling out the form, barely looking at Sean's identification.

"Good. You should take tomorrow off, if you won't get the sack. The only way to lose a rotten cold like you've got is sleep, or else you get dreadfully run-down and it takes weeks. I ended up with pneumonia once, simply because I wouldn't take a day in bed. No one appreciates your loyalty, anyhow."

"You got that right, mate." The young man sneezed quite spectacularly and added, "My boss can sod off, if 'e don't like it. Red or black?"

"Black. Remember to take your phone off the hook, too. Hope you feel better, then."

Sean handed the agent a credit card in the name of Henry Cushman and signed the slip.

"Thank you, Mr. Cushman. Good night." The young man placed a "closed" sign at his station and prepared to leave.

"Nice old bloke, that," he said to a co-worker on his way out.

Sean located the unobtrusive black sedan in the parking lot, and stowed his luggage on the rear seat, but not before booting his laptop to check the news. He seemed to still be in the clear. He double-checked the map from the rental counter and after showing his credentials to the Hertz gatekeeper, exited the lot. A few hundred yards down the road, Sean removed Mr. Cushman's glasses, but kept the hat on. He drove carefully to Trafalgar Square and parked in a high rise garage, replaced his glasses and walked with his suitcase and briefcase to a nearby pub. Once inside, Sean chose another dimly lit corner and seated himself. It was eleven o'clock, only six in Boston. He had a few hours to kill.

He sat with his back to the bar and set up his laptop on the table in front of him. Sean didn't want to make any new friends tonight and he hoped the computer would discourage fraternization. Eventually the bartender came over.

"Sorry mate, we're short-handed. The floor girl went home with a nasty tooth. Don't envy her that. What can I get for you?"

"How about a pint of your best and a menu, if the kitchen's still open."

"Yeah, it stays open 'til closin'. Nothin' fancy, mind you. But the grub's good here."

"That's fine. Thank you."

The bartender returned in a few minutes, with Sean's pint and a menu.

"Just holler when you're ready, mate."

"Right-o," Sean replied, managing to sound like a Brit.

Sean sipped his beer and went online for the Salem News. He was still in the clear, but Sean would rest easier after reading the morning edition. He took his time finishing the pint and signaled the bartender for another. When it arrived,

Sean ordered a ham and cheese on rye. True to the bartender's word, the sandwich was surprisingly tasty. The ham was thickly sliced and lean. The cheese was an excellent cheddar and the mustard selection that accompanied the plate was superior. Even the accompanying fries, or chips as they were called in England, were irresistible. Sean ate them with vinegar, not wanting to request ketchup, a sure way to start a conversation.

"So you're a yank, then mate?" he could imagine the bartender saying.

Sean left the pub around half past mid-night. The rain was heavier than before and he flagged a cab.

"The Cosmopolitan, please," he said to the driver.

While in the dark rear seat of the British hack, Sean removed Mr. Cushman's hat and glasses, stowing them in his coat's inside pocket. He was positive the driver had not noticed the gray fringe on this dark, wet evening. It was time to become Sean Rogers again.

Sean and Grace had stayed at the Cosmopolitan on their honeymoon. Sean remembered it as an elegant European hotel and wondered if he would find it changed. The entrance was covered by a portico and the doorman, complete with top hat and gloves, opened the taxi's door for him.

"Checking in, sir?" he asked reaching for Sean's bags.

"Yes, thank you."

They walked through the deserted marble lobby to the registration desk, where an impeccably dressed, dark suited, tall, trim man was on duty. His nametag read Mr. Smithers, Reservations Manager. Sean guessed Mr. Smithers was in his early thirties.

"May I be of assistance, sir?" he asked with an aristocratic accent and slight nod of his well-groomed head.

"I hope so. I don't have a reservation," Sean replied, using his well-rehearsed disarming smile.

"That should not be a problem, sir. Did you have a specific accommodation in mind?"

"Nothing too noisy. Maybe overlooking the side street." The Cosmopolitan was located on a corner.

"What size bed do you prefer?" Mr. Smithers asked, typing on his computer.

"Queen or king. Either one."

"How long will you be with us, sir?"

"Three nights at least. My plans are a bit up in the air."

"Not a problem. Just tell us when they're settled. We have quite a comfortable executive room on the sixth floor. Our executive rooms are larger than standard, but not suites, and include rather nice amenities, including an oversized loo. How does that sound?"

"Great." Sean handed him his own credit card and filled out the registration card. In return, Mr. Smithers efficiently rang for the bellman and handed him the key.

"Enjoy your stay, Mr. Rogers."

"Thank you, Mr. Smithers."

Once Sean was installed in his room, he used the bathroom, disturbed a few towels, and messed up the bed, as though it had been slept in. He put Mr. Cushman's hat and glasses back on and took the side elevator back to the ground floor. He remembered the second set of elevators from ten years ago, and was pleased they still existed. He also knew that this bank of elevators avoided the lobby and led to a door on the side street. With a momentary pang, Sean recalled passionately kissing Grace each time they found themselves alone on these elevators.

He exited the building carrying his briefcase and suitcase and walked across the side street to the Lenox hotel on the next corner. He remembered the Lenox bar from his honeymoon, intimate, with polished wood, a piano and gleaming brass. The hotel itself was less elegant than the Cosmopolitan, but the little bar had suited him and Grace for a late nightcap, before returning to their suite across the way. The bar had a door on the street and another into the lobby. Carrying his luggage, Sean walked through the bar to the lobby registration desk. Under the name of Henry Cushman, he secured a sixth floor room facing the Cosmopolitan. Sean had purposely left the lights off in his room at the Cosmopolitan. If they were turned on before dawn, he would know to get lost. If not, his alibi was established.

Sean showered before ordering a pot of coffee from room service. He set up his laptop on the table by the window and turned out the lights in his hotel room. It was twenty minutes before two in the morning. The shit hit the fan at precisely three fifteen. The lights went on in his room across the way and he could see Mr. Smithers standing by the open door like a mother hen, while two trench-coated detectives checked the closet, under the king size bed, and the extra large loo, to no avail.

Chapter Twenty Two
Magnolia

The smell of coffee and bacon coaxed me down the stairs at seven forty-five. Alec was in the kitchen eating a breakfast fit for the New England Patriots when I scuffled in wearing my bathrobe and slippers. As soon as he saw me, Alec said,

"She's not out of the woods, but she's conscious! She can talk. She has no memory of the crash, but other than that her mind seems to be in tact. Thank God!"

"Tell me everything," I said helping myself to the coffee, bacon and eggs Alec had left for me.

"She woke up about an hour after I left here. I'm sorry I didn't call."

"That's all right. What does the doctor think?"

"He's concerned about the two head injuries in a relatively short period of time. And he wants to assess the extent of Elise's head trauma with the skull fracture. The fracture is high on the right side of her skull. I can't believe that's all that happened. I drove to the police impound lot, where they're keeping your car, on my way here. That was some crash. Your car's totaled. That imbecile Larry Coffin was the one who crashed into her, which spun the car into a huge tree, and knocked it over. He was late to work, so Einstein decided to speed with his siren going and couldn't hear Elise blowing the horn."

"Did he lose his job?"

"Don't know, but as a lawyer, it would be a tough call to make stick. Elise couldn't use your brakes. The car was pretty much out of control."

"Is she in a lot of pain?"

"Hell, yes, but she's a brave one. She even cracked a joke. She looked me in the eyes and said, 'I can't move my legs.'"

"How long will she be there?"

"Too soon to tell. They have tests scheduled this morning. It's important that she stays still and calm."

"What about visitors?"

"With doctor's permission."

"Does she know what John LoConte told me?"

"Every word. She can't wait to see you, but the doctor says no more visitors until six tonight because of the tests, and he wants complete rest this afternoon."

The front doorbell rang and I answered it.

"Oh, hi, Skip. Come on in."

"I thought I'd stop by and drop off your purse and Elise's luggage. Something's wrong with your phone. I wouldn't blame you for taking it off the hook. How are you feeling, Laura?"

"Much better. And Elise has regained consciousness, too. Thank you for bringing our things, Skip. That's very nice of you."

"It's the least I can do, all things considered. Do you have a minute to talk? Is Alec here? I see his car outside."

"Yah, he's in the kitchen. Come on in. I'll make more coffee."

We sat around the kitchen table. I put out the plate of leftover bacon and made enough cinnamon toast for all of us.

"I don't know why I'm so hungry," I said.

"It's because of yesterday. When your body uses adrenaline, other functions shut down. I bet you weren't hungry at all through your whole ordeal, and it went on a long time. It's the same reason people often faint or, excuse me if I'm being indelicate, lose control of those other two bodily functions in an emergency. You're back on track now and your brain is telling you to eat," Skip explained.

"Well, you learn something every day," I said.

"I'm glad to hear about Elise. I was scared to ask. Tell her I don't think I need to talk to her any time soon. Between you and Flash Coffin, I think I've got everything I need."

"How is Flash?" Alec asked without smiling.

"Much better than he deserves, is all I can say."

Skip reached for a piece of cinnamon toast and dunked it in his coffee.

"You have something to tell us?" Alec asked.

"Well, it's more like an update. About ten hours ago Scotland Yard searched Sean Rogers' hotel room in London. He didn't do anything to hide his tracks. He must think that you two ladies are dead. Anyhow, he wasn't there and neither was his luggage. The Brits are reviewing security tape from Heathrow and the hotel. Hopefully, they'll come up with something."

"What about John LoConte?" I asked.

"Another dead end, I'm afraid. The New Hampshire police are scouring the woods off of ninety-three and the story is running on radio, television, and in the papers, too. You must have seen it. Has your phone been ringing off the hook?"

"Actually, no," Alec answered. "We haven't seen today's paper, or even put on the television. I guess we've been thinking about Elise." He paused a moment, "Oh, Lord, Laura I forgot. When I called the security firm from the hospital yesterday, they suggested changing your phone number and delisting it. It totally slipped my mind. Elise would use my cell if she needed me, but we better tell the boys."

"And my kids," I added.

"The security detail is doing a good job keeping reporters away. They tried to stop me," Skip added. "Anyhow, all the publicity ought to give us a few leads on Mr. LoConte. Just nothing yet. I'll keep you posted. You better give me the new phone number, too. I won't pass it along."

"I'll have to call the security office," Alec said reaching for the phone. "I don't know the number either."

"So what's going on with the Carlisles? Are they part of this?" I asked.

"Yes and no," the Chief answered. "They know the players all right, but so far, their involvement seems to be greed, not murder. The consensus is that Sean talked them into the money laundering mortgage company, but he didn't meet much resistance."

"What will happen to them?" I asked.

"Nothing yet. We'll get further not tipping our hand, but the Feds are keeping tabs on the Carlisles. They're criminals, but, so far, no proof that they're murderers. Hopefully, they'll lead us to others."

"Is there any reason to keep my home on the market?"

"No. We accomplished more than we bargained for with that ploy. There's nothing else to gain and plenty to lose. You don't want strangers coming and going. I'm assuming Elise will recuperate here, and we certainly don't want bugs planted or any other snooping. There's also the danger of retaliation. LoConte let himself in with a key the first time you were kidnapped. He was probably following orders from at least one of the Carlisles, most likely Mister. This crowd doesn't have female bosses, as a rule. There are a thousand reasons for you to de-list, Laura. Do it today and change the locks. Keep the security people on. Maybe the Feds can be persuaded to provide security, gratis, considering who we're dealing with."

"What I don't understand Skip, is how did John LoConte know our theory, which turned out to be wrong, that the Reverend and Mrs. Parker were the murderers? We discussed it here, but this place has been swept for listening devices and there aren't any. I never talked about it over the phone. Did you, Alec?"

He shook his head no.

"I had the same thought last night when I was explaining developments to Elise. LoConte knew what we had discussed, and he knew we were wrong, but he tried to use our mistake to his advantage and convince us we were right. And it worked, too. We'd still believe it if you and Elise hadn't been unlucky enough to surprise him and Sean yesterday morning."

"What about Stephen and Donald? Their phones, apartment and cars need to be checked. Donald's office, too. I'll get on it. Do you know where Stephen is now?" Skip asked me, getting to his feet and taking his parka from the back of the kitchen chair.

"It's Friday. He's teaching at the Work Ethic."

Alec hung up the phone and handed the Chief a page from his yellow legal pad with my new phone number on it.

"Thank you, sir. Give my best to Elise. Call if you think of something. I'll do the same," he said before letting himself out.

"You bet."

After Skip left, I called Stephen on his cell to give him my new phone number. He said my kids had phoned him earlier in the morning looking for me, and he had invited them for dinner at his place. We could eat after I visited Elise. I knew Alec wanted to sit with her as long as he could, but I would only stay a few minutes, per doctor's orders. Alec might show up at the boys' or I'd see him back at my house later tonight. Next I left separate messages for Abbie and Dave on their machines, but before I was finished the doorbell rang again. Alec opened the door.

"Is my mother here?" I heard Dave say.

I hung up and walked out of the kitchen in my bathrobe. Abbie and Dave were standing in the living room with Alec. Abbie looked at me, smiled and raised her eyebrows.

"Hey, Mom," Dave said, "I hear you've been busy."

"You might say that," Alec answered for me. "I'm Alec McBride, Stephen's lawyer. Glad to meet you, Abbie, Dave." They all shook hands. "I've got to run. If I don't spend the next few hours in my office, I'll have a mutiny on my hands. I'll see you around six at the hospital, Laura."

Alec closed the door behind him and the three of us hugged. Dave was tall like his father and Abbie was short like me. They were handsome and adorable, respectively, and no longer kids. They had inherited Greg's calm and common sense and I liked to think that we all shared a sense of humor.

"Ma, I turned on the radio when I got out of the shower this morning and they were talking about you. I picked up the phone and you've been disconnected, so I called Dave and he had just done the same thing."

"We got here as fast as we could from Boston. I picked up Abb and we called Stephen en route, so we know some of this. It's unbelievable."

"You've got that right. I can't tell you how good it is to see you."

We had seen each other less than a month ago, but hadn't talked since just before I was kidnapped for the first time, two weeks ago. We had been playing telephone tag. Abbie and Dave told me they had each taken a "personal day" from work and were planning to sleep in Magnolia tonight.

"There's breakfast stuff still out," I said. "I'll just go upstairs and get dressed."

Abbie looked at my bandaged hand and said,

"I'll wash your hair. Dave can do the dishes, and we'll take you out for lunch."

"That sounds better than perfect. Just pick a place where no one knows us."

All things being equal, we would have chosen Sugar Magnolia's, but the three of us knew the owners, staff, and half of the regulars. Given my recent notoriety, the chances for a peaceful lunch with my son and daughter were nil. Instead, we chose McT's, another Gloucester eatery that catered mostly to tourists. It was much larger than Sugar Mag's and located directly on the fishing docks. This time of year, mid-week, they would be slug slow. There was no line waiting to be seated, so the hostess showed us to a prized window booth and handed us one of those huge menus that keeps opening and is printed on all eight sides. The only vessels in the slips along the dock were fishing boats. It was still much too early in the season for pleasure craft. I was overwhelmed by all the choices and asked Abbie to pick a salad that I'd enjoy. I certainly intended to save room for Stephen's dinner. My adrenaline feeding frenzy had passed.

Abbie and Dave asked me lots of questions and I told them what I knew. Finally, Dave put his head in his hands and started laughing.

"Mom, this is crazy. What is wrong with these people? Having you in the middle of it all is hilarious, now that it's over. You flipped yourself out of the trunk of a Coupe de Ville? I can't believe it. This lawyer LAWYER, not postal worker, not pervert, not maniac activist, not psycho, decides to frame Stephen STEPHEN, of all people, and you're caught in the middle. Some hitman HIT-MAN ties you up and you escape when he takes a WIZZ, on the car door, no less! I'm sorry for laughing. Abb, we should never have left Mom and Stephen alone without supervision."

Lord, it felt good to laugh, laugh 'til you cry laugh, lose your breath laugh, wet your pants laugh. I picked my head off of the table, took a deep breath and was on the verge of starting all over, when I noticed someone vaguely familiar out of the corner of my eye, walking past the restaurant's window along the dock. I turned my head and there in front of me was John LoConte carrying a brown grocery bag and a six-pack of Bud. He had a black knit cap pulled low over his forehead and his head was bowed, but there was no mistaking the big lug. In the summer, the sun beats into McT's, and with the fishing vessels out of their slips the reflection off the water is blinding. Accordingly, the owners had put in tinted glass several years ago, which shielded the customers from the glare, and prevented all of the promenading summer tourists from staring at the diners. I knew he couldn't see me, but I started shaking.

"Call 911," I whispered.

Chapter Twenty Three

Despite my vehement objection, Dave pursued John LoConte, but thankfully the restaurant's door was on the street side of the building and LoConte had already disappeared in the half minute it took Dave to reach the dock. Abbie phoned Skip Doliber and he met us at the restaurant. After listening to our tale of woe, Skip made a few phone calls. We waited an hour in McT's for three F.B.I. agents to arrive. We listened as the four law enforcement officers drew up a plan to patrol within a half-mile radius of McT's. Because LoConte was on foot and carrying his groceries, they suspected he was holed up nearby.

Skip drove us home and instructed Detective Miller to drive Dave's car to my house. On the way, he told us that a listening device had been found in the Ferrari and left in place. We would use it to trap LoConte. One of the men guarding my home, handed me a new set of keys when we drove in. The locksmith had already come and gone. I went inside to call June Carlisle.

"Hello, June. It's Laura English," I said when we were connected.

"Oh, Laura, you're lucky to catch me in. Dick and I are waiting for some heavy hitters from San Francisco. They need to be bi-coastal. Price is no object, privacy and ocean view mandatory. Obviously, they'd have no interest in your house. They found us on the internet and have insisted on being able to pick both our brains. They're 'can-do' people and are fully prepared to close within days. What do you want, by the way?"

Either she was the only person in town not to hear of yesterday's ordeal, or she was determined to avoid the whole subject.

"I want to take my house off the market."

"You might as well. With all the trouble you've gotten yourself into, people are thinking that place is jinxed, anyway. It doesn't do our reputation any good to be handling your property, either. I'll mail you the keys."

"Thank…" I didn't finish because June had already hung up.

"That woman is unbelievable," I said to Skip.

"Mom, you were going to sell the house?" Abbie asked.

"No, not really. I was pretending in order…Oh, never mind, it's better you don't know. I'll tell you when this is all over."

"Do you think it's safe for my mother to stay here, Chief?" Dave asked.

"It's safe enough. This is the last place Mr. LoConte would come. I think he's only in the area because he already had a hideout and he wanted to eavesdrop on what gets said in the Ferrari. But judging from June Carlisle's reaction to your mother just now, they may all be leaving town soon. The only reason that woman wouldn't fight tooth and nail to keep a listing is if she didn't expect to be around for the commission. Can I use your phone, Laura?"

"Of course."

Skip called the Treasury agent responsible for investigating the Carlisle's money laundering scheme.

"I think your realtors may be getting ready to take a powder, Mike."

Skip listened to the agent for a good five minutes, occasionally making a short remark and hanging up by saying,

"Good idea. I'll be back to you."

"Do you know Donald's number at work, Laura?" he said with the receiver still in his hand.

"Sure, six one seven, five three six, zero zero zero zero. Extension one."

Howie dialed as Abbie, Dave and I watched like the three "see no evil, speak no evil, hear no evil" monkeys from our position on the sofa.

"Donald, Skip Doliber…No, everything's fine. I need a favor from you…Great. Could you leave work now and come to Laura's house with the Ferrari…I'll explain when you get here. See you soon."

Donald stopped what he was doing and left his office. This was the second time today that he had spoken with Skip Doliber. The first time was just before he left for work this morning when Skip told Stephen and him the Ferrari and apartment needed to be checked for listening devices. Donald doubted their apartment was bugged. The building would be very difficult to break in to and Arrietta was a vigilant landlord and neighbor. He and Stephen tended to be rather tidy and Donald knew they would have noticed something askew if John

LoConte had managed to invade their home. But he should have considered the possibility that his car might be bugged. LoConte had probably done it when he planted the hatpins in the glove compartment.

The F.B.I. agent had been waiting for Donald in the garage when he arrived at work. After probing the car, the agent had come into the office to relay his discovery to Donald in person. Donald would be glad when this nightmare was over and judging from Skip's two calls today, Donald had the feeling that it might not be long now. He drove in silence to Magnolia, savoring the hum of the Ferrari's engine, and arrived a little after four.

Skip, Abbie, Dave and I were waiting for him.

"Hey, team. What's up? Anybody pregnant?" Donald asked.

"Hey, Donald. Good to see you, man. What have you let my Mom and Stephen get in to? I count on you to keep them out of trouble," Dave joked, shaking Donald's hand.

"Well, as of last night they're both grounded."

"Nice threads, Donald. Machine wash and dry?" Abbie said hugging him and running her palms up and down his back, over his cashmere sports jacket.

"Chief," Donald said nodding at Skip. "What's up?"

"We need to make a plan. The Carlisles don't know we're onto the money laundering, but Laura's adventure with LoConte yesterday must be making them nervous. They aren't sure what, if anything, Laura knows, but it must have occurred to them that, if LoConte were ever arrested, he might spill the beans to avoid the death sentence. I doubt they know where he is. Their phones are tapped and we're following them the best we can in a small town like Magnolia. We need to trick LoConte into coming out of hiding. Dollars to donuts, he's in Gloucester, near McT's. I was hoping we could come up with a staged conversation for the Ferrari and hope LoConte takes the bait. What do you think?"

"I think we could do it. I suppose that I know him best. He's got a hair trigger, so to speak. If we could get him angry enough, he'd come after us," I said.

"I don't think so, Laura," Skip answered. "But the anger angle is good. You didn't say anything to LoConte about the phony mortgage scam, did you, Laura?"

"Nope, not me."

"I think Laura should go to visit Elise at six, as planned, with me in tow. Is it all right if she uses your car Dave?"

"Of course."

"Then, you give Abbie and Dave a ride in the Ferrari to your apartment for dinner," Skip said looking at Donald. "On the way, you guys thank Donald for going out of his way to give you a ride, because your Mom needed to borrow your car. Mention that your house is off the market and keep emphasizing how much fun Mr. and Mrs. Carlisle made of John when the three of you went to reclaim the keys at the real estate office this afternoon. Lay it on real thick. My guess is John LoConte will come out of hiding and show up at the Carlisles. We'll continue looking for him in Gloucester, but there will be police waiting at the Carlisles, just in case we miss him."

"What if the Carlisles are home? Won't they cause trouble?" Donald asked.

"They won't be home. Those heavy hitters from San Francisco are federal agents."

"Couldn't happen to a cuter couple," I said cheerily.

Donald, Abbie and Dave practiced their act for the next hour. When we all felt they were worthy of an Academy Award, they were sent on their way with simple advice from Skip.

"Don't over-paint the canvas."

I, however, insisted on kisses and hugs all around. I felt a little like I did on my children's first day of Kindergarten.

Once inside the car, the performance began.

"Thanks for giving us a lift," Abbie said.

"Donald, have you seen her car?" Dave asked.

"Your Mom's? Yes, and it's really a wreck. I've never seen such a mess. No wonder they had to airlift Elise to Boston."

They had decided to float a red herring regarding Elise's whereabouts.

"What did you and your mother do today?"

"Not much. Talked about all the shit that's going on, and we decided to take the house off the market. Abbie and I don't want her to sell yet and she's fine with that. I don't think she ever really wanted to, either. Kind of got talked into it. We all went to the real estate office to pick up the house keys, before she changed her mind again," Dave said.

"Do you know the Carlisles, Donald?" Abbie asked.

"Just by sight. Why do you ask?"

"Well, Dave and I don't know them either, but Mom's had a really scary couple of weeks and all they could talk about was how stupid John LoConte is. They never even asked how Mom was feeling or anything. They just made it mighty clear what an imbecile low-life he is, not that they actually know him, except for a piece of property or two. 'Who'd want to?' they both said, and then Mr. Carlisle called him 'dumber than a sack of hammers.'"

"They were unbelievable," Dave added. "They made it sound like anyone could have gotten away from him. Mrs. Carlisle actually said, 'Laura, you've got nothing to worry about. If the big ape comes back, throw him a banana and he'll forget why he came.' She said he was too stupid to even buy property that appreciated."

"Then she made an extremely crude remark about his sexual prowess," Abbie added.

"Oh, do tell, Abbie. We're old friends, sweetie. No fair keeping secrets," Donald pleaded, going out of his way to sound effeminate. He suspected being laughed at by a homosexual might not sit well with John LoConte.

"I'm not saying it. You can tell him, if you want to Dave."

"She said, 'If it wasn't for his right hand, he'd be a virgin.'"

As rehearsed, the three of them laughed, but no one louder than Donald.

Inside his apartment at the fish factory, John LoConte made a decision. It was time to get out of town. His landlord would return soon from fishing and he was bound to see a newspaper and recognize John's picture. He just had one small piece of business to take care of first. He wondered how smart the Carlisles would look when Dick's head was bashed in by a hammer and June was strangled, with a banana in her mouth. LoConte smiled. If he had the time, he might place the banana somewhere else.

John easily located a hammer and a few other tools inside the factory. He grabbed the three bananas he had bought earlier in the afternoon at the grocery. He gathered his few belongings and walked outside to the green pick-up truck. He could steal something else, or maybe he'd just swap plates and get the truck repainted. John had never been inside the Carlisle's home, but he had been asked to wait outside more than once. The first time that prick Dick Carlisle had told him not to bother coming in, Sean said,

"You're making a mistake, Dick. None of this works without John."

Dick hadn't even shrugged, like LoConte had no feelings. As a rule, John took no pleasure in killing people, but these two would be different. If they weren't home, he'd let himself in and wait. The Carlisles lived on a high rise of land, facing a cove in Magnolia. John reconnoitered the stretch of road that they lived on. When he didn't notice any activity in the posh neighborhood, he parked in a grove of trees, in front of a neighbor's house. With his gun in his belt, banana in one parka pocket, a few tools in the other, and the hammer in his right hand, John LoConte proceeded cautiously to the rear of the house. Despite the dusk, no lights were on inside. He didn't see any cars through the garage windows, so he sat leaning against a tree and waited. Nothing happened. John decided to let himself in.

The bulkhead door was usually best in big old houses like this. People rarely bothered replacing the old original doors and they were difficult to wire for an alarm system. Pelting rain, snow, and ice sliding off of the roof in winter all set them off. He knelt next to the bulkhead and easily saw the inside bolt through the crack where the two sides of the door no longer closed tightly. John removed the chisel from his jacket's pocket, placed it above the bolt and fiercely struck it with the hammer. The bolt landed on the inside cement steps. John could hear the three loud clangs as it rolled down the stairs. He lifted one door, and closed it after himself. The inside door wasn't even locked. A faint, hint of light filtered through the casement windows and John found his way to the stairs leading to the first floor. He crept up them with much creaking and slowly turned the door handle at the top. He was carrying the hammer in front of him and used it to push the door open. He and his hammer were silhouetted in the quickly diminishing light.

"Drop it, Mister," a man's voice yelled.

It didn't sound like Dick Carlisle, but John couldn't be sure. He sure as hell wasn't letting that wussy prick get the better of him. John dropped the hammer, but slowly reached for the gun under his belt. Unfortunately, the hammer landed smack on his big toe, the one with a painful bunion. John yelled, "Goddamit! Fucking toe!" at the same time as the first F.B.I. agent shouted, "F.B.I.," and the second agent loudly warned his partner, "Gun!"

It was the second agent who killed John LoConte, but afterwards they were both puzzled by the banana in his pocket.

Chapter Twenty Four

Alec was already with Elise when Skip and I arrived at Gilbert Hospital.

"Can you tell me which room Elise Sanderson is in?" I asked the nurse at reception.

She checked the roster and asked,

"Names please?"

"Elise Sanderson."

"No, I mean your names."

"Oh, Laura English and Skip Doliber."

"Yes, Doctor Hodgeson said Mrs. English could visit, but no more than ten minutes. There is no mention of you Mr. Doliber. You'll have to wait here."

"That's fine. I'll wait here Laura. There's nothing I need to ask."

"Ms. Sanderson is to remain calm and still. I'm setting my timer for fifteen minutes and if you haven't left, I'll send an orderly to fetch you. If you care about Ms. Sanderson's recovery, you won't make me do that. Be sure to check out with me when you leave. She's on the third floor. Room 307."

"Thank you," I said, feeling as if I were leaving the principal's office.

The door to Elise's room was closed when I got there. I tapped softly and in a moment Alec opened it.

"Come in. Come in. There's someone here who can't wait to see you."

I walked over to Elise and kissed her hand. She was lying flat on her back with just one pillow under her head. Except that her eye was still bruised from two weeks ago, and she was paler than Casper the Ghost, her smile untied the knot in my stomach.

"Oh, darling girl, it's good to see you," I said. "I'm not allowed to stay more than ten minutes and if either of us misbehaves, I'll be forever banished. So, I won't cry if you won't."

"Deal."

"First, how's your head?"

"It hurts like the devil and the room spins when I raise it."

"I guess that means a cocktail is out of the question. How did the tests go?"

"Horrendous. The only people I'd wish them on are my brother-in-law or John LoConte. But the results are good. No spinal fluid in my brain, or is it brain fluid in my spine? Anyhow, the brain swelling is minimal and subsiding."

"Oh, Elise, I'm so glad. I just wish your head didn't hurt."

"Me, too. Anyhow, Alec told me about your trip to New Hampshire. Not much foliage this time of year, I guess."

"Don't make me laugh, or Nurse Ratchett will have my head. Any chance of being sprung soon?"

"A week, knock on wood."

"Can I bring you anything tomorrow?"

"Lip gloss, blush, and a hand mirror."

"Done, done, and done."

"How are you, really, Laura? What an ordeal you had yesterday. They're going to start calling you Pauline."

"Look who's talking, but I do have news. I better make it fast. Abbie and Dave took me to Gloucester for lunch and we saw John LoConte."

"You're serious?" Alec asked.

"Yes. He didn't see us, thank heavens. Dave chased him before I could do anything about it, but he disappeared. The F.B.I. has three men looking for him in Gloucester and Donald and my kids are trying to trick him into coming out of hiding using the bug they discovered today in Donald's car."

"The Ferrari's bugged! That's how LoConte knew our hypothesis about the Reverend and Christine Parker," Alec said.

We were interrupted by a knock on the door. Alec opened it and Skip Doliber walked in.

"Hi, Elise, how are you doing?"

"Better by the minute, Chief."

"Glad to hear it. They sent me to get you, Laura, but I thought you might like to hear my news. I just received a phone call from the F.B.I. coordinator and they've arrested the Carlisles. John LoConte has been shot dead by the F.B.I. breaking in to the Carlisles' house, and Sean is still among the missing, presumably in London."

Elise, Alec, and I were dumbfounded, but Skip quickly added,

"Give Elise your new phone number, Laura. If you ever want to come back, you've got to leave right now. That nurse used to be a marine."

"I already wrote it down for her," Alec said.

"I'll see you later then, Alec," I said. "I'll be at Stephen's for a few hours. Stop by for a bite, or I'll see you at home." I turned to Elise. "Precious Angel, I'll be back tomorrow with Estee Lauder herself." I bent over, gently kissed Elise's cheek and whispered, "Thank God you're going to be all right."

As soon as Stephen opened the door into his apartment, he hugged me.

"Can you believe it? Our brilliant thespians pulled it off."

"Are they all right with the outcome?" I whispered in his ear.

"Fine, I think. I mean the guy was such a low life, Laura, right up to his last gasp."

"You don't have to tell me, mon amour."

Donald greeted me with a glass of wine.

"Thank you, my dear and congratulations on a job well done," I said raising my glass to him, Stephen, Abbie, and Dave.

"It's a good thing there wasn't a hidden camera in the Ferrari," Abbie said. "I was so nervous that I had to close my eyes. I felt like I might start laughing hysterically and Dave would have to slap me."

"Well, you were all magnificent. Skip told me that LoConte showed up armed with a gun, hammer and a banana."

"That's a scary picture," Stephen said. "Do you think the Carlisles will be inclined to be co-operative?"

"Hard to say. I wonder how much they really know beyond their direct role in the money laundering. The police already know about Sean, and the Carlisles probably don't know any one else beyond John LoConte," Donald said.

"Sean is the one who knows all the players. Now, how was Elise?"

"She's hurting, but alive. Alec was there. I bet we don't see him for dinner. He didn't look like a man who was about to leave voluntarily. Dr. Hodgeson thinks she'll be hospitalized about a week."

Stephen had disappeared into the kitchen and returned to announce that dinner was ready. He had prepared my kids' childhood favorite, chicken parmigiana.

Judging from their appetites, my children were suffering no serious side effects from today's events.

"To getting that bastard Sean Rogers," Stephen said raising his bottle.

He, Abbie and Dave had decided on beer tonight. Donald was seated opposite Stephen, at the other end of the table, and I couldn't help but notice how deeply they were gazing into each others' eyes.

"To getting that bastard Sean Rogers," we all repeated.

Chapter Twenty Five
Five Thousand Miles East of
Magnolia

Five thousand miles away, Sean Rogers, a.k.a. Henry Cushman, was a man with a plan. He patiently waited in his hotel room until eight Friday morning. The lobby would be bustling at that time and no one from the night before would be on duty to recognize him. He donned Mr. Cushman's hat and glasses and carried his own bags through the lobby. The doorman whistled a waiting taxi and helped him into the car. Sean was glad it was still drizzling. Taxis would be busy today and he doubted the driver would have much recollection of this small fare.

"I'm just going to the other side of the Square. A little pub. Forget it's name, but I left my umbrella there last night. Good though. Think they're open for breakfast, too."

"I know the one. Do you want me to wait?"

"No need. I'll have an egg in the hole and flag another car when I'm finished. Thanks all the same." Sean's British accent was improving.

The trip took several minutes with the morning traffic. The Brits may not indulge themselves with simple luxuries like central heating, but they certainly knew how to design a hackney, with plenty of leg room, usually eliminating the inconvenience of placing luggage in the trunk. Sean liked the head room and the slight step up into a British taxi, especially today, when he was on the lookout for police. After paying the driver, Sean entered the pub and ordered tea and scones to go. He walked with his luggage and small brown bag next door to the car park. After locating the rental car and stowing his luggage on the rear seat, Sean studied the map in the glove box, as the Brits called it. He looked at his watch. Three thirty Friday morning in the States. No need to check his laptop for news. Obviously, at least one of the women was alive and talking. The details wouldn't change anything.

Sean studied the route from London to Folkstone, where the English mouth of the Chunnel was located. The drive was roughly a hundred miles. He had considered taking the Eurostar train from London to Paris, but had decided not to. The train would be considerably faster and easier, but if something went wrong, Sean was wary of being trapped on the Eurostar. He would have more maneuverability driving himself. The Chunnel was about thirty miles long, and he judged Paris to be at least two hours from Calais on the French side, over four hours in all, if he took his time. Sean had no desire to be stopped for speeding.

Customs was thankfully uneventful. Henry Cushman was a dull, unassuming professor of Christian Legal Ethics, on sabbatical from Gordon College in Wenham, Massachusetts. Gordon was only a few miles from Magnolia and Sean had driven past it countless times on Grapevine Road. The school boasted an idyllic New England campus and attracted mainly upper middle class straight-arrows. Christian religious instruction was included in all course work. Sean had carefully researched the school and was familiar with the names of its deans and the rest of the information in Gordon's most recent catalogue. Most importantly, an academic, traveling alone, never seemed to attract much attention.

The rain persisted all the way to the Chunnel, but when Sean emerged in Calais, the sun was out. The countryside was greening and buds were perched hopefully on bare branches. He decided to leave the main auto-route and find a spot for lunch. There was no need to keep Henry Cushman's Burberry hat, with its gray fringe of hair, on his head. He detoured into Champagne and found himself following a luxury l'autobus. It was painted a high gloss black with extremely tasteful gold lettering, which declared it to be *Le Tour Relais et Chateaux*. In smaller letters beneath was *Relais Gourmands*. This group would certainly know where to have lunch and they'd also serve as camouflage.

Sean followed the tour bus south along A26 for over an hour. They seemed to be headed for Reims. Just as he decided maybe the bus was not planning to stop, it signaled a left turn off of the highway, and in only a few minutes, Sean found himself at an elegant turn-of-the-century chateau, set in the middle of a glorious parkland. A bronze plaque next to the elegant double French doors announced *Boyer Les Crayeres*. He had no idea what that might mean, but it was secluded.

The proprietors were waiting on the expansive, columned front porch to greet their guests. Sean watched as the tourists got off the bus. He was in luck. They were Japanese. No nosy Americans. No one who would be reading the *Boston Globe*. He observed each guest bow to the owners as they entered the chateau. Sean counted twelve Japanese and two tour directors, a thirty-something year old couple, presumably French. The bus driver helped the chateau's staff off-load luggage. The tour must be spending the night here. Maybe he would, too.

The parking attendant did not notice Sean until the bus was moved, and then he scurried to the black sedan almost in a panic.

"Pardonnez-moi, Monsieur. Je ne vous vois pas."

"Pas de probleme, mon ami. Je suis Americain," Sean said, smiling his well-practiced smile.

The attendant laughed, clearly relieved.

"Will you be resting with us long?" he asked with a heavy French accent.

"How long is the tour staying?"

"Just the night," only it sounded more like, "Juiced zee night." Then he added, "Tomorrow it is Geneve for them."

Grace had always been the French speaker in the family, but Sean knew a smattering and he knew Geneve was Geneva.

"I would very much enjoy staying the night, but I do not have a reservation."

"Pas de probleme. I will help you settle."

The attendant escorted Sean and his luggage to the registration area. The tour was already seated in the dining room. The desk clerk smiled pleasantly at Sean, while the parking attendant spoke to him in French.

"Yes, monsieur, we would be honored to have you as a guest. Have you visited us before?" he said in perfect English.

"No. To tell you the truth, I followed the tour bus."

"A very clever maneuver, Monsieur. Relais et Chateau stay only at the finest establishments."

Sean was shown to his room and freshened up before lunch. He could get used to this. His room had three sets of French windows, all looking out on an expanse of lush lawn and formal gardens. There was a boxwood maze in the distance and stables beyond. The room had a high domed ceiling that was painted with rosy, smiling cherubs and puffy white clouds against a blue sky. The bathroom had a claw foot, oversized soaking tub. Unexpectantly, Sean remembered the story of Ira Einhorn, the American hippy from the sixties. He was an unemployed college dropout, living off of his girlfriend. When she found him entertaining another woman in her apartment, the hapless girlfriend insisted that Ira vacate. Unfortunately for the girlfriend, Ira decided he preferred murdering, dismembering, and stuffing her into a foot locker to moving. He continued to live with her at the foot of their bed, and only when the stench became unbearable, causing the neighbors to complain, did Ira flee the country, wisely choosing France as his new home. Ira's mistake had been staying in the same village for thirty years. He had married a French woman, but was eventually tracked down by his dead girlfriend's family. Even then, the unfathomable French blocked his extradition for years. The country's consensus was, "So what? We all make our little mistakes and Ira is such fun now." Sean smiled thinking about it. He was going to be fun, too, but he wouldn't stay in one place for thirty years. He wasn't going to fall in love, but he wouldn't mind getting laid. This was going to work out just fine.

Sean left his suite and was seated in the simple, yet elegant dining room. Paneled walls boasted charming portraits of children, pets, and substantial looking lords and ladies. Lush arrangements of opulent freshly cut flowers spilled from the walls built-in niches. The high ceiling was domed and simple butter colored sconces adorned the many French windows. A perfectly proportioned crystal chandelier hung from the center of the ceiling. The table linen was damask and Sean's napkin was both oversized and hand embroidered. A hand-penned card on Sean's table read *M. Cushman*, in black India ink against an expensive cream-colored stock. As soon as the waiter assisted Sean into the chair, he removed the card with a gloved hand. Grace would have known the chair's style was Queen Anne, but Sean noticed that the striped cream and butter colored padded silk, which covered the chair's back and seat, were immensely comfortable.

"Would you care for an aperitif, Monsieur Cushman?"

"Yes, I believe I would. Could you recommend your favorite Champagne to me?" Sean was in the province of Champagne, after all, and when in Rome…

"Allow the sommelier to be of assistance, Monsieur. Tastes are so individual and we only want your happiness."

He signaled the wine steward, who materialized seemingly from thin air. After asking Sean a few gastronomic questions, he clicked his heels and disappeared, only to return in two minutes with a bottle tenderly cradled in his hands. While he was gone, an ice bucket had appeared table side. The cork was perfectly popped by the sommelier, no erupting explosion ensued. After sampling a swallow himself from the small silver chalice hanging around his neck, the sommelier poured for Sean and held his breath while Sean inhaled and then swallowed the lively pale liquid. He let it slide slowly across his tongue. Sean had forgotten how delicious untraveled fine Champagne could be. He hadn't enjoyed any since his honeymoon ten years ago, but that did not diminish his pleasure. He looked at the sommelier and said,

"Celestial, mon ami."

Tears appeared in the wine steward's eyes. He bowed his head and filled Sean's flute.

"Thank you for letting me be of assistance, Monsieur," he said humbly, before clicking his heels and turning away.

The waiter allowed Sean the perfect amount of time to savor his drink before returning with the menu. Sean refused the menu, saying,

"Would you be kind enough to choose for me?"

"Certainment, Monsieur. It would be my grand pleasure. Do you enjoy the poisson, fish?"

"Very much."

"Then you are about to be truly happy," he said before hurrying to the kitchen.

Sean sipped his Champagne and contemplated the joy he had provided for the two waiters. Yes, he was going to be more fun than a nymphomaniac virgin meeting a convict on his first day out of jail.

Chapter Twenty Six

Sean undeservedly slept the sleep of the just. After forty-eight hours of consciousness, an exquisitely chilled bottle of vintage Champagne, a kingly meal of filet de rouget de roche grille, and a night cap of one hundred-fifty year old Port, Sean surrendered to his tapestried canopy bed's eight hundred thread count linen. The last sound he heard before entering a profound, dreamless slumber was the comforting whoosh of his magnificently plush feather mattress. Whomever said, there is no rest for the wicked, never met Sean Rogers.

Sean did not descend to the dining room until nearly noon the next day. He watched as two waiters meticulously polished the already gleaming silverware, before precisely laying it at each place setting. The air was filled with the unmistakable chiming of sparkling crystal wine glasses softly touching one another, as full trays were expertly whisked to each table. Yet to be distributed, plump freshly cut arrangements of hydrangea and peonies, from the chateau's green house, adorned the sideboards. From what Sean could observe, his fellow travelers had arisen with the birds and had spent the morning walking, golfing, and in one instance, horseback riding. The two tour guides were deep in conversation with the proprietors, presumably speaking of the planned luncheon and future tours, when Sean entered the dining room. Immediately Elyane, the gracious proprietress, left her small group to receive him.

"Monsieur Cushman, I trust you rested well."

"Never better, Madame. I can't remember sleeping this late since my childhood. Have I missed breakfast, or might I have an early lunch?"

"Certainment. Let me seat you, and Gerard will be right over for your dining wishes."

"Splendid. Would it be possible to ask the tour guides to join me for a moment when your business is settled?"

"Bien sur, Monsieur."

Gerard dutifully appeared, offering coffee or tea. Sean chose the French roast and savored it while his waiter adjourned to the kitchen to arrange a brunch of sorts. Sean also savored having the dining room to himself at this hour. He had always been mildly amused by Japanese tourists. They were so busy and serious. What did they do with all of the pictures that they took? And did they ever photograph one another without elaborately posing? He gazed out the French windows and watched a young Japanese husband repeatedly capture his wife as she pretended to emerge from the boxwood maze confused and dazed. They never actually enjoyed the maze. He just shot frame after frame of his young bride emerging, holding her head in her hands, or with the back of her wrist draped dramatically across her forehead. The young woman's acting ability seemed to be a grave disappointment to her husband and Sean suspected that luncheon conversation between the two would not be jovial.

His musings were interrupted by the arrival of the tour guides, who introduced themselves as Judith and Jonathon Kent. They were attractive British siblings and the children of a career diplomat posted to Japan. Their etiquette was flawless and their uniforms were well-tailored dark blue suits. Sean was convinced that neither one of them would ever be accused of flirting with a member of their tour. After exchanging pleasantries, Sean asked,

"Would it be possible for me to join your tour as far as Geneva? Driving on the other side of the road and not speaking the language is more of a challenge than I considered."

"That can be easily arranged. Our tours usually accommodate twenty and this time of year, we'll have no trouble reserving a room at Domaine de Chateauvieux, where we stay in Geneva. Will you be traveling further with us?" Judith answered.

"No. I have a bit of business in Geneva and then I think I'll risk Paris. You wouldn't be headed there, by any chance?"

"Actually, no. We've just left, but the TGV is super from Geneva to Paris. We'll gladly arrange it for you," Jonathon said.

"TGV? I'm afraid I don't know that."

"Oh, sorry. The high speed train. Train de Grand Vitesse. The speeds are close to two hundred kilometers an hour and the ride is so smooth that the open wine bottles don't even need to be secured. The entire train is First Class only."

Jonathon produced a sheet of letterhead from his briefcase and jotted down the services to be rendered to Sean with the price in dollars next to them. He slid the sheet across the table to Sean for his approval.

"That will be fine. Thank you."

"It's our pleasure. You'd be surprised how often this sort of thing happens, but usually the tour doesn't have vacancies. Would you like us to arrange the return of your rental car?"

"Could you? I was planning on asking the chateau to figure it out."

Jonathon made an adjustment to the sheet he had just shown Sean and slid it back across the table for his added approval.

"Of course, we'll handle customs, as much as we're permitted. If I can just borrow your passport, I'll set the arrangements and have it returned to you promptly. We depart at two thirty, and would be grateful if you could have your luggage outside your door by two."

"Thank you both. I feel very fortunate to have crossed your path," Sean said standing up to shake their hands.

"Our pleasure," the siblings said before taking their leave.

Gerard returned with a sumptuous offering. He said the recipe had been created for the British royal family. It consisted of a freshly baked loaf of Brioche, with the crust removed. Two thick slices were then cut, trimmed, and molded into the shape of an oversized teacup, without a handle, and toasted. After toasting, the bottoms were generously covered with succulently fresh, sauteed crabmeat, topped by an egg, which had been poached to perfectly fit into the Brioche basket. The crabs were delivered live daily. Then the entire dish was napped with a heavenly smooth combination of Bearnaise and Hollandaise sauces. The dish was accompanied by impeccably steamed asparagus, and hand-carved rosettes of radish and carrot. A freshly squeezed and strained glass of blood orange juice completed Sean's meal.

He returned to his room as his co-travelers were arriving for lunch. Once inside his suite, Sean went on line. He was amazed to discover that Elise and Laura were both alive, but John LoConte was dead. The Carlisles' speedy arrest was equally unexpected. After reading the articles, he packed his bag and placed it outside the door, glad to have gotten out of Dodge in the nick of time. He would not like to exchange his room at Boyer Les Crayeres for a prison cell.

The tour arrived at the chateau outside of Geneva before dark. Sean had sat alone during the drive and contented himself with watching the countryside as he comfortably rolled through it. Judith came by once as they drove past the five-hundred-year-old walled city of Beaune. She kindly pointed out the mid-evil Hospice, where the nuns valiantly tried to nurse the peasants suffering from the Bubonic Plague. Judith made no attempt to join him, just inquired if there was anything that he might need.

In contrast to Boyer Les Crayeres, Domaine de Chateauvieux had been a former outbuilding to another grand chateau. It was surrounded by idyllic farmland, and managed to be both rustic, and elegant. The inside walls were original stone with walk-in height fireplaces. The establishment was built on top of a hill and Sean could see the lights of Geneva from his room's windows. Dinner was unforgettable. Sean ordered a Breton lobster which was roasted and served on risotto with a white truffle sauce. It was accompanied by home grown vegetables and a remarkable local, well-chilled Rully. The manager supplied him with a flashlight and he enjoyed a long walk after dinner. Again, Sean treated himself to a fine Cognac before enjoying a sound night's sleep.

The next day was Sunday. Sean watched from his window as the Japanese tourists climbed aboard their luxury bus. Each husband had a camera around his neck and the wives all carried festive tote bags, presumably filled with film. They took turns loaning their cameras to Judith and Jonathan, who dutifully snapped pictures of each couple posing in front of the bus. Most of the men posed in profile, choosing to rest a foot on the bus' front bumper, with an elbow leaning on the raised knee, and a fist supporting the head, sort of a variation of *The Thinker* statue. Their dutiful wives stood behind them smiling. Sean wondered if Japanese wives were allowed to use cameras.

When they had departed, Sean felt it was safe to descend to the dining room for breakfast. He was graciously seated and poured a cup of coffee. The gastronomic excesses of the two days with *Relais et Chateau* inspired Sean to order fresh fruit and homemade muesli. When he was finished, the waiter returned..

"Pardonnez-moi, Monsieur. Have you plans for the day?"

"No. What would you suggest?"

"Do you like shooting?"

Sean hadn't been hunting in years, but it was a perfect Spring day and the thought of some activity appealed to him.

"We keep game birds here. They are wild, but we feed them all winter, so they are plump."

The waiter pronounced the word "ploomp."

"The widow of our gamekeeper is a good guide and good with the rifle. She is the gamekeeper now. I could inquire."

"Thank you. I think I would enjoy that."

"Bien!"

Three-quarters of an hour later, the gamekeeper Raquelle called for Sean. Sean judged her to be in her late forties, several years his senior. Raquelle stood five foot eight with broad shoulders and a sturdy build. She wore faded overalls with a well worn sky blue flannel shirt underneath. Her coarse head of short, wild, brown and gray hair formed a shelf at the nape of her strong neck. Sean correctly guessed that she cropped it herself. The hard lines of Raquelle's face were worn proudly. Make-up would be an obscenity on this woman. She was both Mother Nature and mountain woman.

"Bonjour, Monsieur. I am Raquelle Bohon."

Sean held her calloused, rough, large, strong hand in his. It was as capable a hand as Sean had ever felt.

"Bonjour, Madame. I am Henry Cushman."

"I have brought the clothes for you. You did not expect the hunting, non?"

"No, I did not. Merci, Madame."

"Call me Raquelle."

"If you call me Henry."

"Ah, Henri. You do not look like an Henri to me, but you do look like a hunter."

"We'll see," Sean said climbing into Raquelle's old jeep.

They drove in silence. Ten miles later, she turned off the paved road onto a rutted dirt one, which took them into the woods. Soon she stopped the truck and they both got out. Raquelle removed two rifles from the back of the jeep and loaded them.

"Take a few shots. Aim at that big oak," she commanded.

Sean did as he was told.

"Bien. The sights are good, non?"

"Yes."

"Bon. Suivez-moi. Tell me if I go too fast. I am used to my own pace and I know this land. I do not mean to hurry you," she said unhinging her rifle.

Sean did the same and followed. They tramped the woods for hours, fording streams, climbing down ravines, and up again. Raquelle did not speak, but she frequently pointed out does with their fawns, wild birds and hiding grouse and pheasant. She allowed Sean to take all the shots and she knew to slow her pace without being asked. Only when Raquelle thought they had enough, did they stop.

"Come. We will eat. I am hungry and I think you are, too. I will keep two grouse and Chef Chevrier will be happy for the rest."

Again, Sean followed without questioning, until they came upon a stone cottage built on a small rise of land. He had not looked up to notice the cottage earlier, but Sean could see Raquelle's jeep in the gully below.

"This is my home. I will cook and show you how the peasants eat."

Raquelle was flushed from their tramp and Sean couldn't help but notice her smile. It was generous, but somehow sad, and strangely disarming. Her teeth were white as a lioness' in her prime.

"The waiter said you are a widow?" Sean surprised himself by asking.

"You want to know what happened, yes?"

Sean found himself blushing. He couldn't remember the last time that had happened.

"Okay. I do not mind. He was mauled by the bear. It was a false Spring and the bear woke up early and there was my Jacques, a perfectly magnifique feast for that hungry fellow. I fed my Jacques so good that the bear ate him in the woods and did not even take him home to the cave."

Raquelle took Sean's rifle and locked it in the gun rack. She opened a bottle of red wine and poured two glasses.

"To my Jacques. I do not blame the bear. My Jacques was so good that sometimes I wanted to devour him, too." Sean and Raquelle raised their glasses, drank, and shared a comfortable silence.

"Now we will have jambon and an omelette. After, you can help me pluck the birds," Raquelle said standing up and opening the ice box.

Sean noticed for the first time that there was no electricity or plumbing in the cottage. He watched as Raquelle removed a hunk of what looked like ham from the ice box and a carefully wrapped piece of runny brie. She placed the brie in a wooden bowl with a small spatula and loaf of bread next to it. She handed the platter to Sean.

"The bread is fresh this morning from La Domaine. I smoke the jambon myself," Raquelle said, smiling and beguiling. "It is very good."

Next she crossed the room to a bowl full of brown eggs.

"Gathered today," she said, breaking a half dozen into a bowl.

Sean sipped his wine, watching her chop vegetables before she scrambled them into the eggs. She lit an alcohol burner, placed a heavy iron skillet on top, nonchalantly threw in a quarter pound of sweet butter, and waited for it to melt before pouring the eggs into the pan. She quickly sliced several slabs of ham and returned the remaining leg to the ice box. Raquelle refilled their glasses and opened another bottle, so it could breathe. She placed the platter of ham and skillet of eggs directly on her planked wooden table, along with hand towel napkins, and forks. Raquelle motioned for Sean to come to the table and he did. This time Sean refilled their glasses. They ate the ham with their fingers and the eggs directly from the pan.

"Being a peasant is not so bad, eh, Henri? We will have the grouse for dinner. Chef Chevalier can pluck his own pheasant."

After their late afternoon lunch, Raquelle carried the pheasant to her drying shed to hang. She wiped out her iron skillet with one of the napkins and took off her overalls. Her flannel shirt was long, but not long enough to hide the fact that she was wearing no underwear. She looked at Sean and without a word he removed his overalls, and the rest of his clothes, standing naked in front of her. Raquelle did the same. They rutted like wild animals in season. Afterwards, they slept and awoke in the dark. Raquelle lit two lanterns and several candles before leading Sean to her outside pump, where she watched as he rinsed himself in the famous icy cold water of Evian. Sean watched Raquelle as she did the same, and naked, they returned inside.

"Build a fire, Henri and then I will show you how to pluck the birds."

Early Monday morning, Raquelle drove Sean and the pheasants back to La Domaine.

"May I see you again?" Sean asked.

"Anytime, Henri. I am constant. You are the traveler."

"Thank you, for every minute, Raquelle."

"Come when you will, Henri Cushman."

They stood in front of La Domaine and shook hands like strangers, but their eyes said otherwise.

Chapter Twenty Seven

Sean returned to his room dazed. He requested his best suit to be pressed. While waiting for its return, Sean relived the previous day with Raquelle. He wondered if something like this had been the eventual downfall of Ira Einhorn. His suit was returned and he dressed carefully for the day in Geneva. As promised, Judith had arranged for a car and driver to transport him to the city and take him to the TGV when his business was finished. The Kent siblings had wished him pleasant journeys and expressed their hopes to be of service again someday.

A black Peugeot was waiting when Sean emerged from La Domaine. Geneva was a mere five mile trip. Within half an hour, Sean was seated with an officer of the Credit Suisse, Private Bank division. After completing the paperwork, Sean was presented with the equivalent of a ten thousand dollar certified check, which he intended to use to open an account with a bank in Paris. Monsieur Rochefort efficiently arranged for regular monthly transfers from Sean's numbered Swiss account to the French account, but Sean would have to open the French account in person. Sean had read in *Newsweek* that the bank provided the exact same service for Yasser Arafat's wife, when he was alive, only her transfers were considerably larger. Sean didn't begrudge Mrs. Arafat her booty. He couldn't imagine a sum large enough to compensate for having sex with Yasser.

When their business was complete, Monsieur Rochefort walked at a brisk pace with Sean back to the Peugeot. The two men shook hands cordially, and in barely an hour, Sean was en route to the train station, thinking that the Swiss deserved their reputation for efficiency. Sean might have reconsidered had he known that the moment of his departure, Monsieur Rochefort returned to the office and placed a phone call.

"The bird is flying to our nest in Paris," he said, before disconnecting.

The train was not crowded and Sean shared the entire car with only six other passengers, five business men and an attractive brunette with a French braid down her back. She was dressed in tight designer jeans with expensive looking leather boots, which accented her long legs. A short cropped, long sleeved, pale blue cashmere cardigan showed off both her narrow hips and braless torso. The top three buttons were undone and the omission suited her. A leather bomber jacket was on the seat next to her. Sean watched as she stood to stow the jacket in the spacious bin above. A taut, pale midriff was revealed when she raised her arms. Sean helped her close the compartment.

"Merci, Monsieur," she said smiling.

"Pas de tout," Sean answered, noticing a stylish leather backpack by her feet. She seemed too old to be a college student. Maybe she was a graduate student at the Sorbonne.

"Etudiante?" Sean asked.

"Non," she replied politely, blushing.

"Parlez-vous anglais?" Sean inquired.

"I'm American," she answered.

"Me, too. Are you a tourist, then?"

"Sort of. I'm an exchange professor of Ancient Greek at the Sorbonne. My class doesn't meet on Monday, so I visited Geneva overnight. The TGV is so easy. What about you?"

"A little business. A little pleasure," he answered flashing his well-practiced smile. "Where do you teach in the States?"

"Wellesley."

"I'm impressed."

"Don't be. Only a handful of undergraduate colleges offer Ancient Greek as a language. The Classics are currently unfashionable, so the few of us who are qualified to teach, can pretty much choose where we want to be. I thought Paris would be fun for a year."

"You sound disappointed."

"Oh, no, but I like the countryside better. Paris is beautiful, but frenetic. Have you been there often?"

"No. This is only my second visit. I was here ten years ago on my honeymoon."

"Where is your wife? Surely you didn't leave her home. Ten years is time for a second honeymoon."

Sean glanced out the window briefly, before turning back to his fellow passenger,

"She's dead," he said sadly, milking the moment for full effect.

"Oh, dear. I'm sorry. Forgive me."

"Nothing to forgive," Sean paused, then asked, "I realize how brazen this will sound, but could I take you to dinner? You'll have to suggest a restaurant, but you'd be doing me a favor. I would be grateful for your company. Maybe, I could even prevail upon you to suggest a hotel."

"I would enjoy that. My name is Elizabeth Yost. Beth for short."

"And I'm Henry Cushman."

"You don't look like a Henry to me. You look much more fun than a Henry."

Sean smiled. He fully intended on being a great deal of fun. Before the two hour trip to Paris was complete, Sean was seated next to Beth and they were conversing easily. She wrote down the name of a small, but well-appointed hotel not far from the L'Arc de Triomphe that she thought would suit Henry. They shared a taxi from the train station, dropping Henry at the Republic Bank on the way.

"I'll collect you at L'Hotel Louis Quatorze around eight. No need for a tie. My telephone is on the page if your plans change."

"My plans won't change," he said, flashing his well practiced smile.

Sean easily opened his account in the name of Henry Cushman, and established a safe deposit box at the bank to use as his address. Thanks to Monsieur Rochefort, the bank was expecting him. The young officer spoke English and even instructed his secretary to confirm a room at L'Hotel Louis Quatorze for M. Cushman. After his business was complete, Sean exchanged more dollars for Euros and took a taxi to his hotel. L'Hotel Louis Quatorze was intimate and elegant. The lobby was exquisitely marbled and appointed with oversized, opulent flowers. The reservations manager spoke English and efficiently installed Sean in a corner room on the fourth floor. The hotel boasted only fifty rooms and prided itself on its service. Before being shown to his quarters, Sean prevailed upon the manager to send up a light lunch with a half bottle of appropriate wine. Sean had done a lot today, and last night. Even though it was barely past two, he thought he would enjoy a bath and a nap.

After a satisfying salad of poulet, surrounded by artistically arranged crunchy fresh vegetables, Sean indulged himself in an afternoon tub. He soaked in the deep antique bathtub, smoking a cigar. Last night seemed very long ago, almost like a dream. He had never plucked a bird before, let alone by firelight. He felt like the Connecticut Yankee awaking in King Arthur's Court. Sean wondered if Raquelle were thinking of him. He couldn't say why, but he hoped she was. He wondered if she often took men to her bed.

After three quarters of an hour, Sean reluctantly climbed out of the tub and toweled himself off, before sinking into his king-size bed with eleven pillows.

The sun was setting when Sean opened his eyes. He tried to remember the last time he had enjoyed a late afternoon nap and couldn't. Afternoon naps were very European and Sean intended to blend in. He called the front desk and asked them to connect him with the number Beth had left him.

"Allo. Allo," she answered on the second ring.

"Beth, it's Henry. I'm at the Louis Quatorze and it's perfect. Thank you."

"Oh, I'm glad it suits you."

"The reason I'm phoning is to tell you that my business has wrapped up sooner than expected. Would you like to meet earlier?"

"How about seven thirty there?"

"It's a date. I'll be in the bar."

"A toute a l'heure, Henri."

Beth was refreshingly prompt and found Sean sipping a martini. The bar was small and richly furnished in the style of Versailles. She was wearing a short black leather jacket, cinched at her tiny waist, over a mini, tightly fitting, hot pink knitted dress with long sleeves. Her hair was loosely piled on top of her head with a few seductive tendrils trailing down. Designer black stilettos with a matching shoulder bag completed the outfit. Once again, she did not wear a bra, to great advantage, and Sean found himself wondering if her stockings were elastic at her thighs, garter belt, or panty hose.

"You are a vision," he said, helping her off with the leather jacket. It was soft as butter.

"I'm glad you approve, Henry."

"What would you like to drink?"

"I'll have what you're having."

They left the bar after finishing their cocktails and at Beth's suggestion, took a taxi to Au Pieds de Cochon, in the market section of Paris.

"This is where the Parisians go," Beth told Sean. "It's great food with a built-in floor show."

The restaurant was busy and noisy. Gone were the elegant manners and affectations of the expensive establishments. They were replaced by a bustling energy, loud clanging from the open-faced kitchen, and shouts from the impatient waiters. The patrons were dramatic in a typically French manner and ranged from fishermen to Parisian dowagers. Sean and Beth shared a massive bouillabaisse and a sinfully cheap, delicious bottle of wine. Beth suggested walking to a quiet café only a few blocks away for dessert. The night air was mild and the stroll was welcomed. Their conversation flowed so easily that Sean realized his time with Beth must be short-lived. He told her that he was an importer from New York City, and did not mention Boston. Otherwise, it would be way too easy for her to discover something about him when she returned to Wellesley. He added a few lonely details about his sainted wife, who died from cancer, but mainly Sean concentrated on asking Beth about herself, all the time successfully exuding his well-polished charm.

By the time they arrived at the café, Beth and Sean were holding hands. By the time they finished their port and left the café, Sean's arm was around Beth's waist. She felt so good. She smelled like wild flowers.

"Will you come back to the Louis Quatorze?" he asked.

"Only if you take me to bed immediately. I give a three hour seminar starting at eight in the morning. I must leave you by six."

Early the next morning, Sean hugged Beth in his bathrobe before she left the hotel room.

"I must see you again. What about tonight?"

"I have a better idea."

"Whatever you say."

"I'm finished by eleven. Schools aren't open on Wednesdays in France, sort of like Saturdays in the States. I don't teach again until Thursday afternoon. Be downstairs at noon and I'll pick you up. Pack casually for overnight and bring sturdy shoes if you have them."

She kissed him firmly on the lips, holding his handsome face in her hands and dashed out the door. Sean watched as the elevator door closed behind the hot pink mini-dress and wished that he really were Henry Cushman.

Promptly at noon, Beth appeared at the hotel in a taxi. Sean climbed in the back seat with her. Again she tenderly held his face and kissed him on the lips, only this time her tongue briefly flirted with his teeth.

"Chemin de fer TGV," she told the driver.

After paying for the taxi, they walked arm in arm into the station. Beth was wearing jeans, hiking boots, and a deep turquoise turtle neck sweater that matched her thickly lashed eyes. Sean had emptied his briefcase and was carrying a change of clothes in it. Presumably, Beth's were in the leather backpack slung over her shoulder.

"Where are we going?"

"To my favorite place in France. I found it on Sunday and I can't wait to share it with you."

"Is it in Geneva, then?"

"Now, what country is Geneva in?" Beth teased, sounding a bit like a professor.

"Oh, right. Is it near Geneva?"

"It's very close," Beth said mysteriously.

They enjoyed lunch and non-stop conversation en route. As Judith had promised, the ride was so smooth that the bottle of wine did not have to be secured. Sean found himself in Chamonix by two. He followed Beth off of the train and felt as if he had stepped into a picture postcard. The only thing missing was the sound of yodeling. There were no taxis at the station, only horse drawn carriages. Beth spoke to their driver in French when they were settled in the loveseat shaped worn leather seat. The surrounding mountain peaks were snow-covered, the sky was brilliantly blue, the sun was comforting, the wild flowers were beginning to bloom in the meadows that the horse trotted past and the air was alive with purity. Beth spread a reindeer pelt across their laps and kissed Sean again.

"You don't kiss like a Henry, either," she said.

"How many Henrys have you kissed?"

Beth smiled in reply. She did not hold Sean's head in her hands. Instead, she caressed his cheek with her right hand, while leaving the left beneath the pelt, tenderly stroking the inside of Sean's strong upper thigh.

"I hope we're going directly to a hotel," he whispered.

"Not so fast, Monsieur. We are being dropped at the spot I discovered two days ago. We can easily walk to the Auberge du Bois Prin from there. Tomorrow's weather may not be perfect like today and I really want to share my spot with you, so it can be our spot. Do you think that's silly? Don't worry. I promise to have you in heaven before you know it."

"In that case, I suppose I have no choice."

"None whatsoever."

In about twenty minutes the horse halted. Beth and Sean stepped down, and as soon as the cart was out of sight, they embraced.

"Thank you," Sean said.

"For what?"

"For taking me under your wing. For showing me such fun," he paused theatrically, "For making me happy again. Now, where's that view of ours."

"It's a few hundred yards into the woods. I'll show you."

They walked hand in hand through the forest. Sean had never felt so alive. He could smell the damp earth and the pine sap. Their feet made no noise on the pine needles beneath them. Birds were singing and squirrels were jumping from branch to branch, playing their version of tag. The altitude contributed to Sean's dreamlike state. In a few minutes, the forest ended and he found himself on a grassy cliff overlooking a fairy tale valley with Mont Blanc majestically in the distance. He was speechless.

"Walk a little closer to the edge and look down, if you really want to see something."

"Come with me."

"I will. I just want to take your picture. Capture your first expression when you see our special place. I know. I'm being silly."

"No you're not. I love that it's important to you."

Sean walked closer to the edge and saw a magnificent waterfall far below him. The spray caused the most beautiful rainbow he had ever seen.

"Surely this place is the pot of gold at the rainbow's end," he said turning around to find Beth standing a few feet away, with a revolver in her hand. "What are you doing?"

"I think you can guess what I'm doing, Sean. The better question is 'what did you think you were doing?' Do you have any idea whose money you stole? Do you know who the Big Boss really is?"

"The Gambini's? I'll give it all to you. I haven't spent any yet. You can have it."

"Oh, there's no doubt we will have it. We already have it. We just used it to get you. Have you ever heard of the White Man? That's whose money it is. He's my father. Nobody steals from the White Man, Sean."

Sean certainly had heard of the White Man. He had run the most successful mob operation in the country forty years ago. They were known as the Summer Hill Gang. The White Man had single-handedly controlled most of the Boston F.B.I., and continued doing so for decades, even after he had disappeared. Over the years, dozens of corpses had been discovered in remote burial grounds, their whereabouts revealed by thugs hoping to cut a deal with the authorities. They testified that the White Man had killed most of the victims. He thought nothing of murdering girlfriends if they displeased him, or if he simply tired of them. Judging from her age, Beth could be the daughter of one of the corpses, or maybe the White Man had married after going on the lam. His brother had been a powerful politician in Massachusetts and still wielded plenty of clout. There had been occasional sitings over time, and many rumors that the White Man was living in Europe.

"How do you think my father has survived for thirty-five years? He's still the Big Boss. He pays well for his loyalties, and no one lives to betray him twice. When you stole from your boss, you were really stealing from my father, too. My father won't live forever, and he has taught me well. Who do you think will take over when he dies?"

"Beth, we…"

"Shut up," she said, before gently squeezing the trigger.

The shot echoed through the valley below. At least a hundred panicked birds took flight. Beth fell forward and her face planted into the soft earth. Behind her, Raquelle stood with a hunting rifle at her shoulder.

"There are a few things we do not know about each other, non? Come, I will put the color back in those cheeks of yours, but first we must undress our prey, and throw her over the cliff. The grizzlies love that waterfall, but they do not eat clothes."

Sean and Raquelle worked quickly to strip the corpse. When they had finished, Sean held Beth's still warm wrists, while Raquelle took Beth's delicate ankles in her deadly, capable hands. They had rolled Beth's body over to undress her and mud covered her face.

"God did not make those bosoms. She is just so many sticks, n'est-ce pas?"

Sean did not answer.

"Un…deux…trois," Raquelle counted slowly, as the duo swung the body higher and higher, before flinging it over the cliff. They stood side by side and watched while Beth soared naked through the air, silently disappearing into the waterfall. Sean wondered if it had really been her favorite place, and who else's body might be down there.

"You will like the peasant living, I promise," Raquelle said, as they walked back into the woods. Sean was not so sure, but he wisely remained silent.

Chapter Twenty Eight
Magnolia

Elise was released from the hospital a week later. Alec had hovered over her every day. I offered to collect Elise, but Alec insisted on doing it himself.

"Nothing personal, Laura, but I can't trust you two together," he told me.

"Very funny," I said.

I loved having Elise and Alec under my roof again. I had grown accustomed to their company and their absence reminded me how much I missed Greg. Elise was under doctor's instructions to rest and avoid all activity for at least another three weeks. I was not proud of myself, but the doctor's orders suited me just fine. Alec commuted to work from Magnolia, and could not have been kinder in his appreciation to me, especially considering there was little else I'd rather be doing. I realized that soon enough I would have to come to grip with my future, but in the meantime, I happily procrastinated. Stephen and Donald often joined us for dinner, frequently doing the cooking. They invited me out twice a week, which gave Alec and Elise some privacy.

The second Sunday that Elise was home, Skip Doliber telephoned.

"Any chance of getting the five of you together sometime today?" he asked when I answered my phone.

"Sure. What's up?"

"Plenty, but I'd just as soon spell it out to everyone at the same time."

"Fair enough. How about coming for supper? Nothing fancy, just pot luck."

"What time?"

"How does six sound?"

"See you then."

Skip was never one to mince words. Stephen, Donald and I had seen him and Dorothy Andrews having dinner at The Lyceum, Salem's most delicious and historic restaurant, one evening when the boys invited me out. I was glad Dorothy was getting on with her life, and told myself that I would do the same.

I relayed Skip's message to Alec and Elise, then called the boys. The five of us were gathered by five thirty and had to wait a half hour for the Chief. No one wanted to miss a word, so I had made lasagna during the afternoon and was keeping it warm in my oven. The boys brought salad and garlic bread. Spring had officially arrived and the local fish market was again open on Sundays. Alec provided us with two dozen jumbo shrimp as an hors d'oeuvre. He made his own cocktail sauce, using lots of extra hot horseradish and fresh lemon juice. Elise even got dressed for the occasion.

Skip arrived promptly and blessedly didn't waste time on pleasantries.

"They found Sean's luggage in a hotel room in Paris. The best they can figure is that he had martinis in the hotel's bar with a real looker the night before he disappeared, two weeks ago tomorrow, and she left his room early the next morning."

"Sounds like Sean," Elise said quietly.

"He left the hotel dressed real casually at noon the next day. The front desk manager thinks he got into a cab, but he wasn't sure. The French authorities checked into it, and they found a cabbie who remembers being flagged down by an extremely attractive brunette in her late twenties on the Left Bank before noon on that Tuesday. She was dressed in jeans and a sweater. He drove her to the hotel and some man, who could have been Sean, came out and got in the cab. The driver didn't pay much attention to the man. He drove them to the Paris train station, but has no idea where they went from there.

"Three days ago the hotel manager called the police. It seems an American, Mr. Henry Cushman, had been missing from his room for nine days. The hotel prides itself on discretion, and they waited nine days to report the disappearance in case Mr. Cushman was just having a little extra-marital fling. After all, they had an imprint of his credit card and they'd seen his passport. He left expensive clothes, luggage, and a new laptop in the room, but nine days is nine days and they were getting nervous. The police in Paris weren't too worried, but they checked it out anyway. Our State Department has no record of issuing a passport to any Henry Cushman at the address given, which doesn't exist, by the way.

Now Interpol gets involved and they come up with a Henry Cushman who rents a car at Heathrow on the same day Sean flew to London. They also have a record of a Henry Cushman, who spends one night at a London hotel, across the street from where Sean was registered. The two rooms faced one another across the side street. Customs shows a Henry Cushman driving the Chunnel to France the day after Sean arrived in London. The rental car was returned near Reims two days later when Henry Cushman seems to have joined a tour group in Reims, but only for one night. After arranging a car and driver for Henry Cushman, the tour left him in Geneva. The driver transported him to a private bank in Geneva first thing two Mondays ago, and then dropped him at the train station. Later that day Henry Cushman shows up at the hotel in Paris, spends the evening with a beautiful mystery woman and they disappear, apparently together, the next day. There the trail goes cold."

"No wonder you wanted to tell all of us at once," Alec said after a stunned silence.

"That Sean. Wasn't he the busy bee?" Stephen added.

"How about we talk about it over dinner?" I asked, carrying the empty shrimp bowl into the kitchen.

We bombarded Skip with questions during dinner. Were there any clues in Sean's luggage? Who returned the rental car? Had the tour staff and hotel employees been interviewed? He patiently answered our questions, but none of the answers put us any closer to solving the mystery.

"What's your theory, Skip?"

"My guess is he's dead. You don't cheat the Mafia and live to tell about it."

"Unless the mystery lady provided him with yet another identity," Alec said. "Do you know if Sean did much traveling alone over the last few years, Elise?"

"I don't think so, unless he did it while my sister and I vacationed on the yacht."

"Chief, can you and I look into that possibility," Alec said.

"Sure, but I wouldn't waste too much time worrying about Sean," Skip said. "Something will break. If it doesn't, dollars to donuts, he's dead. Coming back here would be plain suicidal, and Sean Rogers strikes me as a man who scrupulously takes care of number one."

We thought of little else for weeks. Elise healed and Alec flew with her to Chicago. They returned ten days later with her condominium under agreement and started a search for a home of their own in Magnolia. An autumn wedding was planned. Alec introduced Elise to the girl in the wheelchair from Amherst. The three of them spent increasing amounts of happy, productive time together and I was not surprised when Elise told me that they were applying to become Mary's foster parents. Grace's ashes were collected and resided temporarily in my guest room with Elise and Alec. After all, Grace was the one who had brought them together.

Stephen and Donald faded from their unwanted limelight. Elise and Alec were not the only newlyweds on the horizon. With the advent of Massachusetts' controversial gay marriage legislation, my two dearest friends had hopes of uniting under the approval of the law. I was convinced they already had the Lord's blessing. A romantic honeymoon at a gourmet French Chateau near Mont Blanc was in their future.

I went to the pound and with Stephen's help, chose a darling, sandy colored, shaggy mutt. I guessed him to be a Lab/Westy mix. He had a black button nose and intelligent bright black eyes. He was extremely mellow, humorously clever, and the mere thought of me caused him to levitate with joy. I named him Bob Barker. The two of us often visited my father, and when the darling man died peacefully in his sleep, Bob mourned with me. And still there was no word about Sean. Slowly, we began believing that he really was dead and our nightmare was truly behind us.

One afternoon I was home with Bob, when my doorbell rang. I opened the door to find a vaguely familiar, nice looking man, whom I judged to be in his mid-sixties.

"Mrs. English," he said, "My name is Hopkins Stone. My friends call me Hoppy. I recognize you from Oakwood. My mother was there at the same time as your parents."

"Oh, yes, of course I remember, the Lorna Doones."

"Yes, she loved your parents' little Cairn. Piper, wasn't he?"

I smiled and nodded.

"Is your father still there?"

"No. He died a few months ago."

"Oh, I'm sorry to hear that. He seemed such a gentle man."

"He was, thank you."

"I hope I'm not being too forward, but I remember seeing that your home was on the market a while back. I take it you changed your mind. I don't blame you. It's such a lovely spot. I've always thought this looked like a friendly house. My wife and I had friends, the Seymours, down the street, but they've retired to Florida now. Anyhow, whenever they invited us over, Jan and I would pass this house and admire it. 'That looks like a happy home, well used,' she would always say.

We lived in a Victorian white elephant on Eastern Point for thirty-five years. I still do, but Jan died a few years ago and it's time for me to move on. I couldn't talk you into changing your mind, could I?"

I looked at Hoppy Stone and smiled. He was the sort of man to inspire a smile. He was attractive with clear blue eyes and white hair. Hoppy was nicely dressed and held his cap in his hands. His teeth looked real. Bob looked up at him and started wagging. I've always put faith in a good dog's judge of character. Hoppy immediately squatted to stroke Bob behind his alert little ears. It was a much more genuine gesture than bending over.

"Hello, handsome. What's your name?"

Bob barked once.

"That's Bob Barker," I said.

Hoppy laughed. He had a wonderful laugh. Three weeks later Hoppy had met Abbie, Dave, Stephen, Donald, Elise, and Alec. Everyone approved and we officially became an item.

Five thousand miles away, Raquelle's cooking had already put twenty pounds on Sean. He was growing into Jacque's mountain man clothes. He had also grown a massively impressive full bushy beard, and doubted that his own mother would recognize him. With unplanned irony, Raquelle told La Domaine that her brother was staying with her, while he struggled to overcome the tragic death of his young wife. Under her tutelage, Sean was laboriously learning French, but for the time being, he could not risk going out alone. Sean was penniless, and a virtual prisoner. He missed indoor plumbing and electricity. He dreaded the thought of winter in the French Alps, trapped with the insatiable Raquelle, and he hated chopping wood. Sean no longer found Raquelle beguiling, but he could not survive for long without her protection.

For her part, Raquelle was content. She had a younger man, who did what he was told, and in return she smothered him with food and lust. Raquelle was convinced that a few more pounds, and a few more years were all Sean needed to resign himself to her. He would forget those ridiculous girls. What were they compared to her? Merely piles of bones, with useless narrow hips, and store bought bosoms. Raquelle would prevail, or die trying.

Coming Soon from Nancy Jelliffe Bruett
FIERCE FRIENDS
Chapter One
Indian Territory, 1879

Oklahoma Territory was on the far side of wild in 1879. Cruel and down right mean was a more apt description. Settlers of the territory learned to act the same way, or they died trying. Mean was what kept you alive, and the meanest men of all lived in Indian Territory. Indian Territory did not abide by white man's laws. It attracted the desperados, who preferred being scalped to the certainty of the hangman's noose. No one knew what had driven James and Rebekah McDoulet into Indian Territory, and no one dared ask.

Anna, their third child in as many years, was born in the midst of a savage dust storm. While the birth progressed, the useless dirt sifted between the shack's miserable slats and into the windowless, one room catastrophe that served as a house. Calvin and Martha, the newborn's toddling brother and sister, knew not to complain, but instead covered their own small mouths with filthy little hands, watching through an unclean haze as the squalling baby's breath sucked the dancing dust into her tiny lungs. Anna McDoulet's first taste of life was dirt and the tumultuous existence that followed her was hardly a bolt from the blue.

Anna was not the baby of her family for long. By the time she was ten, Anna would have six younger siblings, but she would always be her father's favorite. Anna was obedient and undemanding, but so were her older siblings, Calvin and Martha. No, Anna became the apple of her father's eye when she was four and her family settled near a Pawnee village on what is now the Oklahoma—Kansas border. Anna was the only flaxen haired, blue eyed member of the McDoulet family. Her hair was as fair and soft as the corn silk on the cobs grown by the Pawnee women, and her eyes were startlingly blue, as though the Great Spirit Tirawa had plucked two pieces out of the vast Oklahoma sky, just for Anna to see through. The Pawnee were a superstitious nation and no one in their village had ever seen hair or eyes like Anna's. Never one to avoid easy exploitation, James McDoulet was quick to notice the awe on the Indians' faces whenever they saw Anna. While the rest of the McDoulet tribe was squalid, James insisted that his wife Rebekah keep Anna's hair clean, brushed and free from vermin.

Pawnee men were great hunters. At first, James McDoulet allowed the Indians to trade game and vegetables for simply a touch of Anna's hair, and he may have been content to leave things that way, if fate had not intervened. For Anna's part, she quickly made friends with the Indian children. She lived to ride their ponies and by the time she was five, only her fair skin, blond hair and blue eyes betrayed the fact that she was not an Indian. Anna learned the Pawnee dialect and preferred sleeping in the Indians' grass houses, which they covered with mud in winter, than with her own family. She had no desire to wear skirts and dressed in the soft leathers worn by her friends. During the merciless heat of an Oklahoma summer, Anna rode both bare back and bare-chested. She was thrilled by the thundering speed and sheer freedom of galloping the countryside with her playmates.

August, 1885, produced raging temperatures on the Oklahoma plains. Bands of heat emanated from the scorched earth, like a frying pan left empty over a camp fire. Most days, Anna and her friends Oochin and Fwapa rode to the Territory's poor excuse for a river. The Arkansas meandered through the countryside, but was a mere trickle by summer's end, except for one spot, where a bend in the river caused the water to pool. Oochin and Fwapa were nine, three years older than Anna. Oochin's father was Chief of the Pawnee village, and Fwapa was his cousin. The children spoke infrequently on their ten mile journey, preferring to point at distant circling buzzards, or look for prairie dog holes, hoping to spare their ponies injury.

The day was too sultry to ask the ponies to race. Just plodding through the torrid air was effort enough. Young as they were, the trio created a dignified, almost regal, impression. Anna was flanked by her two friends and rode half a pony length ahead. The children had bows and quivers of arrows across their bare chests, sitting alert and tall on their bareback steeds. Though only six, Anna was the same height as her friends, but where Oochin and Fwapa were broad and sturdy, Anna was long and lanky. Her colt-like legs were deceptively powerful and firmly secured her to the pony. Her light frame and natural ability to seemingly become a part of her horse when the children raced across the prairie, left Anna the undisputed champion. The boys did not begrudge their friend's prowess. Although never discussed out loud, they knew she had a gift from the Great Spirit, and took joy watching her bent at the waist, chest flat on the pony's back, with her cheek pressed against the animal's neck. Her long flaxen hair would stream behind her like a magic cloak, and anyone close enough to see the expression of concentrated joy on Anna's face could only admire her.

As the children approached their spot in the river, they were overjoyed to see the water was still high enough to swim. They helped their ponies to climb down the steep bank upstream from the pool and left them wading in the shallow water, while Anna, Oochin and Fwapa proceeded to leap gleefully from overhanging tree branches into the delicious wetness. Sheer indulgence caused them to lose track of time, and only when they noticed their ponies nervously pacing on the river bank, did the children reluctantly leave Shangri-la.

"What has you so nervous?" Fwapa asked his horse.

"Maybe he's hungry," Oochin offered.

They were wearing only loin cloths, and as was their habit, Anna and the boys turned their backs to one another while removing their dripping wet, skimpy attire to wring it out. Anna finished first.

"Safe to turn?" she asked with her gaze lowered, when she noticed the rattler slithering across tree roots, less than five feet from the boys.

Without thinking, she dove for the snake, grabbing its tail and flinging it into the river, before her friends realized the danger. The boys turned in time to see Anna sprawled on the ground and the snake quickly retreating across the top of the water.

"That's why the ponies are nervous. Let's get out of here before the mate appears," Anna said.

"Wait until I tell Father, Anna. He will kill a buffalo for the hungry McDoulets."

"I'd rather live with you," Anna said.

"Fine. Half the time with us. Half the time with Fwapa. Fwapa's mother and sister may not be too pleased, but maybe we can implore Tirawa to change their hearts," Oochin joked as the three friends mounted their ponies.

"These ponies are still scared," Anna said looking around on the ground and also into the branches of the trees above them for the rattler's mate.

That's when she noticed the threatening funnel cloud in the distance. This was not Anna's first encounter with a tornado and before Oochin and Fwapa could suggest trying to outrun it, she dug her heels into her pony's side and cantered in front of them.

"Follow me," she shouted with an authority that belied her age.

Oochin and Fwapa did not argue. Anna led them a few hundred yards downstream, to the deepest section of the almost dry riverbed, urging their ponies down the steep bank.

"Lie flat, underneath your pony, but do not hold them. We don't want to be dragged if they bolt."

James McDoulet had never come by a horse honestly, but he respected them. Twice before Anna had watched her father set an ill-gotten horse free, and both times the horse had returned unscathed after the monstrous wind had gone. He called it horse sense.

The Indian ponies stood like statues straddling the children. Anna took this as a good omen. The air above them became eerily still, just before they heard the beginning of the roar. Anna closed her eyes, covered her ears and prayed to the Great Spirit. The McDoulets were not a god-fearing family. At a time like this, Anna chose to put her faith in Tirawa, the Pawnee's omnipotent spirit ruler.

Five minutes is an eternity when you expect every breath to be your last. Eventually, the children dared to peak, cautiously through one eye and then both, they found the sky blue and the air perversely calm. They walked their ponies up the riverbed toward the swimming hole, only to find the water gone, sucked out by the murderous wind. The trees had vanished without a trace. Not even a single leaf remained. The tornado's path of devastation led west, away from the Pawnee village. The children found themselves involuntarily shaking and they sank to their knees. The ponies watched as they drew Tirawa's symbol into the earth with their fingers, because no rocks or sticks remained. Solemnly, the three friends arose on steadier legs and circled the symbol in a ritual dance. The children chanted while reverently and rhythmically stomping their feet. They alternately bent low, allowing their hair to touch the ground, and then stretched tall with their faces heavenward. Before riding home, the trio placed their right fists over their hearts and beat their chest three times to show Tirawa their love for her. Once mounted, Anna, Oochin, and Fwapa rode as if they were the wind. The tribe's search party encountered the children two miles outside the village. Oochin and Fwapa's fathers broke rank and galloped to meet their sons. They swooped them off of the ponies and into their strong bronze arms without even slowing down. No one in the McDoulet family was thinking about Anna, let alone searching for her.

"You have done well, my son. The Great Spirit has chosen to keep you safe," Oochin's father, the Chief, whispered.

"It was Anna, Father. First, Tirawa sent her the snake to warn of evil, and then she led us to safety. Even the ponies knew to follow."

"Ah, it is how I thought, then. This Anna with the sun for hair and sky for eyes is from Tirawa. She is one of us."

Anna hung her head to hide her tears. When she was able, the young girl held her head up and started to speak. She wanted her friends' fathers to know that she was not from Tirawa, but with one motion of his massive arm, the Chief forbade her to speak. Fwapa's father did the same, causing Anna to hang her head again and let the search party lead her back to the village. When the Pawnee heard of the snake and Anna's bravery, they knew that she was a gift from the Great Spirit. The Chief ordered the tribe's squaws to prepare a grand feast of thanksgiving to Tirawa for sending Anna to them.

"Come with us, Little Spirit," Fwapa's mother told Anna.

She followed her friend's mother into the special hut reserved for women, usually brides being prepared for their wedding ceremony. Here the women gently rubbed Anna with sage and basil before rinsing her in cool spring water. Her long flaxen hair was gently washed, rinsed with pine scented water and brushed until it was dry. Anna was not embarrassed by her nakedness, but she was unaccustomed to the reverence that the women showed her. She tried to help them with their tasks.

"No, no. You must not, Little Spirit. You have saved our sons and not to honor you would surely displease Tirawa. It is foolish not to enjoy a celebration. There are not as many as before. Our bison and our land are disappearing. But we can still celebrate the lives of Fwapa and Oochin, thanks to you."

Anna looked into the faces of the women and rather than seeing the lines of hard work and sorrow, she saw only the kindness deep in their dark brown eyes, something her own mother seemed to lack.

"Okay," she said in the Pawnee dialect, "Make me magnificent."

The women giggled and proceeded to streak Anna's now gleaming hair with the red ochre that was the mark of their tribe. They also added ceremonial feathers, dressing her in a short girdle of red-tailed hawk feathers with necklaces of beads and fluffy white baby hawk feathers, gathered from their first molting. When Anna was properly prepared, the Pawnee women took her hands and walked Anna to the rock lined pool of water near the hut's grass wall. She looked down on her reflection in the still water, amazed at her transformation. Staring back at her was a Pawnee princess. The women watched as Anna moved one hand, to ensure that the reflection was truly her own.

"Is it really me?"

Oochin and Fwapa's mothers smiled.

"To night you will not be Anna from the hungry McDoulets. You will be Rala Lhushn."

Anna placed her open palms over her heart and lowered her head, but this time not to hide her tears. She was thanking the omnipotent Tirawa for saving the three friends' lives, and honoring her as Fooling the Wind.

Anna did not return to her family's shack for two days. When she did, Oochin and Fwapa's fathers accompanied her. Anna rode her very own pony, a gift from the Pawnee. The Chief and his brother silently presented James McDoulet with the hide and meat of a freshly killed bison. James nodded acknowledgement and the braves rode away. Anna still had the red ochre streaking her hair. She was dressed in her own shabby shirt and pants, wishing to leave her precious Pawnee clothes with the tribe.

"I don't know what you did Anna, but whatever it was you don't look the worse for it. I take it from that Pawnee crap in your hair that they think you're one of 'em now. Good. That's going to be very useful to this family and I expect you not to ferk it up."

"I won't, Pa."

"Rebekah! Calvin! Martha! Get out here. We got meat to preserve and a pony to feed," James bellowed, as he and Anna walked inside.

He never did ask his six year old daughter what had happened, and Anna volunteered nothing.

About the Author

Nancy Jelliffe Bruett is living her adult life in a town on the New England sea coast. She has been married to the same man for over thirty years, and is blessed to have her two adult children nearby. Her incorrigible, eclectic friends provide the author with both inspiration and tasty food for thought.

"Please visit www.bruettbooks.com"

978-0-595-38748-9
0-595-38748-9

Printed in the United States
52964LVS00004B/163-189

9 780595 387489